Praise for Jackpot by

Keller, then, is bilingual when it comes to the discourse of emotion: she understands both the language of bland social accommodations and the language of excessive despair. The former shouts at us like an alibi, jarring in its cheerfulness. The latter is inarticulate and sulking....It's as if this book were written both by a Henry James and a Hubert Selby, Jr.: a glittering chronicler of social mores, where exterior and interior worlds interweave a rich tapestry, and a poete maudite, who savors the most abject and perverse treasures of the human condition. BRUCE BENDERSON/THE BROOKLYN RAIL

Jackpot, Tsipi Keller's third novel and the first book in a trilogy, reminds me of Jean Rhys like no book I've read in years. I love Rhys; that's high praise. It's also a consumer warning: This book is a study in self-destruction. It's addictive, intense-a psychological page-turner that doesn't miss a beat... An exceptional work of fiction. JESSE KORNBLUTH/BOOKREPORTER.COM

Keller travels a delicate emotional line. In Maggie, Keller has captured a quirky, worthy sensitivity. Jackpot flows to its conclusion with a straight-ahead style that serves to keep the nerves on edge. JANYCE STEFAN-COLE/ AMERICAN BOOK REVIEW

Jackpot is a compelling, shocking novel. The story of Maggie, *Jackpot*'s main character, achieves a Dostoevskian power that unsettles the soul. In Maggie we see reflected our own humanity, vulnerability, and darkness. Tsipi Keller is a novelist whose artistry and vision command our admiration. JAIME MANRIQUE

The problem with novels of degradation is that the depressing nature of the narrative slows down the reading. If you like the character, then you'll not like seeing the character take a trip down the big swirly. Keller gets the reader past this with her present-tense prose and the wealth of understated humor inherent in her perspective on her character... The publisher of Keller's novel, Spuyten Duyvil is not exactly a household word, but they have a huge line of original fiction available in these attractive trade paperback editions. RICK KLEFFEL /AGONY COLUMN

At less than 200 pages, *Jackpot* would not seem to be a demanding read—but I warn you, Keller's Maggie has the power to take you along with her. This slender volume is, like Maggie's planned seven-day vacation, deceptive in the duration of its effect." PAT CUMMINGS/BLOGCRITICS.ORG

It isn't very long before you realize that Keller has caught you in a deceptive web of shallow ideals and insanity that in no way resemble the bland Ally McBeal psycho-babble you were prepared for. As a matter of fact it's closer to the ever-descending rings of hell of Hubert Selby's *Requiem for a Dream*. Unlike the intensity of Selby's work, Keller's story has a hypnotic, seductive quality that pulls the reader further into Maggie's escalating disintegration.   Paul McDonald/ Louisville Courier Journal

"She is on a roll, nothing and no one can stop her." By the time this illusory revelation occurs to Maggie, while she is in a tropical island casino surrounded by gamblers ("They seem to be in a hurry, oblivious to the small wins, waiting for the long, sharp wail of a jackpot win."), we know she's just kidding herself. This is gambler's logic, and Maggie is about to wager everything-money being the least of it-on a single, perilous spin of her life. Talked into going on this holiday by her glamorous, wealthy, but ultimately callow friend Robin, Maggie abandons her unsatisfying, if safe and quiet, life quickly and fiercely once she reaches Paradise Island. I guess you could call *Jackpot* a beach read's worst nightmare, in the best possible sense: sun, sand, and palm trees cannot begin to mask the dark corners of this paradise.   Robert Gray/Fresh Eyes

Tsipi Keller's new novel *Jackpot* is a skillfully plotted story of a character's unravelling, so gradual and inexorable that you move from comfort level to comfort level without realizing how uncomfortable you're getting, like the proverbial frog in the pot...One thinks, oddly enough, of *The House of Mirth*. Though Maggie doesn't have to fall as far as Lily Bart, she falls in the same curious stepwise fashion, and wonders where it all came undone. One thinks, too—continuing the theme of the American fallen-woman novel—of The Awakening, not least because Natan Nuchi's cover art shows Maggie staring out to an empty sea...But *Jackpot* is very much a postmodern fallen-woman novel, without any of the moral and social anxieties that characterize even as modernist a work as *The Awakening*.
Tim Morris/Lection

Keller is a skillful writer who is unobtrusive in the practice of her skill. Her observations are keen and she draws a spare but exact picture of a moral decline and the setting in which it occurs.   Bob Williams/Compulsive Reader.com

Tsipi Keller masterfully presents the story of Maggie, who discovers that Paradise Island is paradise lost when her traveling companion's betrayal leads to her own descent into the underworld of greed and illusion. The glittering casino-island within the island-nearly eradicates the sea. And water, primordial emblem, is the only substance that can break the spell of Maggie's emotional and sexual degradation. *Jackpot* is a deeply disturbing and haunting novel.   JAN FREEMAN

Jackpot is a daring novel of particular interest.The genius of the narrative is its vivid and hypnotic prose, which makes the incremental unraveling of the self seem not just plausible but logical. Unsettling and profound.
JANE DELYNN

If you've ever been gambling in the Bahamas, thought about gambling in the Bahamas, or wondered what a Bahamian vacation can do to a single woman-read this. I see this book as the anti-thesis of Marion Keyes. And we need some of that.   VALERIE MACEWAN

OTHER BOOKS BY TSIPI KELLER

FICTION
Jackpot (Spuyten Duyvil, NYC 2004)
Leverage (Sifriat Poalim, Israel 1997)
The Prophet of Tenth Street (Sifriat Poalim, Israel 1995)

TRANSLATIONS
Last Poems by Dan Pagis (QRL 1993)
And I Wrote Poems by Irit Katzir (Carmel 1999)

RETELLING

A NOVEL

TSIPI KELLER

SPUYTEN DUYVIL
New York City

Cover art by Scott Neary

Author photo by Judy Somerville

ISBN 1-933132-19-1

Portions of this novel appeared in the Brooklyn Rail and Prague Literary Review.

Library of Congress Cataloging-in-Publication Data

Keller, Tsipi.

Retelling : a novel / Tsipi Keller.

p. cm.

ISBN-13: 978-1-933132-19-8

ISBN-10: 1-933132-19-1

1. New York (N.Y.)--Fiction. 2. Psychological fiction. I. Title.

PS3611.E43R48 2006

813'.6--dc22

2005028367

Printed in Canada

Yourself walked in the room tonight
and it wasn't you. Your way of
being here isn't another's way.
It's all the same somewhere maybe,
and the same old thing isn't you.
All the negatives in existence
don't change anything anyway.
Robert Creeley, *Away*

"...even the very clouds are doubted."
Gilbert Sorrentino, *Splendide Hotel*

AH, TO BE ALIVE, I THOUGHT. Not a small miracle, considering the events of the past few weeks and the growing uncertainty I sensed all around me. Breaking 'miracle' into its components I counted seven letters and three syllables, numbers which, momentarily at least, reassured me some, bearing, as I saw it, a favorable message. I was alone in my small neighborhood park, saturating my eyes with the lush sparkling green of young leaves; their exuberance cheered me and I sat there, drawing on their energy, when a light rain began to fall. Go home, I pondered, or wait for the drizzle to stop? Concentrating, I trained my gaze on the gray spaces between the drops and saw through the mist Elsbeth shimmering among the trees. She wore a severe and haunted expression on her face but her white strapless dress, her wispy blond hair, and her smooth bare shoulders softened the overall waif-like image. As always her beauty moved me deeply and my whole being swelled with gratitude for the gift of this luminous visitation. I wanted to stand up and call to her, yet I knew I mustn't move or even blink if I wanted this fleeting gossamer apparition to last a little longer. She had come to console me! the thought blazed through my mind, bringing self-pitying tears into my eyes and drowning the cherished image. A steady rain was falling, mingling with my tears, still I remained on my bench, willing Elsbeth to reappear. In the distance, the three fountains roared up to the sky, then came down in a loud greenish splash. How strange, I thought, that Elsbeth was "there" and I was "here." Walking to the gym early this morning I noticed a clan of pigeons peacefully squatting in a puddle from last night's rain. Light and shade trembled in the perfect circle of the sidewalk puddle, and as I stood and marveled at this still life a sudden urge to leave everything and go away somewhere overwhelmed me. Lately, a kind of permanent bubble encircled my middle, a heaviness of heart that encumbered my step and dampened my spirit, a disquieting apprehension about the future, about the meticulous day-ness of it. Maybe it was a cloud and not a bubble that followed me around and life, or my control over it, seemed to be slipping from my hands. My nerves were on edge and people, merely by existing, infuriated me. A stranger on the street who walked too slowly and blocked my way, or else a neighbor on my floor who let his door slam shut, causing my door to echo and vibrate. Why can't people be more *considerate?* I fumed. Why must they be so *noisy?* This inner aggression, carried to extremes, worried me, and I regretted and feared the vicious scenarios that sprang of their own accord in my head. For brief spells I experienced subtle reality shifts as if I existed, simultaneously, on two or more fault lines and could not always trust what I thought I saw or heard. I began to doubt small ordinary things, and before inserting my key in the lock I paused to make sure I was on the right floor, facing my own door. I listened raptly when I heard myself address inanimate objects, like a spoon or a fork, apologizing for having dropped them to the floor. During meals I suddenly opened my mouth and let out a long, hard burp, then blushed, flashing a discreet apologetic smile, begging the indulgence of imaginary guests. Everything seemed comic somehow, not quite real, or, if real, a bit off. Is it me, or is it me? I wondered. When I recalled something particularly annoying, like Mr. Daley's positively grotesque head, I paced the rooms and hurled curses at the walls, worrying about the neighbors listening from behind their doors, then calming myself with the thought that they didn't know I was alone. Still, I felt uncomfortable when I encountered them in the elevator, confirmed in my belief that people were wary of those of us who lived alone, just as those of us who lived alone were wary of other neighbors who lived alone, suspecting them of the same misdeeds and thoughts we knew ourselves capable of. Such moments of doubt were disconcerting, not to say debilitating, and I often caught myself wondering if I even knew who I was. Last night I tossed and turned in my queen-size bed, tormented by the belief that I was being punished and that the worst was yet to come. I tried to hold onto the thin veil of sleep, but Lydia kept creeping into my thoughts and I, helpless, considered the tyranny of friendship. Lydia used her sting sparingly and yet so effectively, just being around her sometimes was enough to make me question my own and Lydia's mental and emotional stability. She was an only child, as I was, and it occurred to me that we recognized in each other certain peculiarities which bound us like sisters and yet grated on our nerves whenever we met. During dinner last night she made one of her characteristically insensitive and blunt remarks about Elsbeth, and I, who should have known better, responded in kind. It all began when I suggested, ever so tentatively, that everything seemed tenuous to me, that the world "as we know it" was gripped in a downward spiral. Look around you, I said grandly, if emptily, waving my arm. At the slightest provocation people pounced on one another with an explosive ferocity that was both scary and fascinating to me. This inner tension,

I said, this aggression, could be, and sometimes was, alleviated when a stranger on the street smiled and shrugged, as if to say: "Go figure!" but most New Yorkers didn't bother any more. I smelled fear, I said. The collective fear of small animals trapped in a cage. And why—I asked her—why, in our mad pursuit of success and material comfort, were we so intolerant of those around us who after all were engaged in the same pursuit? As I was talking, Lydia's face took on a stony expression, an expression I knew well, and for a fleeting moment I considered stopping right there but, perhaps perversely, I insisted on my right to complete my "sermon," sweeping in its condemnations as it was. I didn't mean to spite her, I don't think, I was only trying to understand how people like Lydia could remain so earnestly complacent in face of the small yet alarming signs. Our world is falling apart, I said, and even before the words left my mouth I knew what Lydia was thinking. She was thinking that maybe *I* was falling apart, or that my world was falling apart, but not the world at large. The world of taxis and cell phones and urgent appointments, the world of rising markets and luxury items, in short, her world and the world of her colleagues would continue to exist in spite of weaklings like myself. After all, Lydia was in the thick of things, making tons of money selling condos and townhouses to the newly rich, whereas I was depleting my capital, "eating up" (her words) my inheritance, while trying to complete my dissertation. In Lydia's estimation I was behind the times, hopelessly old-fashioned in my aspirations, and she saw it as her burden to open my eyes and save me while there was still time. I was too passive, she said, and in her fervor basically discounted whatever I thought was significant in my life. Naturally, I was filled with such corrosive resentment toward her, I often decided never to call her again, but she was one of my oldest friends and, I knew, she did care for me in her own singular way. Additionally, when I listened to her tightly reasoned arguments and considered her impeccable makeup, her impeccably ironed clothes, I imagined her neat closets and felt a twitch of envy, wishing I had it in me to become as organized and sure about things as she was. She couldn't help it, I thought. She believed that success was our supreme duty and that money was the key. I believed she was simply in love with making money, even consumed, or maybe addicted: the more she made, the more she needed to make. She had been trying to convince me to sell my co-op and move into a new luxury condo with marble baths. My apartment, she argued, was old and much too large for just one person—why not sell it and get better value for my money? When I tried to tell her that the walls were dear to me because my mother had lived in and still permeated the rooms, she said that such devotion was both misplaced and sentimental, and that even my mother would want me to move on.

FOR BETTER OR FOR WORSE, I knew what she was thinking when I said that the world was falling apart, yet she didn't respond, not right away. She looked at me with her exotic almond-shaped eyes and continued to chew with her strong, picture-perfect teeth. Only later, while daintily dipping her spoon into her chocolate mousse, she said: "Your apocalyptic vision has nothing to do with reality and everything to do with Elsbeth. She was a bad influence, Sally. I tried to warn you but you wouldn't listen. I don't mean to sound heartless, but in a way you're lucky she's gone, she ruined your life." Lydia's brutal assessment of the situation hit me hard, setting off tiny explosions in my head; stunned, I watched her as my brain went about its work, sifting through the rubble of her words. I had to come up with a cutting response but couldn't think where and how to begin. "How dare you say such things to me?!" was one option, but I knew it wouldn't satisfy my need to retaliate. I also needed, urgently, to demolish her assertion that my life was a ruin. And yet, as often happened in such situations, I was too enraged to find just the right retort and so I attacked her instead, saying (perhaps in too loud a voice) that she was obnoxious and that her life, no matter how much money she made, was a waste and a sham. I also said that I didn't appreciate her sly insinuation that her vision of reality was truer and more valid than mine. More venom spilled out of me, although I can't recall its exact content, while Lydia blanched all over her makeup and cast a quick glance at the couple seated at the next table. The man and woman, approximately our age and very successful-looking, had obviously overheard, and delighted in, my little speech, which made everything even worse for Lydia who abhorred the disgrace of "public scenes." We paid our bill without saying another word, and each of us went her way, seething with indignation. Outside, I did try to make amends, for I regretted my outburst and felt sorry for Lydia whose face, when I sneaked a glance, revealed her distress. She was quite defenseless, really, even if she pretended always to know what was best. I reached for her and said, "Lydia," in a conciliatory tone, but she waved her arm in rejection, shot me a look full of hurt and walked away. And so all night, exhausted and victimized, I lay spread-eagle across the bed, opening myself up and wishing for calm to descend from above and smother all doubt like a soft soothing comforter. I hated conflict, any kind of conflict, and still it annoyed me that it was I, yet again, who had tried to patch things up, to no avail. Why do I even bother? I asked myself. Lydia, I concluded, was evil and passive-aggressive, and yet, at the same time, I couldn't help the sneaking suspicion that it was I who was evil and passive-aggressive. Nonetheless—I argued—even if I was evil and self-ish, at least I was willing to admit it! At least I questioned my motives and behavior, whereas Lydia, hardheaded and inflexible, never gave the matter another thought. In all likelihood, she was sleeping soundly, while I, as usual, was battling the deepest misgivings and regrets, trying to figure out why such trivial clashes took place in our universe at all. What ultimate purpose did they serve in the celestial scheme of cause and effect? Unless, of course, they

were subtle warning signs and it was up to us to rec-
ognize what we were being warned about.

WHEN I FINALLY LET GO OF LYDIA, or Lydia let
go of me, I continued to toss against the mangled
sheets, embroiled in a long, agonizing dream where I
couldn't find my keys, even though I looked for them
everywhere. In the dream it was Thanksgiving week
and there was nothing in the mail except for a musty
manila envelope from Nili and Ethan, containing a
crinkled plastic sheet with small bubbles on it, and a
cardboard drawing depicting a spectral yellow moon
on a black backdrop. In the bizarre way that dreams
are sometimes coherent, the yellow moon looked like
a drawing one of their children might have made.
Usually, even when flustered and distraught, I liked
myself better in the reality of dreams: I was sullen
and aloof, just as I used to be in my teens, acting out
my feelings instead of hiding behind a sociable
veneer. This realization led me to theorize that we
never really truly change, that the core personality
we develop in our teens remains with us forever and

emerges in the night when we dream. With a sigh I turned on my side and shut my eyes. The cardboard moon drifted away and for a brief magical respite I found myself walking among the stalls of the Farmers Market in Union Square, buying vegetables and fruit—an all-absorbing activity, devoid of malice and contention. But soon I was jolted to wakefulness again and sat up coughing in bed, filled with derision for my weak, smoking self. I worried about the coughing but couldn't imagine going on day after day, bereft of my sole and always reliable tranquilizing angels. Cigarettes allowed me to be alone with my thoughts, and even as I sat in bed coughing my guts out, I had a romantic vision of myself sitting at my desk near the window with a shot of whiskey and a cigarette, taking long satisfying drags and watching the tip glow in the ashen pre-dawn light. Cigarettes gave me something to do and kept me company when I needed it most, very much so these days when belligerence and hostility had become my habitual survival aids. On the whole, I was in good shape, radiating health and a sturdy physique, never mind what my periodontist in his soft, periodontal voice said yesterday when I came for a cleaning, warning me about nicotine and the damage it wrought. It thinned the blood in the tinniest vessels in my gums,

g decay and gum disease. It was never too
_ _id, to worry about such things, and need
he mention the stains that yellowed my teeth and
darkened my lungs? No, he needn't mention it, I
said, I knew all about it. Tobacco, I had read, caused
arteriosclerosis, ulcers, halitosis, and was the main
culprit when cancer proliferated along the "smoke
alley," namely, the lips, the tongue, the lining of the
mouth, the jaw, the esophagus, the windpipe, and
lastly the lungs. It was in Nazi Germany, I read further, where the connection between nicotine and cancer was first established and Hitler, a reformed heavy
smoker himself, stoked the fires of the anti-tobacco
and the anti-Jewish campaigns, blaming Jewish cap-
italism for the prevalence of smoking in Europe.

IT WAS A HOT DAY. EARLIER, one of my neighbors, an old man a little odd in manner and dress,
spoke to me in the elevator. "My mother," he said,
"has always hated the hot weather. The colder the
better she says, and she's a hundred years old, God

bless her, and three months. Her friends loved the hot weather, and now they're all dead, but she is still here, strong as an ox." He grinned, and I observed his gray toothless gums with mild revulsion. "That's wonderful," I said, waiting for the man to say more, perhaps reveal yet another tidbit about longevity, but he continued to grin, as if inviting me to speak, so I offered with a small, apologetic smile, "My mother died at fifty," and the man looked at me, then shuffled away from me and turned to face the door. I watched his back and for an eerie moment wondered if he'd addressed me at all. In the pool, pushing from the tiled edge with a practiced kick of my feet, I did the crawl in slow rhythmic strokes, luxuriating in the soft caressing feel of the water, and in the easy response of my muscles. My thin brown arms glistened in the sun that pierced through the octagonal skylight, and I imagined my mouth gaping like a fish's when I came up for air. I flipped over and did the back stroke, devising a way out for Lydia and myself. When we met or spoke again on the telephone, I would suggest that the two of us were viciously trapped in a blind corner of our own points of view, and the only thing to do was to forgive and forget. Lydia was stubborn, and in her long drawn face often reminded me of a mule. Yet at times Lydia did back off, and I for my part was willing to concede that when it came to Elsbeth I tolerated little or no criticism. Pleased with myself, I pretended to squint against the sun as I nodded at the man who had just taken the next lane. The two of us, it seemed, kept the same schedule, swimming a few mornings a week. He looked vaguely interesting and seemed vaguely interested in me. After the nod I gave him a grim smile that reflected my ambivalent feelings and my uncertainty as to whether or not I should give him the green light. Approaching middle age he was solidly built, reminding me of the men my mother used to date after my father divorced her. The fact that I might be interested in this man made me think that my mother and I had the same taste in men, that we attracted the same type of men. The attraction I felt for him, if attraction it was, was of a dark and twisted sort, nearly querulous in nature, feeding on shyness, pride and mistrust which, I imagined, I must have imbibed with my mother's milk. Thinking these thoughts I realized I was just about the age my mother was when these men came around the house to take her out. They looked ancient in my eyes, and therefore lewd and degenerate, and yet, I had since calculated, they couldn't have been more than forty years old. At the time I sullenly begrudged the men's hold over my mother, but had since felt nothing but the deepest sorrow for her, fervently hoping she had enjoyed her men and had good sex with them. At least that. A few moments of total abandon in a life so humiliatingly short and filled with regrets. What's the point of living, I thought, when the exit is so bitter? When your last moments on earth are so painful? "Are you a sad person?" someone approached and asked me at a party. I had a ready reply but I took a moment to think and then said (enigmatically, I hoped): "When I listen to beautiful music I am." I had an image of myself, dancing and crying: "Oh life, life!" The party was given by this woman named Julia, whom I had met only once or twice, and who was one of Elsbeth's many professional connections. It turned out to be what Elsbeth liked to call a DSP, a Desperado Sardine Procession, where the door was kept open and people in black came and went in a steady flow of cool ennui. Tara, Julia's roommate, kept shouting: "Who are these people?" and Julia laughed. They both looked quite pleased that so many had turned up for their "small soirée." As usual, the guys were loud and rowdy, while the women teetered on their high heels, straining to keep up. Some of them, the awkward ones, seemed lost, perhaps uncertain as to their right to be there at all. They had nervous hands and darting eyes, especially those with the very short skirts and somewhat heavy thighs. Every so often they flashed a smile that froze on their faces before fading away, and my heart ached for them and for myself. Why do women do the things they do? I wondered. I stood near the door, waiting for Elsbeth, and then, like a ray of sunshine, she appeared and swept me to the center of the room. Shaking with excitement I felt wanted and alive, knowing that all eyes were on us; Elsbeth, so tall, so blond, and so very slim, always stood out, and I blossomed in her shadow. She whispered in my ear, confiding she was wearing a corset she had just bought, an old-fashioned one like her mother used to wear, and I asked if she could breathe all right. "Sure," she said, "it's only around my belly to tuck in the fat." "You— fat?" I almost gagged with disbelief. "You know me," Elsbeth said, and I smiled. I loved Elsbeth. Whatever she said I drank with infinite zealous thirst. "They met last year," I reluctantly told the detective, "when Julia threw a party to celebrate the winter solstice." "The what?" the detective said, and I looked into his eyes. The guy was obtuse, maybe new on the job, and it irked me that a moron had been put in charge to investigate Elsbeth's death. He was young and his head was shaved skinhead style and a permanent scowl, it seemed, dominated his expression; this guy, I sensed, never gave his face a break. He either didn't hear me, or pretended not to have heard me, or had no clue as to what the solstice meant and why people would throw parties to celebrate it. He disliked me on sight, I could smell it, and I gloomily disliked him back but dutifully sat in the chair he had pointed to. They were interviewing all of Elsbeth's friends and, filling out a form, he asked for my office telephone number. When I said I didn't work in an office, I worked at home, he said in a haughty dismissive tone, "What type of work do you do at home?" "I'm writing my thesis," I said, a reply that clearly went over his head, for he mumbled something I didn't quite catch. "Excuse me, I couldn't hear you," I wanted to say, but decided it was wiser not to acknowledge his animosity. I considered lightening up the atmosphere by initiating small talk, maybe even get him to laugh, but I couldn't muster the necessary strength to surmount the wall of his resistance. To my dismay, I felt myself shrink and cower in his presence, not so much his presence as the authority of his position, the fact that he was on that side of the desk, and I was on this side of the desk, and the only thing to do was to cross my legs and lean back in my chair, simulating ease and composure. "It was also her birthday," I said, raising my voice just a notch. "Her thirtieth birthday." "Whose birthday?" the detective asked; it took effort on my part not to broadcast my impatience by rolling my eyes and re-crossing my legs—plainly, the guy wasn't listening, why was he wasting my time? "Julia's," I said. "The solstice and her birthday. Two birds in one." I grinned. Piqued and disappointed with my answers, the detective heaved a sigh, and I calmly perceived that I might enjoy ruffling him. "And then?" he asked. "And then Elsbeth arrived," I replied, sort of dreamily and with a touch of wonder. I left the somber detective at his desk and followed Elsbeth into the bedroom where she shed her leather jacket and hung it in Julia's closet rather than tossing it on the bed with all the other coats. "Middle-class germs," she said and laughed, so I pulled my jacket from the pile and hung it next to Elsbeth's in the closet. "She arrived alone, but left with Drew. She didn't have a boyfriend at the time," I explained, watching the detective rub an itch out of his nose. "She always had boyfriends," he stated/asked. "More or less," I confirmed even though I didn't appreciate the implication of his words. "She was very popular," I added. "Did you see them leave together? Elsbeth and Drew?" he asked and I shook my head. I didn't see them leave, but I did, all at once, notice Drew—tall and dark and with strong, slanting cheekbones. I had hoped that he would notice me, but then Elsbeth arrived and quite swiftly moved in on him; he didn't stand a chance, neither did I. In retrospect, it seemed fated that Elsbeth and Drew would cling to one another like two rhesus monkeys. On the other hand, had I and Drew stuck together, none of this would have happened. It was amazing, I thought, how events in our lives, down to the very smallest, happened exactly as they did, and yet, at every given moment, they could have taken an altogether different path. "You didn't see them leave?" The detective made a notation in his notebook. "No." I looked at his bowed head. The top had an odd shape to it—straight as an ironing board except for a small freakish dent in the center—and even though phrenology had lost favor long ago, I thought it might still be relevant in some cases. "But someone later said they had left together." "Who said?" "I don't remember," I said, then wondered why what had happened at that party six months ago was so important to the detective. Maybe he thought I was lying, but then, why would he? He hardly seemed interested, scribbling in his notebook, and I itched to know whether he wrote down exactly what I said word for word, or just scribbled his interpretation of what he thought he heard me say. His spelling, I guessed, was primitive. "It's all sort of fuzzy in my head," I said apologetically, eliciting no response. Evidently, in his mind all civilians were aliens. Elsbeth knew this about cops, she used to say they were dead inside. "You and the victim," he finally resumed, picking up then putting down a sheet of paper. "You were close friends." "Yes." I flinched at the term "victim" so casually applied to Elsbeth. Elsbeth was dead, but there was drama and violent beauty in the way she went. This was something the detective, his empty arrogance notwithstanding, would never understand. Elsbeth and I, like Siamese twins, were joined at the navel, we took care of each other, and now Elsbeth was gone, and I was abandoned all over again. "Yes," I said. "We were close, we had a special code." "What do you mean?" the detective asked, all at once fully awake. "The things we said to one another," I continued, pleased that I got his attention. "We never repeated them to others. It was just between the two of us." "What things?" "Like—" I tried to remember but couldn't, not with the detective's eyes scanning me. "I mean, general things, like the meaning of life, stuff like that, we always tried to figure out how our brains worked. We had made a pact to tell each other everything and be each other's reality check. We used to try to remember how a day began and then ended."

ELSBETH IN HER TIGHT T-SHIRTS and the rings in her nipples. Where was she now? In Heaven? Her rings showed through the nearly translucent fabric of her shirts, and it appeared as though she had two sets of small, hard nipples on each breast, one on top of the other. It certainly seemed, I considered telling the detective, that women, daily, hourly, died at the hands of men. Even little girls weren't safe. Women—always looking for contact, for a soul mate. When they tried to act as carefree as men, they got hurt. At the time of her death Elsbeth and Drew had been dating for several months, much longer in fact than I had thought they would, and so I got it into my head that the two of them had felt sorry for one another, and this feeling sorry had kept them together. "I hate my life," Elsbeth complained, "I'm a walking disaster." "No, you're not," I protested, "don't talk like that." Elsbeth smiled. "I'm useless, Sally, I produce nothing of value. I wish I were poor and had a simple life." We were lounging on her bed, sipping tequilas and trying to decide where to go. I knew what she meant, but I also knew that as soon as we went out and sat somewhere where there were people and noise she'd be herself again. "I saw the super's wife schlep two heavy bags to the laundry room, so I offered to help, I actually insisted, and the poor woman let me carry one of the bags, all the while apologizing to me, while I wanted to apologize to *her* for my useless life. She stuffed dolls into pillowcases and sealed them and threw the bundle in the wash, and when I asked what she was doing, she said that you had to put the dolls in the pillowcase, or they would tear. My mother never taught me things like that." "Your mother," I said, "never did the laundry." "True," Elsbeth said, "like mother like daughter. Useless." "You may go now," said the detective, somewhat abruptly, pushing his pad aside and rising to his feet. The brute was even taller than I thought. A Neanderthal. I can do this, I said mutely and stood up. I had feared the interview, but now that it was over, I felt I had handled him, and myself, pretty well. "I'm afraid I wasn't much help," I said, managing a smile that put a strain on my cheeks. The window behind him was streaked with dust; the old airconditioner resumed grinding the air. He was moving files on his desk, aimlessly it seemed, as I stood there, fixed on his fingernails. They were pale and thin, lifeless, as if unfinished and crudely embedded in his flesh, and I remembered that I associated such nails with shifty men of weak character. "Well, *thank you,*" I enunciated, but if he got my sardonic intent, which was doubtful, he hid it well. The moron just looked at me and said, "We'll call you if we need you." His name was Mr. Frank Daley, and I was determined to blot him and his empty hostility from my mind. Summer was around the corner, and I thought I might get away for a little while, leave everything behind and go traveling. Somewhere far and peaceful, where I would be a stranger, a nonentity. A change of scenery, I hoped, would alter the landscape in my head and enable me to go back to my life, finish my dissertation and then maybe engage in something as normal as looking for a job. It was good, I thought, to change one's landscape, the frame of one's thoughts. All I had to do was pick up the phone and book a flight, but somehow, lacking the necessary focus, I didn't, not for a while. Days came and went. I let my hair grow, I cut it short. I went to the gym where I greeted the regulars and was greeted by them. On the StairMaster, I got a whiff of someone's sweat, which instantly transported me back to adolescent sex, not sex exactly but the animalistic scent of the boys I was infatuated with and whose closeness thrilled me in new and mysterious ways. All around me burly men grunted and moaned as they lifted heavy weights, and when a moan was particularly soft, I glanced at the man and imagined him during sex. What if I took him into my bed? the thought wickedly slid into my mind. Would he feel compassion for me, would he offer me asylum, or would he use my body as if doing me a favor and then discard me? Day by day time was running out, even if my body performed responsibly according to long-established laws. Now that Elsbeth was dead I adopted a new approach to life, endeavoring to bring myself out of myself. It seemed an impossible task and yet, if I persevered, I could perhaps unbox myself and set new parameters. I studied street behavior, the way women carried themselves when they thought they went unobserved, just another harried face in the crowd. Eagerly I watched for the personality lurking behind the face, endlessly marveling that each woman I scrutinized was different from the next. There was something airy and unfathomable about them, a sagacity that suggested a life experience that I felt I lacked. Like a predator I watched for the budding breasts on young girls' chests, girls whose faces would soon gain in carnality and settle into womanhood. My brain was active, I was doing research, trying to decode *femininity*, and breasts and their conspicuous, manifold manifestations were of particular interest. Larger than life, breasts filled up precious retail space on billboards, posters, screens, and flashed in neon in Times Square. Nipples, I discovered, were often erect, pointing every which way, having to do, I surmised, with the hasty manner the breast was stuffed into the bra; little did women know the kind of mischief their nipples practiced on them. I didn't discriminate, I watched all women, beautiful and otherwise, aware that the homeliest of women could boast a pair of exquisite roundness under her shirt. Large bouncy breasts were in vogue again and as if overnight a whole breastology campaign had been unleashed, promising to "enhance" the female breast "the natural way" with ointments and herbs; wonder bras from *Victoria's Secret* also helped. I myself did not participate in the orgy, delighting instead in my small pointy breasts and old-fashioned bras. Women, I wrote, internalized sex and it showed on their faces. Even women who went for long periods without sex exuded mysterious depths. I pondered the hidden wisdom of creation, the fact that women were born with a hymen, a useless membrane until you thought of it as a symbolic barrier fraught with psychological overtones. In Greek mythology, I noted, Hymen was the god of marriage. Women, I wrote, harbored the same violent impulses as men but, lacking the physical frame to support it, suffered from an early age bouts of impotent rage, which conflicted with, and yet informed, their sexual urges. I rehearsed words like: Vulva. Cunt. Pussy. I cherished their irascible yet docile impudence and rolled them on my tongue, while men on the street stared at my crotch through the protective spandex of my pink shorts. A babe, ah, little pussy, their eyes glittered. Hispanics and dark-skinned men, and only rarely whites. Whites, somehow, were more reserved, possibly uptight. When men stared at me, I understood in a flash how they could work themselves up to the required frenzy to gang-rape a woman. I felt meek under their gaze, and hated myself for feeling meek. They sneaked glances or smiled affectionately at my triangle, each according to his own weakness, while I pretended not to notice. And I continued to wear my tight shorts. Ever so innocently, daringly, women courted danger. I could have worn longer T-shirts

that came down to my thighs, but I didn't. I attracted the gaze of men and, through their lusting eyes,
felt a renewed, revitalized affection, even reverence,
for my sex. At times, though, feeling too exposed, I
did take off my baseball cap and let it dangle from
my hand, covering the guilty part. How much of her
anatomy could a woman cover? Or should she?
Some days random strangers on the street, men and
women alike, would smile at me in greeting, and I
assumed it was the open, perhaps naive, expression
on my face that had invited their goodwill. In the
sauna room I lay down on a bench and did my
stretching exercises, squeezing and releasing my
vaginal and rectal muscles, initiating tiny sensations
of proximate pleasure. The clitoris, I had read, was a
bundle of eight thousand nerve fibers. I had one, too,
lying hidden in the fleshy folds of my vagina. In bed
in the early morning, in a semi-awake state, I experienced a terrible aching desire for the male form, for
a hardness I could press against and feel in my
womb. A taut erect penis bursting out of its skin
stood in my field of vision: I wanted to lick it. If
only—I thought, lost and soaring in "perverted self-
love," in the words of revolutionary Voltaire. My
head was filled with academic verbiage, and I wondered if it was the Pillar of Civilization I wanted to

embrace, or the personification of God's might on earth, namely, Man. I was confused. In semi-awake states I experienced powerful yearnings that delighted and saddened me. Elsbeth hovered in a corner, and the man, I secretly admit, was as dark and ominous as Drew, yet considerate, taming his nature and tempo to suit mine. In the evenings I went to the park and watched the men play chess late into the night. They punched their little clocks and moved the pieces with amazing speed. Nothing else seemed to matter, and I shook my head in silent admiration for their obsessive dedication, for the single-mindedness they devoted to a game. Their obsession had become mine, and I found myself going there night after night. I was the only female among them, perhaps a voyeur with hidden designs, but no one seemed to pay me any special mind. In the mornings, on the same bench, I ate grapes and drank coffee while gazing at the oak and sycamore trees and waking up to the day. After the grapes and coffee, I lit a cigarette and blew clouds of smoke up to the blue sky. Nearby, young mothers discussed diapers, and toddlers, bearing sleepy expressions on their small faces, observed the world from their strollers. Once in a while one of them would wail in a plaintive, nasal voice, and his peers would join. The grapes I brought from home, the coffee I bought in a coffee shop near the entrance to the park. "Black coffee?" the Hispanic owner working the counter greeted me every morning, and I would nod, or say, "Yes, thanks," feeling guilty. He used to ask me: "Anything else?" before putting the coffee in a brown paperbag, but eventually he stopped. Maybe that's why I felt guilty, ordering only coffee. The coffee shop wasn't particularly clean or inviting, but people from the neighborhood always sat at the counter and at the few tables along the mirrored wall, eating breakfast or lunch. One day, having to pee, I asked the Hispanic's permission to use the bathroom, then climbed down the narrow steps to the basement where I sat on the toilet and parsed two lines of poetry carved in the chipped white paint on the wooden door: *now i sit here all broken hearted/ came to shit but only farted.*

A NEW MOTHER ARRIVED and sat down a little apart from the others. She unbuttoned her shirt and breastfed her baby while tapping a number on her cell phone. People, I thought, no longer knew how to be quiet, how to concentrate on one thing alone. Sweetly oblivious, the baby continued feeding on the breast, one small finger tucked in its mouth, manipulating the nipple according to its sucking needs. I was eternally awestruck by the nonchalant ease with which mothers seemed to accept the miracle they held in their arms; if I had a baby, I would be anxiously watching its every move. Momentarily, the sun hid behind the clouds, and everything around me turned gray and soothingly calm. "We had stimulating conversations," I said to the detective. "I remember one afternoon when we took a walk to Battery Park and sat on the grass facing the water and Elsbeth talked. She never tried to *cohere* or make sense in any ordinary way, but I understood her all the same. You get up in the morning, she said, and bend over the sink and brush your teeth, vaguely aware that it's a weekday and that you're a small particle of dust in the traffic of life. The sun is already high in the sky, your rooms are flooded with nourishing light, and you stand there naked, the scent of sleep seeping out of your pores as you gawk at your own furniture. You know you're young and that the world is waiting, and you feel a sudden uplift, a sudden need to go out and make your presence known. Things like that, that's how she talked,

but only with me." The detective nodded, waiting.
Even he, it seemed, understood at last. I stretched
out my legs on the stone chess table and pulled my
arms behind my back. As usual, I had my books with
me, but couldn't bring myself to take them out of my
bag and do my work. It was so much easier to lean
back and empty my head. A large, mustachioed man
went past, pushing twins in a stroller, and I felt my
facial muscles relax into a smile. The twins stretched
their tiny legs on the rail of the stroller and looked
very cozy and smug, with a delicious air of conspir-
acy about them. I wanted to call to the man and say
something nice, something about the twins, but
nothing concrete came to mind. I noticed an old,
gray-haired lady a few benches away, holding up a
pale blue parasol against the sky even though she
was sitting in the shade. She had a dignified profile
and I watched her for a while, making a composite
image of the gray of the hair, the blue of the parasol,
and the green of the leaves. Finally, I brought my feet
down with a sigh and reached for my books. I read
about the Futurists at the turn of the century, about
Marinetti who wrote in 1909: "We stand on the last
promontory of the centuries! We will glorify war—
the world's only hygiene—militarism, patriotism, the
destructive gesture of freedom-bringers, beautiful

ideas worth dying for, and scorn for women." This was something I could show Lydia, if she ever condescended to talk to me again. I went home and fixed lunch, then turned on the TV and followed the stock market ticker as it zoomed by at the bottom of the screen. All the indices were down and the various experts and analysts proffered advice, discussing the market as if it were a living thing, assigning to it mythical powers as to an oracle. In the afternoon, just as I was about to leave and go to the library, Lydia called. "I'm sorry that I upset you," she began, and I, enormously relieved, was quick to reciprocate, "That's all right, I'm glad you called." "I'm not good at hiding my feelings," Lydia said, "but I never liked Elsbeth." And she never liked you, I thought darkly, but said nothing. "I tried to warn you," Lydia continued, "but you wouldn't listen." "Warn me about what?" I asked. "She was cold and calculating, she knew the gestures of love and friendship, knew how to make people believe what they wanted to believe. You were so blinded by her glamour, or by what you thought was glamour, you didn't see how deranged she was. And devious, too. She was a disaster waiting to happen. I even told the police." "You told them what?" I felt myself grow pale and numb. "That I'm actually not surprised that she drove someone to the point where killing her seemed the only choice." "You mean Drew," I suggested. "No, I mean *someone*. We don't know that it was Drew. Who knows who else she was involved with. But, I won't say anymore, she was your friend, and I respect that." I went to the library but couldn't concentrate, and in the park the next morning I still felt out of sorts, and yet, in some part of my brain, inspired as well: hope flickered at the edge of confusion. It was a new day, the sun reappeared, warming my ankles and toes; my skin glowed. A man who made his living collecting recyclables and discarded books from the buildings around the park said hello. I said, Hi. I liked him, I liked his pleasant demeanor. He wore his usual dungarees and white T-shirt, and everything about him—his calm face, his smooth brown skin, his smiling brown eyes—suggested a sound equilibrium: I imagined him with a wife and a couple of small children. Once, sorting out the books he had just collected, he handed me a 1950 book of Edvard Munch's reproductions. "Take it," he said. "It's a valuable book." He couldn't sell it, he explained, because the cover was torn. I thanked him and put the book on my shelf, even though I worried about worms. "What a perfect day," he now said, and I agreed. The sun went behind the clouds and

the wind picked up. In the gym, someone had said
something about rain. A tall, narrow-waisted
woman walked past, her huge bosom packed into a
tight mauve T-shirt, the letters L-O-V-E emblazoned
in bold red ink across her chest. An invitation, I
thought, wondering if the breasts were real or
pumped with silicone. On my own I was tough and
self-reliant, but around people I felt myself pull back,
especially now that Elsbeth was dead. Now that
Elsbeth was dead, life rushed at me in its myriad
frailties, and I sensed uncertainty and disaster in the
air. Everything glimmered with a menace, and I
remembered I hadn't written a will. Nor could I
name a beneficiary, now that Elsbeth was dead.
There was blood everywhere, good blood gone to
waste, spilling from Elsbeth's veins onto the white-
bleached floorboards, the white walls, soaking the
sheets and mattress. Drama and violence in the way
she went. Two gardeners in blue overalls stood a few
feet away, chatting loudly in a foreign tongue. The
one with the very large belly held a shovel in his hand
and I had a vision of him digging a grave, like in that
awful movie I saw years ago where a guy, as if spell-
bound, sets out to find his girlfriend who had vanished without a trace. He leaves his life behind and
crisscrosses the highways of Europe, only to end up

getting buried alive in a grave he himself digs. The libido never dies, a 74-year-old woman assured me. The woman, a neighbor, was in hospital, recovering from a rare muscular disorder, and when I came to visit I brought her a Chinese hand puzzle and an everything bagel with cream cheese, as she had asked. I sat and watched the cheese ooze from the bagel as she bit into it, and my stomach turned. The notion of food in hospitals nauseated me, reminded as I was of the hospice where my mother had spent the last month of her life, and where I vainly tried to get some food into her mouth. Ice cream was the only thing she would swallow, and I fed it to her, she the child and I the mother, the mother hoping that the child would communicate her pleasure, but the child's eyes remained dim. My neighbor finished the bagel, and I wheeled her out of the hospital to a coffee shop across the street where we sat and sipped iced coffee. She asked if I had a boyfriend, and I said, No. I said I had a few girlfriends, but no boyfriend, and she said that the libido never dies and that my day would come, that I would meet the man who was right for me. One of the guards patrolling the park drove by in his small vehicle. Politely, he asked me to take my feet off the table. "I don't mean to bother you," he added, and I smiled, swiftly bringing down my feet. "I know," I said, meaning that I knew I wasn't supposed to put my feet on the table. He was cute, saluting me and smiling before driving off. How sweet, I thought. Calm reigned in my heart. On the night Elsbeth died, the three of us had gone out to dinner. At one point, Drew got upset over something, and he left the restaurant without any warning. I wanted to run after him to bring him back, but Elsbeth stopped me and made me sit down. Inwardly, I trembled with possibilities. "He can't go far," Elsbeth said, a strange smile on her firm, carved lips where a beautiful permanent sadness resided. "What do you mean?" I asked. "I'm pregnant," she said, smirking in a way that made me uneasy because Elsbeth, for a split second, looked like a different person, someone much older and conniving, even cheap. "You can't be," I blurted, and Elsbeth laughed. "Why not?" she asked, mocking me with her eyes. I reached and touched her belly. "It doesn't show yet, silly." She pushed my hand, perhaps a little harder than she had intended. I removed my hand and put it in my lap, taking time to adjust. It came as a shock that Elsbeth was pregnant and that she was keeping the child. "You hardly know each other," I finally said, thinking that maybe this was the reason Drew had acted peculiar all night, more so than usual. "Does he even want the child? And what about your modelling?" I asked, alarmed. Elsbeth shrugged. "I can do maternity for a while, I won't be pregnant forever. It might be a blessing in disguise, maybe I'll change careers, maybe I'll go to Hollywood and shoot a picture." "What picture?" I asked, bewildered. "I don't know, we'll see." None of it made sense, but I let it go. "We've had so much wine tonight," I cautioned. "You must quit smoking and drinking." "I will," Elsbeth said. "But I feel so strong and powerful, nothing could harm my baby. My hormones are rooting for me." I nodded absent-mindedly, imagining hormones busy at work, cushioning Elsbeth's womb. Elsbeth's womb, so elastic and vibrant, preparing for the inevitable. The detectives never brought it up, and neither did I. Even Elsbeth's mother, when she came to town, never mentioned it. Her first grandchild, from her eldest— and once pure and obedient—child. Another perfect baby-daughter in a line of breeding beauties. Maybe, in the end, it had all been a mistake, maybe Elsbeth had miscalculated. Today, for the first time, I noticed testicles on a squirrel. They seemed enlarged, swollen, perhaps a growth, perhaps not testicles at all. He climbed up the tree and I lost him in the top branches. I don't know why I stood up that night, prepared to run after Drew to bring him back to the table. Maybe I felt guilty for sitting there between them, maybe I whispered in Elsbeth's ear and he felt excluded. He was four years younger than us and always acted as one who had to prove something. Still, the more I observed him, the more inscrutable he seemed. He never tried to put me at ease or make me feel like I belonged with them. "He doesn't like me," I said, and Elsbeth shrugged. "It's not you," she said. "He's leaving on a trip tomorrow, and I don't want him to go." "Why not?" I asked. "Because," Elsbeth said. Elsbeth, people agreed, was cold and withdrawn, and yet I clung to her as if wishing to be there when the transformation occurred. I used to imagine Elsbeth and Drew doing it, Elsbeth faking it in her usual fashion, and Drew, somber and efficient, driving himself in hard furious strokes. Maybe a baby would do it, I thought that night. The next day, I called Elsbeth, but Elsbeth never called back, a fact that registered in my mind for a few days as something incomplete, but not as a cause for alarm. Maybe she went with him on that trip, I thought. Elsbeth and Sally, everybody said. They're inseparable. Always Elsbeth and Sally, never Sally and Elsbeth. Some people shine, I reasoned, and Elsbeth shone. Bathed in coldness, she stood apart, exuding a shimmer which protected her from unwelcome intruders. Acute jealousy was never a thing between us, even if Elsbeth did guard her territory. That fatal night, Elsbeth talked at length about having left a brand new cardigan in a restaurant. When she went back the next day to claim it, it wasn't there. She loved the cardigan so much, she ran to the store, hoping to buy another just like it, but they had sold out. And so, Elsbeth said, she had wasted a whole day, trying to retrieve a cardigan. "How tiresome it is to think that you've wasted time, as if time and what you did with it mattered in the long run." Waste and futility, I thought. One day a woman gets all worked up over a lost cardigan, and the next day she is gone, dead forever. A woman like Elsbeth, whose incarnations populated my thoughts and dreams. Elsbeth of the beautiful skin, the intelligent smile, the long, willowy limbs. Elsbeth the sorceress, straightforward and yet enigmatic. Elsbeth of the thousand voices, always troubled, never a tranquil moment of truce. Always I sat and listened as Elsbeth, almost out of breath, tried to put one and one together. Periodically, she would embark on binges of self-immolation, telling me she was no good and rotten to the core, and I sat and marveled that life for some was so painful—a continuous, unbroken chain of agony—and I burned to know what was the source of such deep-seated, absolute despair. Was it pure self-indulgence? Was it genetic? Cultural? Was I so immune I didn't even get it? On such occasions she wouldn't allow me, nor would I try very hard, to offer my vacuous refutations. Usually, we were both a little tired, maybe a little drunk, and we understood it was excess she needed to expunge, very much, I thought, like in voodoo ceremonials. I remembered the old adage: "Live every moment as if it were your last," but never remembered to heed its wisdom. At home, I now resolved, I would listen to the new CD I had recently bought. African music from Algeria or Nigeria, said the sales clerk at the new *Virgin* store. On the way home I'd stop at the post office to pick up a package—there was a notice in my mailbox. Small errands, conscientiously executed, made up the fabric of my life. Like well-placed markers dotted along the way they pointed my days in the direction they eventually took. Small errands and random chats, now more random than ever. "Nothing left to mythologize." Elsbeth downed her wine and filled her glass. "In my next life I'm going to find me a nice little fireman and live happily ever after. No hangups, no career considerations, just a nice quiet life in the suburbs somewhere. I'm tired of the city, I need to get out." "Why a fireman?" I asked, suppressing an urge to look at Drew. "Because, my dear Sally, firemen are different. Tough on the outside and sweet and tender on the inside, they know what a family is all about, they understand loyalty, they're men of honor in the old-fashioned way. Other men don't come even close." She lit a cigarette, and I sat there, fascinated, waiting to see how Drew would react. "You're a walking cliché," he said, perhaps prompted by my silence. "Anything in a uniform turns you on." "Wrong," Elsbeth said. "I hate cops and men in suits, but fire-men, I don't know what it is about them, they're drop-dead gorgeous." I chortled nervously and looked at Drew. Such comments, I knew, drove him nuts. I remembered Debenedetti's *Eight Jews,* and his famous line about a Nazi soldier's uniform, which, airtight like a zipper, locked in the man's body and, above all, his mind. Drew, I mused, would look good in a uniform, Nazi or otherwise. He gave Elsbeth a look as if to say he found it incredible that anyone could be so dense, and Elsbeth, noticing his look, went on, digging deeper. "I love how they hang out the windows of their truck and look at us like they were tourists in their own hometown. Cops never do that, they're like blank, like dead inside. For them we're pests, we're all potential criminals."

ALL THE THINGS THAT ELSBETH used to say now intersected in my head. I wasn't much use, said the detective during our second interview, and it stung me a little when he said that. He said, in effect, that I was useless, which surprised me. If anyone could profess to having known Elsbeth, as much as such a claim were possible, it was surely me. So I brooded about the language the detective had chosen and wondered what kind of use he had hoped to make of me. I wondered if he had meant to offend me, or perhaps shock me out of my apparent lethargy and get me to say things. He was rough in his manner, intimidating, and I imagined him practicing in front of the mirror like De Niro in *Taxi Driver*. His face was pockmarked and a deep scar ran down his left cheek; I wondered if he got the scar before or after he joined the force. Thanks to him I now disliked all cops, I who used to feel safe when I saw a police officer on a street corner, a police officer who would protect me with his life if duty called. Now I wasn't so convinced that he would protect me with his life. More likely, in a crisis situation, he'd pull out his gun and shoot hysterically, indiscriminately, killing me in the process. He seemed angry, the detective, as if the whole business with Elsbeth were a bother he hoped to sweep under the rug, just in time for lunch. "Elsbeth's father," I said, "also committed suicide." "Suicide?" The detective raised his brows. "This was no suicide," he said slowly, scrutinizing me. "I know," I said, momentarily disoriented. "So why did you say suicide?" he asked, scribbling something on his notepad. What is he writing? A new fear seized me. I ached to be outside, on my bench in the park, where I didn't have to think so hard about Elsbeth and about what had happened that night. "It's just something that came to my mind," I said. Elsbeth's mother was back in town, this time to clear out Elsbeth's apartment. She couldn't bear it, she said, the thought of Elsbeth's apartment just sitting there, empty, gathering dust. She invited me to have dinner with her in an exclusive restaurant near her midtown hotel. "To think that she lay in her blood for days," Mrs. Williams murmured. "The superintendent still has nightmares, such a sweet man, and very kind." "Yes," I said, thinking of his wife and her laundry techniques. The mother's eyes were dry, which did and did not surprise me. Sitting across from her, I watched her openly, maybe brazenly, trying to find Elsbeth in the mother's face, trying to find the mother in the woman's face. Strong-willed women, I believed, gave birth to daughters, and yet, it was hard to imagine how such a refined, slender lady had deigned to give birth at all. She was anti-Semitic, Elsbeth had said, and yet she married a Jew and bore him three daughters; did she know I was Jewish, I wondered. "My mother"—Elsbeth laughed—"wanting to address one of us, would, in her haste and distraction, call out our names in the descending order we came out of her belly: Elsbeth, Millie, Sandy. I always came first." Elsbeth smiled smugly, and I, who had always wished for a brother or a sister, nodded. Like the detective, Mrs. Williams was annoyed with Elsbeth's timing: there were so many things she had to attend to at home, and now this. She hated Elsbeth's apartment, she hated the East Village. "I told her it was unsafe," Mrs. Williams said, "to live in a tenement." "It's not a tenement," I said, "it's a co-op." "It's a tenement fancying itself a co-op. There are no decent co-ops in the East Village." Mrs. Williams shook her head. "I never understood why Elsbeth insisted on those dreadful nipple rings, or whatever you call them." Elsbeth was always difficult, the mother concluded, her beautiful green eyes wandering away from me. She seemed absent-minded, a trait I associated with the superrich who relied on servants and so developed an amnesia for details. She had been a widow for a year now, and I wondered if she allowed suitors into her life. "We were best friends," I reminded the mother. "I know, honey," Mrs. Williams said. She still looked young, and expensive, in her soft, blond curls, in her cream linen suit and pearls, attractive in her narrow shoulders and admirable posture. She had long, expressive hands and, I remembered, she played the piano. She put tiny morsels of food in her mouth and chewed with her lips shut tight, barely moving her jaw, and I imagined her in her kitchen in the wee hours of the night, wolfing down a greasy sandwich or a candy bar. When the bill came, Mrs. Williams, waving off my attempt to pay, brought out her platinum card. Her gesture said: Don't be ridiculous. Or, presumptuous. Many consumers, I reflected, held a platinum card, but somehow, in Mrs. Williams's elegant hand, it seemed more weighty. I wanted to like her, I wanted her to hug me so we could both cry, so I could compensate for her loss, but it was clear that she would discourage, even repel, any attempt at physical contact. So I resented her, I resented her superior, aloof manner, her great wealth, which allowed her to disregard the feelings of others. Are you grieving? I wanted to ask, but held my tongue. I recalled my own mother, small and insubstantial on her hospice bed, as the head doctor and I stood at the foot of the bed and watched her sleep. Even though my mother lay in a hospice, I didn't believe she was going to die. I invested all my powers in her health, confident that she would dupe the doctors and would soon recover. I believed in miracles, in willing them to happen. I asked the doctor a question, and he, before I could stop him, reached down with the nail of his thumb and scraped the sole of her foot. My mother shivered all over and, waking, let out a cry of anguish, glaring at the doctor with hurt, fearful eyes. If I had known he would do such a thing, I wouldn't have asked him the question, it wasn't that important; I, too, glared at the rude doctor, hating him for disturbing my mother's sleep just to prove a point. Every time I grimaced with pain, like when I bumped my big toe against the metal base of the coffee table and stood there, absorbing the shock, a peculiar physical sensation would overtake me and I would feel as though my mother had entered my body and became me, or that I became her, down to the last, minutest physical and mental detail. It seemed logical, I thought, that the two of us should connect at moments of distress. It was ironic, Mrs. Williams said, that Elsbeth died so soon, eleven months to be precise, after her father, Mr. Williams, had committed suicide. I thought the choice of "ironic" strange, so I asked,

"Why ironic?" and Mrs. Williams shrugged. "Maybe not ironic," she said, "maybe just oddly coincidental." "That's what I told the detective," I said, "she loved her father very much." Mrs. Williams looked at me. "Nonsense," she said, "he was a weak man." She stood up, it was time to kiss goodbye. She straightened out the narrow skirt of her suit and offered her cheek. How cool and composed she is, I thought, but maybe troubled as well. You couldn't tell about a person just from looking at them. "People think my mother is strong," Elsbeth used to say, "but she is frightened and insecure. It's the only thing I can say in her defense. Once, pulling into our driveway, she ran over Spot, our dog. The poor thing had run out to greet her, and she killed him." "She didn't mean to," I said, and Elsbeth's eyes darkened. I thought she was going to cry, but she didn't. "Who knows what she meant," she said. Elsbeth had been her mother's favorite, and yet Elsbeth couldn't stomach her. She wanted to love her mother, but some deep disaffection, and a hardness that came from pride, didn't allow it. Her sisters, whom she couldn't stand, only exacerbated the situation: Elsbeth felt a strong and instinctive aversion to the three of them, which, in the end, hurt her more than it did them, for she was the one out in the cold.

Being disconnected, *alienated*, from your own family, I thought, was the worst predicament, inflicting the deepest wounds. An hour later, at home, I was hungry again, for I had hardly dared touch my food, sitting across from ethereal Mrs. Williams. I made a cheese omelet and devoured it, standing at the kitchen counter and stuffing myself, feeling a little lonely, *miserly,* in my pleasure. Sharing food with another, Elsbeth said that night, was an intimate act. She tilted her head and smiled that curious smile of hers, a smile she attempted when wishing to appear sarcastic, or mysterious. Drew narrowed his eyes and focused his gaze on her as one seeking a meaning beyond the words, a meaning that Elsbeth presumably had intended for him alone, but I soon realized it was nothing of the kind, as Drew was far from understanding. "Oh, yeah?" he said testily. "What's so intimate about food?" Elsbeth and I exchanged a quick, knowing glance, and I wondered what she was doing with a guy who didn't understand something so basic. "I'm not talking about food, I'm talking about mouths," Elsbeth said. "I'd never eat with a guy on a first date." "You're full of it," Drew sneered, "you ate with me." "No I didn't," Elsbeth said. "Not on our first date." Sitting between them I felt a little sorry for Drew, trying so hard to assert his dominance as the only male at the table. He couldn't help himself, I thought. He was the type who only made matters worse. We had ordered oysters and a large antipasto, and by the time we were ready for the main course, we had finished the bottle of wine and ordered another. From the start there had been tension at the table, and I sat there wondering why Elsbeth had insisted that I join them. At times she clung to me, which made me feel needed and yet imposed upon, especially if Drew were to be present. But I loved Elsbeth, there was nothing I wouldn't do for her, even if it meant putting up with Drew and his condescending, petulant manner. Some people developed into masterworks; Elsbeth was one, naturally. Elsbeth, cold in manner but fundamentally, if reservedly, generous. "You're a dangerous woman," Elsbeth said one night, and my flesh now crawled with the memory of it. It was an absurd accusation, uncalled for, and the shame and injury of the incident still lingered. We were walking somewhere and I, talking about my dissertation, threw my hand to the side and inadvertently hit her in the stomach. It was a hot, humid night and Elsbeth, it turned out later, wasn't even listening, she was off in her own world. I hit her and she screamed and we both stopped in the middle of the street. Elsbeth was shocked by the "assault" as she called it, I was shocked by the scream. Passersby stared at us as Elsbeth verbally assaulted me. "Why did you do that?" she hollered, and I, terrified, tried to explain, to apologize. "You're a dangerous woman," Elsbeth said, and even though a few minutes later we continued as before, the phrase kept reverberating in my head. I thought Elsbeth's choice of words bizarre, not only the "dangerous" part but the "woman" part too. I had an image of the two of us as two bitter, old females quarrelling on the street. Elsbeth's beautiful face was white and distorted with rage, and I can only imagine the shock and terror that had registered on mine. She was taller than me and probably stronger and for a moment I thought she was going to hit me. If she hit me, I knew, I wouldn't defend myself. If I was dangerous, I thought, I was dangerous first and foremost to myself. The squirrel with the swollen testicles climbed down the tree. I threw him a peanut, then another, and watched as he sat on his haunches and cracked the shell. He looked like a tiny human, greedy and efficient when it came to his food. When he saw that no more peanuts were coming, he wobbled away. Maybe he's diseased, I thought. Maybe prostate cancer. Both my parents died young, barely making it to fifty. Their deaths were gruesome and yet, in a way, because so young, glamorously tragic. My father died of prostate cancer, my mother of ovarian cancer. No one knew this about my parents, except for Elsbeth; I had been too embarrassed to admit to such messy afflictions in my family. When asked, I invented a heart attack for my dashing father, and a stroke for my mother. The outcome, after all, remained the same: I was orphaned at eighteen. It was telling, I feared, that both my parents' reproductive organs were cursed, and I often wondered about the psyche such an unhealthy union had wrought. They should never have gotten married, I should never have been born.

I FELT AN IRRITATION ON my right shoulder and tapped my skin. Something awoke in me. A new sense of awareness overtook me, even as I struggled with the need for clear definitions. Everything turned crisp, colors became more vivid, green became my magic domain. The air hung heavy, hot and steamy, and whatever breeze there was before was now stilled. Microscopic insects flitted about, small ants climbed on the bench. A very round man walked past, puffing on a cigarette. His breath came quick and shallow, and I watched him, thinking: This man is killing himself. Last night I summoned my courage and played chess with one of the regulars, an old timer who wore a white straw hat. I expected to lose, and I did. Boys and men played here every night, but never a female; as far as I knew it, I was the first. "I haven't played in years," I warned the old man who had invited me to play since all the other players were already engaged in a game. I wasn't a worthy opponent, and I worried that he would be bored, wasting his time with me. But he didn't finish me off quite as fast as I thought he would. I even had the sense that I could have beaten him had I not been so timid and so ready for defeat. These men, who have read all the books, were programmed to play by the rules, which, I thought, should give me an advantage precisely because I didn't know and didn't play by the rules. But I couldn't be sure: for all I knew, they were so far ahead of me, I couldn't even begin to fathom the distance between us. Most of them were pudgy and carried in their bodies the evidence of a sedentary, long-term marriage. Each of these men, it suddenly struck me, mounted a woman who opened her legs for him. They dropped their pants and mounted their women as a matter of course. Briefly, this thought thrilled me, then I refocused my attention on the board. Every night I listened to their banter and quickly caught on to the technical/military terms they seemed so fond of: "open fire," "deep penetration," "block the driveway." I loved the way they shook their heads, repeating, "problem, problem," when they saw a threat develop, a threat I didn't even suspect, and the way they mumbled, "weakness around the King," or, "take take take," or, "run run run," or, "attack attack attack." When they laughed about something that took place on the board I joined in the general mirth even though I wasn't sure what the joke was all about. "Oh baby, baby, is this a friendly game?" one of the players, a regular, asked rhetorically. "Supposed to be, supposed to be," the men on the sidelines responded in a chorus, "but don't listen to advice." It was the Fourth of July weekend, unbearably hot and humid, and the sunscreen lotion felt sticky on my arms and shoulders. I was sitting in the shade, eating grapes and sipping black coffee: this was a new kind of breakfast for me since summer began. From season to season I re-improvised my diet—that was what aging was all about, I mused: perfecting one's diet for health and wholesomeness. Alfalfa sprouts and tofu which were favorites with Elsbeth now featured regularly on my shopping list. Now that Elsbeth was dead it was up to me to keep myself in shape. Now that Elsbeth was dead. Consecrated to God, dead at twenty-eight. We had plans for the Fourth of July weekend, we always spent it together, but the plans had died with Elsbeth. Now I, too, feared Death. I'm too young to think about death, I thought, and yet it pursued me, I felt *It* following my steps, watching me with a thousand eyes. I saw peril and open warfare everywhere, and crossed the street like a much older person would. Even when I had the right of way I was careful and hesitant: one careless, absent-minded step, and you were gone. Drivers, blinded by rage, didn't even see you. They were kings of the road and you, in your smallness, didn't count for more than a cockroach. We were becoming more and more frantic, frenetic—when and how will it all end? I asked when I witnessed yet another murderous exchange between driver and pedestrian. It was the end of the millennium, and fear and anger, the cheapest commodities, were the common denominator, available to all. How I envied those who went to church every morning! It would be nice, I thought, to start each day with a prayer. Routine, I hoped, would save me, even if Elsbeth despised routine. "My life," she said, "is a hopscotch variation." "How so?" I was intrigued. "The lines are drawn but I avoid the squares." I nodded, visualizing the image Elsbeth had depicted so vividly. "You're so whimsical," I said, and Elsbeth laughed. Elsbeth, who loved alfalfa sprouts in her salads because they reminded her of little spermatozoa heads. I pulled my hair tight and gathered it into a short ponytail. A sudden breeze shook the trees, bringing temporary relief. Half a year had already gone by with the usual speed. A woman carrying groceries yelled at her teenage son who walked at her side, his head bowed. In the restaurant, Elsbeth and I were merrily laughing when Drew pulled a marble out of his pocket and began to roll it back and forth across the table. We stopped laughing and watched the marble, as if mesmerized. It was small and shiny and it changed colors, from green to blue, from blue to green, as it rolled on the table. How smooth it looks, I thought, wanting to reach for it but it belonged to Drew so I didn't dare. "What are you doing?" Elsbeth finally asked, and the thought crossed my mind that too often women let the man take center stage. Women, I reflected, always sought approval, a means to subdue their male companion. What got Drew so upset that night? Somehow I had missed it, but how was I to know it would be important? The squirrel with the swollen testicles lay on the ground, stretched out on his belly as if about to expire. I watched him with interest; I'd never noticed a squirrel behaving this way. Perhaps he was trying to cool himself off or, I thought, he must be diseased. Even his tail, I noted when he wobbled away, was stringy and not as bushy as a normal squirrel's tail. He was definitely diseased, I decided, suddenly feeling uneasy, even anxious. Emotions coursed through me like meteors. The top branches swayed in the warm breeze, leaves rustled noisily. Maybe it's the heat, I thought, putting one grape in my mouth, then another. Plastic bottles were strewn on the grass, evidence of last night's celebrations. I had watched the fireworks on my small TV and nervously bit my nails throughout the spectacle. I watched the celebrities—the effervescent stars of the new and recent—parade their toothy, ready-made smiles as they waved a slender arm at their adoring crowd. Celebrities! Imagining all the fun they surely had I begrudged them their spotlight, their privileged lifestyles, yet consoled myself with the thought that they had to continually struggle to hold onto their fame, to keep up with what went for success in their circle; in the end, they, too, had to go home to their problems. It was all a matter of degree:

no life was sheltered, no one was perfectly happy for long. A black man walked by, carrying groceries. A red-bearded man, coming from the other direction, also carried groceries. Today, a day of an extended holiday weekend, men were sent to the store for yet more food. We are a wasteful nation, people said, and went to the store for more canned and packaged goods. A shaved-headed guy with a stud in his ear sat down on a bench a few feet away. He took out a pack of Parliaments and lit one. I put on my sunglasses, regretting not having worn my pink shorts. The three fountains in the distance aimed higher and higher up to the trees, offering a visual cooling effect. My right shin had begun to swell when a mosquito or some other insect came in the night and stung me. The infected area was red and warm and hard to the touch, and I worried about poison in my blood. Upon waking, I noticed a disgusting yellow blister at the top of the red mound and considered pricking it with a needle, but the prospect of some yellowish substance oozing out stopped me. I worried about poison and was further upset by the thought that such a small event as a sting took precedence and festered in my mind. And yet, better that it remain a small event rather than a serious infection. I also worried about the detectives and the investigation, all the while delaying a decision on whether or not I should consult with a lawyer. Certain kinds of decisions, indecisions, clouded my thinking, and even though I repeatedly told myself to be brave, to be patient, to put things in perspective, I kept failing at the task, so the question arose: Who in fact was in charge? I touched the blister, sitting like a golden dome atop the mound of corrupted skin, hoping that the poison was now out of my blood and concentrated in the dome of yellow pus. My gaze shifted and I contemplated my toes, thinking it was time to shave my legs. The guy with the earring was clean-shaven. He ignored me, or seemed to, or maybe he didn't ignore me, maybe he hadn't noticed me at all. Life was a series of missed opportunities and aborted attempts. Maybe he was shy, earring and all. I sat in the shade, but here and there bits of sunshine came in through the leaves and pricked my skin. A woman with large droopy breasts and blue flip-flops strolled by. She seemed calm and self-possessed and she smiled at me. I smiled back, realizing that absorbed in my thoughts I often stared at people, and they, assuming I was looking at them, smiled in response. Maybe, I thought, it wasn't as important as all that to figure things out. Maybe leaning too close to things distorted my view. The sycamore trees stood

still and serene, a fat pigeon with a purple neck wad-
dled near. The heat was unbearable, people moved
cautiously, as if dazed by the burden of it all. "Every
once in a while," Elsbeth said, "I have a moment of
clarity, I suddenly see and understand it all, deep
down to the lightning core at the center. It lasts only
a moment but it feels like an eternity, like this is the
way we were meant to see and understand the world.
But soon it is gone and all I'm left with are these
fleeting moments, a glimpse, before I sink back into
drabness. Maybe progress is nothing but a mirage."
I nodded, remembering Gertrude Stein who had said
that sugar was not a vegetable, yet I didn't offer it as
a tidbit of enlightened erudition, I was content to
just look at Elsbeth's face. The more I looked the
hungrier I became, unwilling to interrupt the flow of
my ruminative gaze. The more I looked, Elsbeth's
features seemed to shift and change. Elsbeth's features changed and shifted, yet the harmony of her
face remained steady, reducing me to a hypnotic
state. Harmony, I thought, bred intelligence, or was
it the other way around? I needed to understand how
I loved Elsbeth and what that love meant. Love and
loathe, I mused, began the same, then went their
divergent ways. No emotions were constant, I
reminded myself, but now that she was dead there

were no hurdles, I could love her freely. I had known flashes of emotion, moments I was flushed with pure delight. Occasionally, like Elsbeth, I experienced moments of clarity when I felt that a certain profundity was accessible to me, that some fundamental secret would be revealed if I concentrated long enough. But as soon as I began to grope for formulations to capture whatever I thought I understood, the feeling vanished and I concluded that such flashes of profound understanding were purely mechanical, caused by certain, perhaps accidental, synaptic clashes. Profundity, I recalled reading somewhere, never clarified the world, but clarity looked more profoundly into its depths. Maybe that was what Elsbeth was trying to put into words. "We talked about things," I told the detective, "important things." "What things?" he asked, but I couldn't remember, not right then. His oddly shaped, shaved head rattled me. "Did you discuss suicide?" he asked. I was in his office again, answering his pointless questions. "We discussed her father and his suicide," I said. "She couldn't understand why he would do a thing like that and leave her behind, but she also admired him for taking matters into his own hands. She mourned him for a long time, she even went to temple to pray for his soul." The phone gave out a shrill ring, and for a brief moment both Mr. Daley and I were focused on the same thing. He reached to pick it up and it stopped ringing; I stifled a groan. "From dust to dust," I said softly. "From dust to dust?" he repeated, still focused on the phone. "For dust thou art, and unto dust shalt thou return," I quoted the Bible for him, putting a stress on the *thou*. "That's what the rabbi said before the open grave. Elsbeth loved the phrase so much, she would repeat it every once in a while just for the sound of it. It became like a mantra." "You went to the funeral?" Mr. Daley asked, ignoring the mantra connotation. "Yes," I said. "She wanted me there, so I flew home with her." This, it was evident, surprised him, even if he tried to hide it. Encouraged, I continued. "He was Jewish, you see, and Jews are put in the ground without a coffin. Mrs. Williams wanted to bury him in a coffin, but he had specified in his will: No coffin. She married him for his money and now it's all hers, or that's what Elsbeth said." "You sure know a lot," the detective said, stumping me; I felt my cheeks burn. "Talking about money," he said. "Elsbeth gave you money, didn't she?" "She did not," I said. "I never took money from her. If anything, I gave her money." "Is that so?" Daley frowned. "Are you saying she was destitute?" "I'm

saying that sometimes she didn't have cash on her."
"We know," he continued as if I hadn't spoken, "that she picked up the tab when you went out." "Who told you such nonsense?" I was incensed. "Sometimes she picked up the tab, sometimes I did. We weren't petty and calculating with each other." "It was Drew, actually," said the detective. "He told us." "Drew." I spat the name. "He's the one to talk! I never took money from her, maybe he did. Drew is a liar. Elsbeth told me he'd lie through his teeth, he'd say anything to save his skin, Elsbeth told me that." "Oh, she did? Elsbeth said that?" "Yes, she did," I said, realizing, too late, that he had made me tell a lie. "And you remember that? Your memory ain't fuzzy anymore?" He was driving me crazy with his sing-song voice. "My memory is fuzzy about that one night only." "Conveniently," said Mr. Daley. "We were drinking," I said. "I'm telling you, Drew is a crook. You'd better talk to him rather than waste your time with me." "We find you very helpful," said the detective. "It's a sure thing. Sooner or later most people in most situations dig themselves deeper and deeper into a hole."

I TOOK A DEEP BREATH, delighting in the crisp, new day. It was early morning, and the park was quiet. Even the squirrels and pigeons were sleeping in, reluctant to leave their dens. All at once the wind picked up and it began to drizzle. I opened my umbrella, feeling special, "artistic," for braving the weather. What a strange summer, I thought. More rain than sunshine. I was alone with the trees, and I saw a black-and-white photograph of myself, a lone figure sitting at a chess table under the cover of a black umbrella. I was chilled to the bones, I realized, shivering in my T-shirt, and I told myself to go home, imagining how nice it would feel to peel off my T-shirt and put on something soft and warm, like the flannel top of my winter pajamas. The air grew thicker, charged with the gray wetness of drops, and I felt the tickling thrill of danger: I'd catch the death of me, sitting like this in the rain. I thought of Elsbeth, of how she had appeared to me out of the mist. Greedily, she followed me from the beyond, possibly jealous of my physical existence in the world, possibly seeking to harm me. Primitive me! If they existed at all, people in the beyond had no business, nor power, among the living. Besides, why would Elsbeth want to harm me? If anything, she'd protect me, like I would her—we were still twin kindred souls. This realization freed my spirit, and I allowed the possibility that things might be better than they seemed. Good things come to those who wait; the trajectory of my fantasies pointed that way. Naturally, I inclined toward logic and continuity— my friends in time of trouble and dread. The rain stopped, I put away my umbrella. Some distance away, a guard in his vehicle sat and watched me, probably out of boredom. I wiped the table and took out my notebooks, contemplating the burning issue of technology and the human race. Technology, advancing faster than science, may be the end of us all—a few lone voices warned and were generally ignored. Homelessness had acquired new faces, and frenzied comfort had reached ever shrieking heights. On the street, more and more people talked to themselves, until you realized they held a cell phone, or had wires coming out of their ears. Even so, they still talked to themselves, even if they didn't know it. In the gym this one man, a black, began to notice me— I saw it in his eyes the moment it happened. We had been saying hello for months, just a friendly exchange between two people seeing one another in the gym, but one morning last week he suddenly *saw* me. He zoomed in on me as if discovering something he hadn't noticed before, and I now wondered what it might have been. "We're so lucky to have this park," a man said, walking past. "Absolutely," I agreed enthusiastically. The day had begun, people emerged from their homes. The sun appeared from behind the clouds, and I put on my sunglasses, allowing the world to turn softer, rounder at the edges. I felt peaceful, determined not to make plans, not to let the future muddy my thinking. The leaves, still hardy and green, rustled in the wind. If I cut things in half they would last longer, I thought. I embraced routine, yet routine made me question what the point of it all was. I sat still, recalling that my period was due. Even in times of distress my body, as if mocking me, functioned like clockwork. "When you buy shoes," the salesman told me at the store, "make sure they're soft and bendable. That's the secret to comfortable shoes." The salesman spoke persuasively and I looked into his eyes, telling myself to listen. I listened, though not with much interest, and yet it stuck. Now that Elsbeth was dead I became a nomad of the city and like a person possessed walked the streets and bought things, mostly odds and ends, as well as a couple of deep pots in which to cook thick nourishing soups when winter came. Entering the apartment carrying my loot, I felt like a mogul's wife after a shopping spree. I'd scissor off the tags and put everything away: in the kitchen cabinets, the bathroom drawers, the closets. I liked things to be in their logical place so I could easily and instantly find what I was looking for. I had plenty of storage space and no matter how much I bought there always seemed to be room for more. After my mother died, I cleared the apartment, then refurbished it in a sparse, monastic style. "Nothing lives here but you," Elsbeth said, impressed. "Why don't you get a couple of plants or something?" "I prefer it this way," I said. If only Elsbeth could see me now, arriving home with all my new purchases. The woman in the coffee shop, I now realized, had put milk in my coffee. The Hispanic man who usually served me wasn't there this morning. He knew I took my coffee black, and as soon as he saw me come in the door, he'd start pouring. He worked fast and reveled in it, coordinating his movements for optimum speed. He was aware, I thought, of my admiration, especially when he snapped open the folded paperbag with one hand and pressed down the lid on the steaming cup with the other. This morning I was very specific with the woman, even emphatic: "Black coffee to go, please." And the woman went ahead and put milk in it. Maybe even cream, for the coffee had a dense, heavy taste to it. I was upset. I considered going back to complain, but then I was sure to spill it and burn my fingers, now that I had torn open the lid. Why work myself into a state? The woman made a mistake, it happens, I should be more forgiving. Maybe she was distracted when I placed my order. Maybe she had a sick child at home. Tomorrow, if I see her behind the counter, I may say something, but with a smile; better keep a pleasant disposition, achieve better results. "You catch more flies with honey," a city official once told me over the telephone, and I had absorbed the lesson. Coffee with milk was not the same as black, but it shouldn't ruin one's morning, unless one insisted. And I had decided not to insist. Instead, I resolved, I would sit and enjoy, listening to the sound of the mowing machines as the caretakers in the park went about their daily chores. And once I had made the decision it was easy to just sit there, enjoying the sound of the mowing machines, inhaling the astringent scent of the freshly mowed grass. So I sat and enjoyed the freedom to sit there. Time stood still, even if the sun changed position in the sky. My next-door neighbor, a Chilean, had taken to telling me about problems he was having with his wife. As we stood talking outside the building, I concentrated on his darkish lips. They were too thick, I thought, and yet I tried to imagine having his mouth pressing against mine. "But she is very nice," I said about the wife, meaning it. I liked him too, he was always pleasant and friendly, I liked to discuss stock options with him, so I stood and listened as he complained about his wife. She was stupid, he said with a passion that bordered on the comical. Instead of learning new ways and adapting to her new country, in her mentality she remained Chilean, while he, he had become a real New Yorker. "Can't you settle your differences?" I asked with some anguish, and the Chilean shook his head. That same night I saw the wife come home with a shopping cart loaded with groceries. She looked tired, even haggard, and I felt sorry for her, having to shop and cook for a husband who bad-mouthed her to the neighbors. In spite of myself, I felt a little superior, a certain haughtiness, now that I knew something about her which she didn't know I knew. Given the fact that I could have easily gone up to her and divulged all that her husband had said, I thought it incredible that the Chilean would open up and reveal himself as he did. He too worked from home, while his wife, every morning, went to work. Maybe, I thought, he was looking to initiate a dis-creet, day-time fling. An overweight, pasty-looking woman landed heavily on the next bench; soon, I thought, she would talk to me. I lit a cigarette, and she muttered, "Shit," under her breath and moved to another bench, farther away from me. "Good riddance," I thought, yet my feelings were hurt. That a stranger could hurt me vexed me even more. When I got home, my phone was ringing—Lydia was calling on her cell phone from a cab. We had a bad connection, but I understood her to say that she had begun remodeling her apartment and that she would invite me to come over to see all the improvements as soon as all the work had been done. "Maybe I should renovate too," I thought out loud. My apartment felt stale, possibly affecting my state of mind; maybe it would be good for me to change a few things. Even old folk took the time and care to renovate, I ruminated, and yet, it seemed futile to exchange one sofa for another, change the color of the walls. "It's not such a bad idea," Lydia said. "I'll help you." The two of us had settled our foolish argument and we were friendly again. Lydia agreed she was insensitive when she said what she said about Elsbeth having ruined my life, and I agreed it was time I turned a leaf and thought more constructively about the future. "You worshipped the ground she walked on," Lydia said, and I agreed that I had worshipped the ground Elsbeth walked on. "She only had to say it, and you would do it," Lydia said, and I concurred. A few years back I toyed with the idea of joining the police force, or a public service of some sort: I wanted to be in a position to help people. Assisting a stranger in an emergency, I told Elsbeth, would fulfill me. "We all experience such moments when we become helpless and let ourselves be sucked into the vortex of standard operating procedures," I elaborated with some extravagance, trying to emulate the language of my idol. "Get out of here." Elsbeth laughed, and so, effectively, killed the idea. "Frankly, I can't see you wearing a stupid uniform. Are you bored?" "No," I said, "I'm not bored." "So why would you want a job?" "I don't want a job, I want to be useful." "What's your hurry, sunshine?" Elsbeth hugged me. "Besides, you're useful to me, I need you. You can't desert me now, can you?" I thought about it. "Well." I smiled uncertainly. "I guess not." "Was Drew physical, did he beat her up?" asked the detective, and I, instinctively, shook my head. Suddenly, I was in demand, they seemed to value me: Mr. Daley had sought me out, leaving two polite messages on my answering machine, and now, again, we sat face to face in his stuffy office. The sun shone brightly in my eyes, blurring my vision of him. "I don't think so," I said, "but I can't say for sure."

I chose my words carefully. Maybe he did beat her up or smack her around a couple of times like men do sometimes. Men like Mr. Daley. "But," I added earnestly, sincerely, "I just can't see Elsbeth lasting in such a relationship." "What do you mean, lasting?" he asked. "I mean, putting up with it," I stated the obvious. "Why not?" he asked. "Because," I said, getting annoyed with his probing, microscopic insistence. "She had too much pride, and self-worth. No one could get away with treating her like that, not even Drew." "What do you mean, not even Drew?" the detective asked. "She loved him," I said, "so she did let him get away with stuff." "Like what?" "Like," I said, "he would say things, he would insult her in public, and she'd let him." "Let him, how?" the detective asked. "Sort of like, she'd ignore him. Maybe later, in private, she'd say something, I don't know, but when there were people around she'd just ignore him." "Didn't it upset him even more? That she ignored him?" "I don't know," I said, "it was hard to tell with Drew, his eyes were always sort of dull, like foggy. He looked cruel to me, like he was capable of cruelty." I was pleased with my description of Drew, my nemesis. "Did he use drugs?" the detective asked, and I considered: how come I never thought about it before? Drew, drugged out of his mind, stabs Elsbeth numerous times. The drug angle might be the clue, clearing the mystery of a motive. "Maybe," I said, "he might have." "What about Elsbeth?" the detective said. "Did she abuse drugs?" "No," I said, "no drugs. Maybe grass once in a while if a joint came her way in a party situation." "A party situation," the detective repeated. "And you?" he asked as I knew he would. "The same," I said, and the detective didn't pursue it. "So, you think he looked cruel," the detective said, and I nodded. "Maybe violent?" he asked. "Possibly," I confirmed, relieved that the presumptuous detective, at last, was on the right track. I marveled at the broad buttocks of a woman as she went past, pushing a tall, brand new carriage and a brand new baby in it. The day was hot. Things jelled in my mind, then receded. I searched for clarity, for the kind of confidence that would make people stop and listen, taken with every word. A leaf blew to my face and stuck to my forehead. If I perceived presumptuousness in others, why couldn't I see it in myself? Or, if I saw it, why not admit it? "You found a cool spot," a man said to me and I smiled even though it wasn't really cool. I was nice and sweet and accommodating in my responses. I didn't actually feel "nice," and I wondered if others were sincerely nice or if, like me, merely polite, acting out a friendliness they did not feel. Still, it was good that people acted friendly, whether they felt it or not, and it was good for me to spend time outdoors, my skin sucked the moisture from the air. Two middle-aged men I knew from the park stopped for a chat near my bench. "Go figure," one of them said. "That's the way it is," said the other. They were regulars, they lived nearby, and often came to the chess tables in the evening. Lately, the one with the red bandanna tied around his forehead, driving by on his bike, would stop at my bench and talk to me about his ex-wives. At first I resented the intrusion, but as I began to pay attention I found him amusing and a welcome distraction; the more I listened, the more I liked the way he expressed himself. "I don't know what happens to women. They're good in the beginning then they break down, like an old car," he said one morning, and I laughed. His name was Tom and he was a retired detective. The other man, comfortably married, was a history professor, and he too sometimes stopped at my bench for a chat. "Life is like a restaurant," Tom now said to the professor. "It's all presentation." I half-listened, knowing I could join their conversation if and when I desired. Tom, I noticed, had gained a little weight. He was taller than the professor, and they stood facing each other, their bellies nearly touching. "You need new blood in the police force," Tom said. "The streets are not what they used to be. I could write a daily column about the things that bug me." Tom heaved his chest and waved his arms as he talked. The professor, a more subdued conversationalist, bowed his gray head and looked down to the ground. "*The Age of Voltaire*, the best book I ever read," said the professor, addressing me. Tom, too, turned my way, and the wind carried the alcohol from his breath. It must be the alcohol, I thought. The crazy look in his eyes, intense, and yet unfocused. It never occurred to me before, but how simple now that I saw it. Tom said something about Mike Tyson, and the history professor gravely agreed. Idly, I moved my hand up and down my arm, seeing myself in first or second grade, sitting in a hot and stuffy classroom, stealthily spitting into the crook of my elbow and rubbing out the fine lines of dirt that had collected there. Tom was still talking about a friend of his, now making big bucks on Wall Street, but who had been a loser all his life. "He was not plugged into the real world. He was always a day late and a dollar short," Tom said and his audience, namely me and the history professor, laughed. I saw them everywhere, men striking conversations with an ease I coveted. Growing up, I had ingested the precept that only women had the secret to meaningful intercourse, but now I found that I favored listening to men. They were more direct, their language had vigor, their subject-matter varied. "You never know," Tom continued. "One day you're a nothing, you're dirt, you make a couple of bucks and you're God, people *defer* to you. I'm a Brooklyn boy, I go up and talk to people. I grew up blue collar, I didn't know I was smart until I went into the army. I didn't achieve any presence until I was in my thirties." Maybe I should talk to Tom, I thought. Maybe he could help me. "See you later." Tom took off on his bike. The professor looked at his watch and sighed. I liked him, he was shy and very well mannered. "I guess I'll get moving, too," he said, and I nodded. The air smelled sweet, I almost had a taste of it. Later, on my way to the river, I noticed a large, orderly group of tourists walk through the U.N. gates; on impulse, I followed behind, donning my tourist-eyes. A bronze statue of a revolver stood proudly in the plaza, right next to all the flags, and even though its nozzle was coiled into a knot, I found it odd that they had opted to exhibit a revolver rather than, for example, an olive branch. There was a huge statue of a man on a gal- loping horse, like the kind you'd see in Europe in a central square. The horse, I noted, had discreet balls but no penis. Third-World wildlife was featured in the magnificent form of a life-size elephant with a life-size penis that hung, thick and massive, below its stomach. When I first noticed the elephant from a distance, I thought it was sexless, perhaps female, but as I walked toward it I noticed the penis, which, I imagined, was the reason why the elephant had been relegated to the far end of the complex, hidden away in the bushes. And yet the penis, I thought, fit in well with the overall covert aggression of the place, an aggression that perhaps only I inferred, for the group of tourists had remained congregated on the main plaza, busily shooting their videos and cameras. I found a bench in the shade and sat down to rest. In a small, fenced-off area children played and shrieked. They were part of the setup and the message seemed to be: All over the planet, children are children. Same as soldiers. Two Asian women appeared on the path, pushing strollers. I exchanged a smile with one of them whose toddler howled until she picked him up and propped him on her hip. I wondered if the two women were the wives of diplomats or maids of the wives of diplomats. A church bell rang out and I looked at my watch. Earlier, my stomach grumbled and a sharp hunger gnawed at me but, as often happened, if I waited long enough, my hunger dissolved into the rest of me and disappeared. When Elsbeth was hungry she had to eat right away. It usually annoyed me, especially if we were in the middle of something and had to drop everything and rush to a café or restaurant just because she was hungry. "What if you were in the camps?" I wanted to ask but didn't, knowing I'd be going too far. Over the years I perfected my sense of orphanhood and taught myself not to want, but to accept; I had become skilled at depriving myself and considered it an accomplishment. Intermittently, I worried about the constant dialogue that ran in a loop in my head, and yet the philosophical tradition of talking to oneself went back thousands of years and had its moments of glory. When Pyrrho was asked why he talked to himself, he said he was training to become useful. Socrates, too, dragged himself barefoot through the streets of Athens and talked to himself. Today's gurus talked on TV. The future, I heard Greenspan say only a few days ago, was sometimes too opaque. The market went up a little after Greenspan spoke, following days of declines. That the future was opaque everybody understood, so they bought back the stocks, now at bargain levels. It was a game the big investors played with the small investors; I stayed put. An elegant, thin-legged bird hurried past, carrying a long twig in her bill. She stopped and swiftly picked a strip of paper and flew up into the tree. Evidently, it was nest-building time and I wished I had something as useful and necessary to absorb me. I imagined the cozy nest up in the tree and took a deep wistful breath. The birds that came here, did they choose to live in the city, rather than in the countryside? Did they have personality quirks which dictated their uptown or downtown predilections? In Mr. Daley's office, an idea popped into my head and before I could stop myself I was talking— it was before I knew better. "Elsbeth loved her father very much," I said, and Mr. Daley gave me a tired look. "So?" "Well," I said, "when he died, she lost something. You say it wasn't a suicide, but I think it's possible she wanted to die too." The detective wrote furiously in his pad, and I suddenly remembered where I was. "You mean, like a mercy killing?" he asked, barely masking his excitement. "No," I said with horror, realizing I might be, unwittingly, leading them directly to me. "I just thought...I just remembered that she was very unhappy. That's why she taunted Drew the way she did." "She confided in you, she told you what was on her mind." Mr. Daley waited, so I nodded that yes, Elsbeth confided in me.

"And she was unhappy, very unhappy, as you just said," he said, treading cautiously. "Yes," again I had to confirm. "Bear with me." Mr. Daley smiled a rare smile. "I'm trying to get it straight. You believe that someone, someone she loved and trusted, wished to do the right thing by her and help her out, right?" "I don't know," I said. I was shaking all over and, to camouflage my shaking, I threw my arms around me. "It's cold in here," I put a whine in my voice. "I'll turn off the air." Mr. Daley swiveled in his chair and hit the switch. "So." He turned to me. "So that's how it happened." "No," I cried, "I don't know how it happened, it was just a thought." At the U.N. I sat and gazed at the river; a pleasant breeze cooled my skin. A boat sailed by, named *walk-about*, which reminded me of that Australian actor who said "mate" a lot and made beer commercials. I listened to the cacophony of birds: when one group stopped, another began. A guard gave a few piercing whistles and shouted at people to get off the grass. He was a little hysterical, I thought, but, on the other hand, it gave him something to do, something to get excited about, if only for a short while. The guard began to walk back and forth along the path where I sat, and I felt myself tense up. He was a large man, and the paraphernalia that hung from his belt bounced and clanked with every step. A black revolver sat high on his waist in its black leather holster. Then he left and disappeared for good, I thought, until I noticed him again, spying on me from behind the fence of the children's playground. After a while he got bored again and went away. A homeless lady arrived with her bags and cart and settled down on a bench. She was as thin as a rail and appeared to be in her thirties although it was hard to tell for she hid her face under a wide-brimmed straw hat. Her long brown hair came down to her waist and fell forward every time she bent over and searched the various bags in her cart. She moved stuff from one bag to another, putting order into things very much like I did at home, and, I imagined, drawing the same sense of satisfaction when everything was just where she wanted it to be. When she was done, she sat and examined her nails. The woman, I noted, went for color: her socks were red, her bags were pink, and a pink sheet of paper with a hand-written message on it hung from a string she had tied around her neck. Similar slips of paper were pinned to her cart, and I recalled Lowell's poem, "Jonathan Edwards in Western Massachusetts," wondering if these written messages were messages from God. I thought I might go up to her and read the messages, perhaps even start a conversation but, just then, as if sensing my intentions, she began to talk in a sharp angry voice, and I reconsidered. A few days ago, a homeless man gave me one of his possessions. I was sitting on my bench, trying to light a cigarette with a dying lighter, and he called, walking toward me, waving a book of matches in his hand. I hesitated a moment, then stood up and went to meet him half way. "Keep it," he said and for a brief moment, as I looked at the matches and then at the man's face, I had the distinct feeling that a whole world, the man's alien world, was contained in the book of matches, and that he was offering it to me. When I sat down again and lit my cigarette, I noticed two telephone numbers the man had written inside the cover in a strong, assured hand. There were only a few matches left and the booklet was crumpled as if it had sat in his pocket for many days. He didn't ask for a cigarette, so I assumed he wasn't a smoker, unless he felt too bashful to ask for an even exchange: a cigarette for his matches. At home, I put the booklet in my kitchen drawer to keep as a memento.

SOMEONE WAS SHOUTING OBSCENITIES on the other side of the fountains. If I had to, I asked, would I run for my life? The sting mark on my shin had gone down considerably but the whole area was now a blue and yellow stain. Last night the dome had burst, smearing my living-room couch, and it now stood reddish and mushy to the touch with a little hole in the center. Lydia, who knew practical things, said that I should have rubbed tobacco on my skin as soon as I was stung to get the poison out. Next time I'll know, I said. I lit a cigarette and watched the brown tobacco turn into black and white ash. An old Asian woman arrived and sat down on a bench. She dropped her slippers and began massaging her feet. The skin of her legs was very white, and her feet and toes were pink, like a baby's. A leaf fell on the bench, and I noticed the tapestry of yellow leaves already on the ground. It was time, I thought, to dye my hair. Elsbeth hated it when my dark roots showed. Elsbeth, naturally, was a natural blonde; I became one. People asked if becoming a blonde changed my personality and I said that if I became a blonde it was only because I had it in me to become one. A man in a blue shirt stood up from his bench and sat on another; I wondered what made him get up and move. Yesterday, walking down Fifth Avenue, I contentedly noted that the signs: "Don't even THINK of parking here," still amused me. A sudden breeze made me shudder with relief, reminding me it was going to be yet another scorching day. People were advised to stay indoors and avoid alcoholic beverages. The radio urged listeners to make sure their elderly friends and relatives turned on their airconditioners. In a dream I went swimming with friends. We swam naked. We were in some resort or camp where the men and women were segregated by a fence and I stole timid glances at the men. I sat on my bench, alive as can be, and yet Elsbeth, my twin, was dead. Alive resonated with open-ended possibilities, whereas dead died echoless on your tongue. I saw Elsbeth and Drew, so tall and aloof, so dazzling and far removed not even envy could touch them. A couple made in heaven, people said and stared, never having enough. Elsbeth regularly had men attached to her—she looked even more complete with a man at her side—whereas I contented myself just longing for them. Periodically in dreams my longing went beyond longing, and I woke moaning, filled with love for my pillow and sadness for myself. How can you know what you don't feel? I asked. Was love crucial for one's mental development? I stretched out my arms, feeling lazy and quite calm. The sun, I realized, had disappeared and the air felt different, it felt like rain. A fly buzzed at my feet and I told it to go away. The park seemed tired, perhaps forlorn. For days the air hung dense and muggy and people prayed for rain. All the records in the record books were broken. The old paradigms, some ventured to say, didn't apply anymore. The future was opaque, Greenspan had said, even though he had a brand new young wife. "Did you two have a fight?" the detective asked, and I said, "No, we never had a fight." "Never?" the detective sounded incredulous, and I gritted my teeth. "That's curious because it says right here"—he waved some papers in my face— "that you did have fights. You even struck her, at least once that we know of, right on the street." "I did not strike her." I trembled with inner rage. "Who told you such a lie?" "People talk," the detective said. "Elsbeth talked. She told people about you. You struck her on the street, there were witnesses." The detective seemed relaxed; maybe he felt that things, this time, were going his way. "You hit her and she yelled at you because you hurt her." "It was an accident," I said. "There's no such thing as an accident," said the detective and I felt sick I had to throw up. It suddenly dawned on me that the detectives were after me. I asked to be excused and ran to the gray smelly ladies room and leaned over the sink. I spat out acrid spittle but no vomit came. In the park I sipped my coffee and ate my grapes but found no joy in it. The sky had a palish, weepy look, the air felt heavy with moisture. In the gym I grunted with pain under the masseuse's hands. "You're tense, relax," she said, and I tried. Every so often she slapped me lightly on the thigh and told me to relax, and I felt oddly ashamed that I had to be told and couldn't relax on my own. The only part in my body that didn't hurt was my face, and I looked forward to the moment when I would turn onto my back and give myself over to the masseuse who would stroke my face in circular motions and touch her soothing fingertips to my shut lids. I remembered my mother and the abandon with which she let the beautician touch her, an abandon I had witnessed with great fascination when my mother took me along to the beauty salon where she went for her monthly facial. The beautician sat at a small table crammed with beautiful-looking jars into which she dipped her clean fingers and applied various creams to my mother's face throat and chest. After the treatment my mother's skin shone and her face radiated as if it were given a new life. "You look like a bride in a magazine," I said one day, looking up at her with total adoration. "And you are my little bunny." She laughed, kneeling down, and hugged me to her breast. The beautician laughed, too, and I was proud of myself for having said just the right words. There were other women like my mother in the salon. They all wore white robes and lay on white beds next to my mother's. They seemed very elegant and wondrous to me, and they too had their faces massaged with creams. At one point the beauticians placed hot steaming towels over their faces, and the women lay still, like mummies. With a sigh I turned over and lay on my back and the masseuse said she hated to do men because men got erections when they lay on their backs. It was embarrassing, the masseuse said, and some men even had the nerve to beg for special favors. I murmured my sympathy. On the next bench a homeless man was starting his day. I said, Good morning, and he nodded, said, Good morning, back. I thought he might be the same man who had given me the matches. It was Sunday. A group of Asians bowed to each other then stood waiting. The men smoked, the women had their hands on their waists, their large picnic bags at their feet. In the early morning, just before waking, I dreamt I was driving a truck with my father at my side. Something blocked the road, so I had to backtrack and go up the hill. It was a difficult undertaking and there was some urgency involved. We heard the roar of a wild beast and glimpsed its fur as it crossed the field and I told my father to run into the house and alert my mother. My father obeyed, and then I too jumped off the truck and ran into the house, just in time to shut the door in the beast's face. It was a lion, I thought, or a tiger, and it was the first time that I could remember hosting both my parents in the same dream. It began to drizzle but I remained seated. The picnickers walked off with their bags, and I continued to sit, dream-like. An obdurate bird kept chirping. The drizzle stopped and I yawned, feeling refreshed. A man carrying a large musical instrument case slumped down on a bench. In his white shirt and wrinkled linen jacket he looked tired, as if after a night's gig. But soon he jumped to his feet, not tired at all: another man, carrying a similar case, arrived and the two of them briskly walked away. I wondered where the two musicians were off to. Maybe there was a big picnic somewhere with food and music and only I, the recluse, didn't know about it. I took a deep breath and thought I smelled wet manure. They didn't use manure in the park, I didn't think, and yet I smelled it. When my parents and I went to visit friends in the country manure was everywhere. I loved the smell of it, even though, or because, the adults thought it curious. I used to sneak out of the house and step in it with my rubber boots, disobeying my mother who forbade it. I often wondered what made me, instinctively, at such a tender age, fancy the texture and odor of manure, but recently, to my delight, I read that Heraclitus had buried himself in manure, hoping the heat would cure him of an edematous swelling. "One thing I never told you," Elsbeth said. "It's his sperm. Even after I take a shower, I can still smell it. I stink down there because of his sperm. It's like he's marked me with his scent, like a dog." I was so shocked, I blushed for Elsbeth. I could never imagine Elsbeth stinking down there, or anywhere the length of her slender white body. Even though we told each other everything, I was surprised that she would reveal such an intimate detail about Drew. "For how long?" I asked in my confusion. Elsbeth burst out laughing, so I laughed, too. "I mean, what do you do?" I asked, and Elsbeth said she doused her panties with perfume.

I FELT BLESSED, ECCENTRIC. Large white birds flew in the sky among the glass towers. I had risen before dawn and peered at the sky, at the sleepy lights of the island across the river; beyond the island the horizon quivered in a golden, enchanting crescent. At the kitchen counter I had my yogurt, mixed in with protein powder and fresh blueberries, then left the house. Street lights burnt like torches, two NYPD cars zoomed down the deserted avenue. I entered the park and took my bench. A soft wind blew and I savored its crispness. The air had that special, early-morning clarity, a clarity I associated with classical music. I felt a little groggy, still waking from sleep, so I stretched out my arms and rested my head on my shoulder. No man was an island, so the saying went, but I felt like one, content in my self-reliant solitude. It wasn't an all-out feeling of happiness that washed over me, but a small feeling of well-being that was more reliable and perhaps longer lasting. A lone female jogger ran past; I sat, my feet on the chess table, and waited for the city to wake. Just before he released me, the detective said: "Tell me, what did you and Elsbeth fight about?" "You've asked me that before," I said, controlling my temper. "And I'm asking you again." "We did not fight," I said, sounding like an obstinate, sullen child. "I'm asking you to think again before you answer," the detective said. "Did you fight?" For a moment I frowned at him, then pretended to search my memory. It wouldn't kill me to play his game, I thought. I looked up to the ceiling and wrinkled my brow, twisted my mouth, concentrating. "No," I finally said, "we didn't." "That's curious," the detective said, "because it says here, black on white, that you did. You even punched her on the street and she screamed for help before you stopped." "You're embellishing," I said coldly. "You have nothing on me, you can't scare me." I wiggled my toes. A man in a gleaming white shirt and suit pants hurriedly walked past. Seeing me sitting there gave him a start, which, I sensed, he tried to mask. The light began to change, spreading in the sky. People were waking to start a new day, the air was mild and fragrant. I smelled bacon and eggs: someone was standing in a kitchen, frying the family's breakfast in a skillet. I did some work then left the park and walked to the river where I stood and looked hard and deep into the thick, undulating water. Life and death, I thought. Such lofty concepts, and yet so common and handy. A long barge plowed against the current, churning a foamy trail. A mountain of trash sat in its center— the wind brought a whiff of its stench to my nose. An

American flag blew in the wind and a man in a red shirt sat up high in the control tower. He was making a living, people made a living in all kinds of jobs they fell into. The flag looked old and dirty, and I wondered why they bothered to stick a flag on top of a heap of garbage. I sat in the shade and gazed at the cheerfully nostalgic Pepsi Cola sign; down below, on the FDR Drive, a river of cars flowed north and south. The wind shuffled my hair. Sparrows beaked the ground near the fence. Once in a while two birds unfurled their wings and fought and I gathered there were worms in the ground for them to fight over. Birds, for all their apparent vulnerability, were ferocious. Outside the dog run a man in a tan shirt sat smoking a cigarette. His dog, a young boxer, kept busy, exploring the grounds. When the man finished smoking, he threw a small ball and the dog fetched it. The dogs in this area were well-fed, well-groomed and well-behaved, and so were the masters. Advisories in a cased bulletin board instructed owners about proper pet behavior: Barking was not allowed, and holes the dogs dug had to be filled. There was an ad for Petography: owners were invited to schedule a photo session with their pets. A neatly typed note, tied around a tree, told the dogs: Flowers at Work, Please Pee Elsewhere. When I looked again, all the sparrows had disappeared, and I thought ahead to what I would have for lunch. A couple of sesame breadflats, sardines, maybe tofu. A tomato. To entice my appetite, I planned my meals in advance. I was out of breadflats; on the way home, I'd stop by the store and get some. Two women, their legs outstretched, were engaged in a leisurely chat in the dog run. Their dogs, already fatigued, lay at their feet, perhaps dreaming of the next meal, the next treat. The sparrows, I discovered, were now feeding on the other side of the paved walk. One of the women who sat and talked came out through the gate with her distinguished gray poodle. The other woman, very sportive-looking in her white polo shirt and baseball cap, remained inside the dog run, now talking to a sportive-looking blonde who smoked a cigarette. The blonde also wore a polo shirt, a green one, which went well with her blue espadrilles. The one with the baseball cap wore sneakers. Both looked athletically relaxed and well-off. I watched them, marveling how people always found some-thing to talk about. The dog run began to empty out: it was almost time for lunch. I sat on, thinking about breadflats and cheese. A woman called out to her dog: "Arthur!" and I thought, Mmmm, Arthur. Last week, after dinner, Lydia and I went to see her apartment. It had been a rainy night, we were both grumpy, I had no desire to go to her place, but by the time we were done eating the rain had stopped, so I yielded to Lydia who was anxious for me to see the changes. Lydia's new parquet floors gave off a brilliant sheen, and I wished I had the energy and sense of purpose to rid my apartment of old dust. Lydia kept pointing at her new shelves and at her new couch that rippled along the wall in blue-green waves. The shelves, off-white and narrow, blended into the walls and held her collection of tea pots and kettles of every imaginable type and color. She had good taste and a good eye, and the way she arranged the pots and kettles on the shelves impressed me, for you could stand there for hours and gaze at them, just as you would at a large fish tank with colorful fish swimming in it. The shelves were custom-made, Lydia said, and therefore extravagantly expensive but worth every penny. I nodded. The rooms looked very neat, if a little sterile, and I wondered how much money she had put into the place. "I'll give you his number," Lydia said, still talking about the carpenter who was very choosy about the clients and the jobs he took. "He is gay and very artistic," she explained. At dinner, I had ordered linguine with white clam sauce, and Lydia ordered the two-color tortellini with shrimp. We shared a shepherd's salad. The salad was delicious, we both agreed, and the lemony dressing was just right. The linguine sauce was a bit too creamy, but I didn't mind. Lydia, on the other hand, complained that her tortellini was too watery—she wanted to send it back and order something else. "Call the waiter," I said, somewhat impatiently. "I'm afraid they'd spit into my dish," Lydia said. "They do that, you know, if you send something back. I saw a program on TV." I said nothing, but again had to question Lydia's mental coherence. Later, in her house, we sat on the new, wavy couch and sipped brandy from deep snifters. Perched on the couch, craning her long neck, Lydia looked like a swan. She talked about the real estate market, saying she was going to make as much money as she could before it crashed. "Why would it crash?" I asked. I didn't really care, but I had to disguise my boredom. Lydia, I realized, was my closest connection to the real world. "It goes in cycles," Lydia said knowingly. Velvet, the cat, rested in Lydia's lap, and I watched the veins on Lydia's white hand as she stroked the bluish, shiny fur. Velvet, I thought, looked just as spiffy and meticulous as her mistress. Every so often she half-shut her eyes and I imagined the tremors of bliss going up and down her cat spine. When we finished the brandy, I walked to the elevators and waved at Lydia who stood in the doorway with Velvet in her arms. I felt a little empty, ghost-like, as I went down in the elevator, imagining the two of them getting into bed and falling asleep together. I had a similar ghostlike feeling yesterday when I walked home from the river and watched the midtown crowds, smartly and efficiently clad, rush past me to their scheduled luncheons. People, I reflected, led busy, noisy lives. They pressed cell phones to their ears, engaged in a global conference call. I too, I thought, should get a cell phone and pretend to talk like everybody else. This perpetual maniacal busyness, not a minute to waste or lose, made me feel I was outside the loop, disconnected and detached, maybe disadvantaged. Yet, I couldn't help believing they were spewing gibberish into the air, it all evaporated in a matter of seconds, leaving not a trace, not even static, and this belief restored my spirits somewhat. At times, how quick is the mind to come to the rescue! I reflected with gratitude. I remembered Socrates in his old cloak, exhorting the citizens around him: "Dear friend, you are an Athenian, citizen of a city greater and more famous than any other for its science and its power, and you do not blush at the fact that you give care to your fortune, in order to increase it." What about your soul? Socrates had asked. This is what you need to improve, but you don't think of it at all. When I finally got to the store, I bought the breadflats and had a delicious lunch by the window, reading an article about Proust. Before I bought the breadflats, I had stopped at the bank to see Rebecca, my account officer. While we executed a transfer, Rebecca talked about her cousin who had just died. The cousin, Jean, had also worked in a bank and was only forty years old. She had gone out for a smoke, and when she came back into the building she stopped at the newsstand in the lobby and bought coffee, then took the elevator upstairs. On her floor, she stepped out and fell headlong, flat on her face, and that was the end of it. A heart attack, Rebecca said. Just like that. Forty years old. "She was a heavy smoker, though," Rebecca added, nodding her head. "How heavy?" I asked. "A pack a day." "That's not heavy," I said. "But she drank coffee. Black," Rebecca said. "I always put a drop of milk in mine." "A lot of coffee?" I asked. Rebecca was suggesting that drinking coffee without milk was somehow more harmful, and I worried. "I don't know," Rebecca said. "We buried her yesterday." I wondered if Rebecca had a photograph of Jean, now dead at forty. For some reason, I wanted to look at Jean's face. "How long did it take for the ambulance to arrive?" I asked. "Five minutes," Rebecca said decisively. "They were very good, they tried to revive her for half an hour. She had cut her chin, too, and she was bleeding, but it didn't matter anymore." "No," I agreed. She lived long enough, I thought, to buy coffee and die on her floor, among her colleagues, rather than on the street, among strangers. I thought of one of my neighbors who had jumped to her death a couple of years ago. It was early Saturday morning, she rose from her bed, opened the window and jumped from the sixteenth floor. Her husband slept. The police arrived and got the superintendent to identify the body. They went upstairs and woke up the husband with the news. The husband stayed on in the building for a while, then moved away. Rebecca's phone rang, a business call, so I left and went to the store to buy my breadflats.

THE WIND BLEW IN THE BRANCHES and I felt a little chilly. A man in a suit walked briskly by, arguing something to himself. Tall on his bike, Tom drove past and waved to me. He'd been to the market, I knew: his weekly supply of two boxes of wheat grass sat in the basket in the back of his bike. I lit a cigarette—the first of the day. I wished I had brought a small sweater with me, like the one Elsbeth had lost in a restaurant and then spent the whole of the next day trying to find its duplicate. Mine was a small cotton sweater with sleeves to the elbow, just the kind of sweater Elsbeth would love; it was my style, too, in some things our tastes coincided. I wondered what Mrs. Williams had done with her daughter's things. She probably called the Salvation Army and had them cart everything away. "Too painful," she probably told her friends upon returning home. She must have paid handsomely to have the super and his handymen scrub the blood and expedite the cleaning and painting so she could put the apartment on the market. The real estate market was hot; Elsbeth's timing, in this respect, was propitious. So, Mrs. Williams did away with Elsbeth's things. It all belonged to her, she could do with it as she pleased. With all of it. With Elsbeth's paintings, her photography and coffee-table books, her dishes, her towels.

All chosen with painstaking care. I was hoping she would remember to offer me something that belonged to Elsbeth, something small, like a book, a scarf, but she didn't. I wondered if she had kept some things for herself, although I couldn't picture elegant Mrs. Williams climbing the stairs to Elsbeth's third-floor apartment. It was pitiful, I thought, that after all the love and dedication one devoted to one's things, a mother, a stranger sometimes, should come and discard them. Elsbeth's father, a Jew ("Like you," Elsbeth once said, maybe contemptuously, maybe playfully), wished to teach his firstborn the principles and values of his people, but was dwarfed by Elsbeth's mother. "I hate it," Elsbeth said, "that I need to impress people, a disorder I inherited from my mother. It was always: What will the neighbors say." "In every home," I said, "it's always the neighbors." "Still," Elsbeth said, "there are neighbors, and there are neighbors." "I know," I said. "My mother, too, worried about the neighbors, if only up to a point. She did have all these men come into our home." "Did she have sex with them?" Elsbeth asked, even though she seemed bored. "I don't know," I said, "I don't remember." "How can you not remember?" Elsbeth asked. "Because I don't," I persisted. "Maybe I was asleep." "It's so boring,"

Elsbeth said, yawning, "to think that nothing ever changes. Our parents were fucked up, we are fucked up, our children will be fucked up." "There's a poem like that," I said, and Elsbeth looked at me. Elsbeth didn't read much, and didn't like to be reminded of the fact; I regretted having mentioned the poem. "What poem?" Elsbeth asked, and I, still reticent, replied, "There's this British poet who said that our parents fuck us up." "I don't need a poem to tell me that." Elsbeth, suddenly animated, leaned forward and patted my hand. "You were a good student, weren't you, little Sally?" She smiled with what I took to be genuine affection. "Did you get straight A's?" "Always." I smirked, the proud child again. "I can just see you," Elsbeth said, "the little mouse, nibbling on books in the dark." "With a flashlight," I corroborated.

REMEMBERING, I LAUGHED. I felt humorous. I felt humor bubbling up inside of me as a potential for something, as a harbinger of good things to come. Such moments, flashes, came and went, filling me with inexplicable joy. I must have slept well, had a quiet stomach for a change, and the coffee I was sipping tasted especially delicious. The trees shimmered benevolently. "You're a specimen," Elsbeth said, "a true eccentric." No one had ever said such a thing about me, and I was flattered, I wanted to hear more. "What do you mean, a true eccentric?" I asked, and Elsbeth smiled. "A little odd, a little off-center." "Like you?" I asked, and Elsbeth said, "Yes, like me." A street sweeper went past, sweeping. The sun knocked on windows, and people in their beds, alone or with a companion, stirred, their subconscious balking at the intrusion. Soon, I knew, I'd smell the bacon and eggs. An autumn chill stood in the air as if it were September already, as if summer, in its ardor, had spent itself a little ahead of schedule. The sparrows were quiet and out of sight. I wanted to go deep into myself, but didn't know how or what I would be looking for. The slow-motion surface of things intrigued me, the plane where Life, in the form of shadows, walked, talked, shopped for groceries; stationary, I experienced a slight, sea-sickness motion. In yoga class, I learned how to breathe and how to surrender to the whiny, insistent tunes of the CDs the instructor played. The yoga instructor said that her boyfriend had bought these CDs, and I wondered if the yoga instructor and her lover, for all their purity, indulged sometimes and got stoned to the many devotional mantra CDs they owned. The instructor always wore white loose cottons in class and that's how I noticed that I always wore black leotards. Many centuries ago, she said, the great wise men and yogis discovered the power of sound to calm the mind and clean negative patterns. I bought a CD from her and lay on the floor in the living room and practiced breathing, giving myself over to the mantra, which, I read on the cover, would invoke the Primary Creative Power, manifest on earth as Woman. It would eliminate my fears, as well as all the karmic blocks and errors of the past. It would purify my magnetic field and most of my desires would be fulfilled. A first sparrow alighted on a branch, and I watched as it flitted from branch to branch, greeting the sun. Presently, other sparrows arrived, filling the air with their usual chatter. The street, too, awoke with morning sounds. People got into their cars and drove away. I smelled the bacon and eggs. I looked my best when I slept little, when I tore my eyes open and went to the bathroom to look in the mirror and wash my face. Then my eyes burned with the darkness of sleep and the violence of waking. It was important, I thought, to like your face in the mirror, and some mornings I did, I was able to connect with and approve of the face I saw. I finished my coffee and walked to the waterfall tucked in a plaza between two office towers. I watched the water thunder down the rock, it was loud and pleasing, it put me in a lull. I caressed my arm right below the shoulder, at the hollow of my armpit, where the skin was particularly soft and silky. I felt a little sleepy, yet invigorated; the day had a fresh, clean feel to it. A family of three studied a map—tourists, I thought, taking a coffee and bagel break near an artificial waterfall in midtown Manhattan. I watched as the woman bit into the bagel. It looked appetizing, and I considered having a bagel, too, but I'd already had my grapes and coffee, and to start all over again seemed extravagant somehow. A magnolia bush shone in the sun and swayed with the power of the waterfall, while a man aimed his tiny camera at the gray rush of water. I stroked my hair. It was short now, and I liked the feel of it, a straight neat line against my neck. The woman seemed very pleased with her bagel. She sat chewing the last quarter of it, and I could tell she wished it would last a little longer. Her son had a Coke, her husband just sat. When they stood up to leave they dropped, then picked up, the map. I once lost a map in Malaga. I went looking for it in a church where I thought I had dropped it. I cherished the map, I had circled and noted many places on it. I didn't find the map, so I went to the Tourist Bureau and got a fresh one, but it didn't feel the same. The tourists left, and I gazed straight ahead, trying to find a pattern in the way the water cascaded down the rock. I had heard someone say that the rock came from the Berlin Wall, but I didn't know how reliable the information was. I shut my eyes and when I opened them with a jolt I realized I must have dozed off. A bit disoriented, I rose and bought another coffee at the window of the small kiosk and in my haste to drink it burnt my lip and tongue. The wind blew furiously. The city was now in a full, mid-week swing. People everywhere ate and talked. Some lit cigarettes, some were overweight. I smelled garlic sautéd in butter, probably from the nearby *au bon pain*. Combining French and English, I read the name as: At the Good Pain, which reminded me of a makeshift sign Elsbeth and I once saw: Wet Pain. Pain was everywhere, Elsbeth said. And rage. People harbored hidden rages which they let erupt when the rage became unmanageable and could no longer be contained. At home I split open a melon, cleaned out the seeds, then sat by the window and chewed the sweet pulp. "Didn't he die, too?" I asked in earnest when the detective talked about Drew. The detective looked at me through narrowed eyes. "That's what people said," I explained, "that he disappeared." "Never happened," he said curtly. "It would have solved your little problem, wouldn't it?" "I don't have a problem," I countered, trying to think what else to say, but he didn't give me a chance. "You don't, huh?" He banged his fist on the desk, making me jump in my seat. "What planet are you living on? Your friend was butchered in a most gruesome way, wasn't she? Your best friend!" I stared at him. Yes, I thought, they were out to get me. They were loath to put away one of their own kind and would much rather lock me away instead of Drew, a young man who was led astray, getting involved with the wrong crowd, the wrong woman. Like Mrs. Williams, Drew was a charmer, he knew the detectives' lingo, he knew how to talk man-to-man. The detective had the palm of his hand over the banged fist—he had hurt himself. "As a matter of fact," I spoke up, "Drew talked a lot about ending up on Death Row. He even planned the menu for his last meal." "You're a piece of work," the detective mumbled, shaking his head. "Unbelievable, the stories you come up with." "But it's true," I cried, "he talked about it." "So what?" said the detective, "what does it prove? Why make him out to be a monster? Your best friend loved him, you said so yourself. How come she loved a monster?" "I didn't say he was a monster," I shouted back, "I didn't say he was a monster." The detective looked at me. "You didn't?" he asked, and I shook my head. "I didn't." "All right, I believe you." He took a deep breath. "So, Drew is not a monster," he continued, now doodling on his notepad. I knew where he was leading me, and I had to go there with him. "No," I said, "Drew is not a monster." "He's a nice guy," the detective suggested. "He's all right," I said weakly, suddenly exhausted. "See? It wasn't that hard," the detective said, and I looked at him. He seemed pleased with himself, or with me, or with his doodles. "You know why Elsbeth loved him," he continued, and I waited a while before responding. "Are you asking me a question?" I finally said, and he nodded. "He was handsome," I ventured, cautiously. "Elsbeth loved beautiful things, and the two of them looked good together, they were a good-looking couple. Everybody said so. It was important to Elsbeth, she needed people to admire her. Eventually, though, she would have tired of him." "No, no." The detective shook his head. "See? You're wrong again, and stubborn, you won't look at the facts. We heard it

from the horse's mouth, so we're absolutely certain."
He let go of his pen and began to rock in his chair,
back and forth, back and forth. "Do you want to
know what's really going on?" he asked, almost
seductively, and I became aware of my heart beating
in my throat. "Yes," I whispered. "All right," he
said, leaning forward across the desk, "I'll tell you.
You've been cooperating for a change, and I get the
feeling that maybe you're ready to open your eyes.
The morning after the gruesome butchering of your
best friend, Drew left on a scuba-diving trip, a trip he
had planned long in advance, and we assumed,
wrongly, that he went missing. Now we know better,
we know exactly where to look." "But you don't
understand," I said in mounting frustration. "Oh,
we do, I assure you," said the detective, "it's our
business."

THERE WERE MOMENTS OF MADNESS, I
thought, yawning in the early morning chill. Indeed,
it felt like September even though August had just
begun. What pretty names the months of the year

had! Birds were chirping, branches played their music in the cool breeze. It was Thursday, people went to work, sanitary workers, wearing thick gloves, collected garbage from the curb. Yesterday, Lydia came over for a drink; she was in the neighborhood, she said, and hopped in for a visit. Do You mind? she asked, and I shrugged, as if to say, Well, you're here, never mind. Idly, she pulled the drawer of my desk and found the small silver box where I kept my roaches. "What a cute little box," she said, pushing up the lid and sniffing the roaches. I didn't like it that she had opened the drawer, and the silver box, but I held my tongue, not wanting to start the evening on a bickering note. She sat in the chair and crossed her legs, telling me she had no meaningful friendships in her life, implying that I was the only exception. She had gathered her long dark hair and pinned a couple of small and colorful stars to the top of her head. The red and blue stars contrasted well with her natural pallor, and I imagined Lydia in front of the mirror, primping, examining her profile from this side and that. Like a delicate plant, Lydia couldn't stand direct sunlight and used a variety of lotions and moisturizers to protect her skin. She wore pearls in her ears, and in her all-white outfit looked simply stunning. For a brief moment my thoughts cleared and I felt a surge of fondness for her, a sudden delight in our complicated friendship. "You look great," I said, and Lydia smiled contentedly. "You're wearing the colors of the flag," I continued, and her smile broadened. "Oh, you noticed." I didn't mean to, but all at once I heard myself talk about the night when Elsbeth said I was "a dangerous woman." It haunted me, I said, needing to know what Elsbeth had meant. "Why didn't you ask her?" Lydia asked, and I nodded. Sure, I could have asked Elsbeth but when confronted like that my mind usually went blank and something, I didn't know what, prevented me from asking the simplest, most basic questions. "She controlled you," Lydia said. The wind picked up and I didn't have my sweater with me. I thought about cyclicity, about how one thing led to another. I thought about Job who claimed his innocence before God, aware as he was that his own mouth convicted him. I was wearing a tight cotton T-shirt with tiny blue blossoms and the tiny blue blossoms reminded me of a T-shirt I had bought years ago. It was French and very *gamin* and I wore it and wore it and then outgrew it but held on to it for several years more until the day I turned ruthless and emptied out my closets. Lydia said she kept boxes full of clothes she couldn't wear anymore but couldn't throw away because they reminded her of places she'd been to. I said I used to hoard possessions, but not anymore. "You have to be brutal," Lydia said, "to do away with your past, your memories." I nodded, agreeing that I was brutal. It sometimes happened, I said, that I got rid of something and later regretted it, but I learned to live with the loss. "That's what I don't want," Lydia said emphatically. "I think it's because you're an orphan. You avoid attachment." "Maybe," I said. I didn't believe it, yet I liked to hear what people thought of me. In college, reading Pirandello, I suddenly grasped that there was no such thing as the Truth, and that the image I had of myself and of the world was necessarily different from the one others had. Even close friends were knowable only up to a point. At the time, this revelation shocked me to the core, and I went around asking friends what they thought of me. To my surprise most of them either couldn't come up with an answer or evaded the question altogether, but two men, both older than me, did respond. One compared me to a narrow vase, secretive and enclosed, the other said I was bright but superficial. I winced at "bright," but more so at "superficial." The vase image I thought too flowery and rejected it. Back then it didn't occur to me to question the motives behind what people said. I didn't understand that people were prey to tricks their minds played, that even when they strove to be truthful, their minds, like a good machine, checked all the possible consequences and modified the statements that finally issued from their lips. That's why slips of the tongue were so revealing sometimes, and sometimes damning. Even fragmentary truths, I had learned, were rare, maybe impossible. I perceived that no matter how hard I tried to reveal myself, others would persist in their perception of me, and who was to say who was right? People dealt with others on a necessary, limited basis. Shortly before or after I discovered Pirandello, I got pregnant and had an abortion even though the guy and I talked about love. We could have got married and had the child, but I was too young, too uncertain to have a child. Every day I noticed a tiny ant make its laborious way across my desk, and every day I squashed it between my fingers. I marveled at the fact that such a small creature managed somehow to climb up so high in a building, and even though the ant's existence didn't bother or interfere with mine I killed it, absent-mindedly, yet noting, with mild curiosity, that it was very hard to squash an ant to death. There was no blood, no body fluids, like when you killed a mosquito or a cockroach, just a lifeless speck I dropped in the ashtray. Often, after I'd squeezed it, the ant, still alive, would fall from my finger to the floor, and I would let it live. I didn't like killing them, I didn't like the thought that I was merciless toward ants, and therefore resolved, many times, to leave the ants alone, but every time I saw one, I went after it. This morning, after I squeezed the ant and was about to drop it in the ashtray, I noticed that it was still wriggling on my finger. I applied more pressure, horrified at myself and, at the same time, awed by this tiny creature, heroically battling for its life till the last breath. A doe, on the other hand, in the paws of a lion, seemed resigned to her fate even before he sank his teeth in her throat, and I tried to imagine what my state of mind would be when the time came: Would I be a doe, or an ant? When I arrived at the waterfall I bought fresh carrot juice at the kiosk and sat in the shade next to a black teenager clad in fashionably wide shorts and nodding off on his chair. A child climbed onto her mother's knee. A man sat with them but I could tell he wasn't the father, maybe a distant relative, or a prospective suitor. The mother mothered the child, caressing her face, the man watched and smiled. On my left a heavyset man pulled a chair and sat down, his thighs spreading in his pants and filling the seat. He wore a tan uniform rimmed with gold, and I surmised he was a doorman in the neighborhood, out on his lunch break. He shed his shoes and jacket and took out his lunch from a plastic bag. A black thread hung from his white shirt, and I was tempted to reach over and stealthily remove it as he ate his homemade ham sandwich and sipped milk with a straw from a small container. He ate fast, taking big bites and chewing with great vigor and, while still chewing the very last bite, was already folding the wax paper and packing the paper and the empty milk container in the plastic bag. When he was done, he leaned back in his chair and lit a cigarette. He was neat, I thought, well trained by his mother or wife. Or both. An elderly black man swept cigarette butts and other dirt off the floor around the tables and chairs. In the restaurant, Elsbeth laughed: "I saw a strange commercial today. It was an ad, actually, on the roof of a cab." "What did it say?" I asked when I realized that Drew wasn't about to break his silence. "It said, 'Take me to the TV, at the corner of Couch and Lamp.' It was an ad for one of the networks. Cool, no?" Elsbeth tapped her fingers on the table and I couldn't tell if she was anxious or excited. "You're making this up," Drew said and Elsbeth smirked, shaking her head. "Don't be stupid," she said, and I felt awkward sitting between them. Every time I looked at Drew, I remembered what Elsbeth had said about his sperm. Drew, of course, didn't have a clue. I imagined that his sperm was thick, gooey, yellowish, a little like someone's mucal spit on the sidewalk. Men polluted women, and then, adding insult to injury, complained and told jokes about their odor. Some men killed their women, spilling their rich blood on the white-bleached floors, then pleaded innocence. When Lydia came over for a drink, I took her to the park to watch the chess players. She wasn't thrilled about going to the park, but she came anyway. Later, when I walked her to a cab, she said she didn't understand what drew me to the park. It was a waste of time, she said, and the chess players were weird. "They're not weird," I said, resenting having to defend them and myself. "They're all family men, they live around here." "Granted," Lydia said, "they're not druggies, but they're weird. Did you see the guy who kept chewing his hand?" "That's Frenchie," I said, indignant. "He happens to be a very sophisticated player, he is rated at 2100, which is a very high rating. And he wasn't chewing his hand, that's how some people concentrate. He's a very funny man." Lydia's skepticism showed on her face. "He is crazy," she said, and again I experienced that queasy feeling in my stomach. It was either that Lydia's perceptions were crazy, or mine were. People's opinions were merely that, opinions, I consoled myself, glad to see Lydia whisked off in a cab. I left the waterfall and went to the park. The sun filtered through the trees, and I waited for its rays to reach my bench. The scent of fresh laundry came to my nose; people were taking care of business, the business of their lives. "I'm the man with the broom now," Tom said, and the history professor smiled and nodded. The history professor often played a game of chess at the tables, but Tom, like me, only watched. He knew chess, he had read the books, but he didn't play; I had the feeling he couldn't bear the idea of losing a game in public. "Remember when we were kids," Tom said, "and we wouldn't go into a certain yard because a man with a broom would come out running? I am the man with the broom now." He was talking about kids from the nearby projects who came to the park in the evenings and harassed the old people. I liked the way he referred to himself as the man with the broom, chasing thugs. He was a lively and colorful talker and every so often he said things that clicked and resonated in my mind as eternally true. The history professor, I knew, liked to listen to Tom for the same reason. I sipped the last of my coffee. I had my books with me and a few pages of my dissertation and soon, I thought, I would get to work but for now I just sat and watched. A dense layer of leaves had collected on the ground, and in a day or two the gardeners and caretakers would sweep them into large heaps and cart them away. The homeless man who had given me the matches arrived; he was wearing yellow earphones, and I was surprised to see such an item on his person. It was still the height of summer, but you could tell it was about to end. In a couple of weeks people would wonder aloud: Where did summer go? I didn't look forward to winter, even though I liked snow and the trees held another kind of beauty, stark and bare. "God bless summertime," I heard one homeless man say to another and I agreed wholeheartedly. In winter, it would be too cold to come out and sit in the park, even if I bundled up. I could sit in a café and watch the street but it wouldn't be the same. I could go traveling, but that, too, wouldn't be the same. I would have to wait for next summer but by then many other things would not be the same. When I arrived at the precinct a cop was standing on the sidewalk by the open steel doors. He stood with his legs planted wide apart, his thumbs hooked on the large metal buckle of his belt. I was prepared to smile my little smile and say hello, but he looked straight through me, which made me feel awful, worse than invisible. In their eyes, I thought, I was nothing but a skeleton to hang their case on. Mr. Daley led me to his small, stuffy office; the dirty window was shut and the airconditioner hummed weakly. He was polite and measured this time, if in a distant sort of way. Things, he said, were moving at a slow pace, but they were making progress. He asked me about Drew, and I said I hardly knew him at all. Did I know any of his friends? No, I said, I didn't. "You didn't like him," Mr. Daley suggested, and I shrugged. "We've been through this before," I said. "I only know what Elsbeth told me." "What did she tell you?" he asked, and I remembered Drew's sperm. "She loved him," I said. "She didn't want to love him but she did or so she believed." "Why didn't she want to love him?" he asked. "Because," I said, "he pulled her down, he was a depressive, which, at first, Elsbeth thought was cool." "What do you mean by depressive?" asked the detective. "He was depressed all the time, like a façade, you know? He didn't have a sense of humor, he didn't get any of her jokes." "So, she liked to tell jokes." Daley nodded his shaved head as if he'd just understood something, and I couldn't tell if he was serious or was back to his old tricks, goading me. Then another detective came into the room and took over for Daley. The new detective was a Mr. Maddox, and I briefly wondered why they switched detectives on me. "Let's start from the beginning," Mr. Maddox said, smiling pleasantly. "I hope you don't mind," he added. I did mind, having to start from the beginning, but I liked him, he seemed so much nicer and gentler than Daley, and better educated. "You and Elsbeth were close," Mr. Maddox began, and I wearily affirmed yet again that Elsbeth and I were close. "You were physical with each other," Mr. Maddox said. "What do you mean?" I asked. "You know, like women are when they feel close to each other, stroking, hugging, kissing?" Where is he leading me? I wondered. "Yes, I guess we were, physical." "Did you take showers in her house?" "Showers?" The question amused me. "You mean, with her?" Mr. Maddox gave me a small, roguish smile. "With or without her," he said. "No," I said, "I don't think I did." "So, did you or didn't you?" "No, I didn't." Now that he insisted, I became irritated. "But you loved each other," Mr. Maddox continued in the same calm voice, "and Drew, how did he fit into the picture?" "He was her boyfriend," I said, and the detective made a notation on his pad. "It's a pity," Mr. Maddox said, "that she had to die like this, and so young, too. As you can imagine, we see all kinds of brutal deaths, we hear all kinds of stories, but this case is unique." "Really?" I said. "How?" "Well," Mr. Maddox said, "we're so close, so close, like, you know the feeling when you can't come up with a certain name, but it's right there, on your tongue, it's the same thing here. We have so many verifiable leads, we have such a clear picture of the sequence of events, and yet none of you people would do the honorable thing so your friend could rest in her grave in peace. You know what I'm saying, right?" Mr. Maddox smiled, waiting for me to speak, but I couldn't come up with anything. I thought I understood where he was going, yet all I could concentrate on was the tingling sensation in my cheeks growing numb and the mist that began rising in my eyes. I mustn't, I thought, let them trick me. "Do you have any idea how hard it is?" he coaxed and at this I shook my head, No. "You know," he continued, "I've been thinking about this a lot. You might say, I'm interested in the subject from the psychological point of view. Friendship is a complex affair, very delicate in fact. Like you and Elsbeth. Maybe she hurt you on some deep level you're not even aware of, but it's there, eating at you like a cancer. Maybe little hurts along the way, the kind of hurts that accrue, causing subtle damage until they find an outlet. Don't think I don't know how you feel, or how you must have felt. Some people seem to have it all, while the rest of us...." Maddox leaned back in his chair with a sigh. "She was beautiful, wasn't she?" he said wistfully. "I saw the pictures, and it breaks your heart to think that such a beautiful woman, a girl really, is dead. And yet, it is also true that beautiful people are, or can be, very cruel." "She wasn't cruel," I murmured. "She was generous with all people, even strangers." "I'm sure she was generous, and cruel. She never hurt you?" Mr. Maddox asked, and I nodded. "Sometimes, but we forgave each other." "Forgiving is one thing, forgetting is another," Maddox said. "Your subconscious doesn't forget, your subconscious remembers the good and the bad. If you want to look at the scars, go to your subconscious." His words reached me as if from afar. I tried very hard to focus on what he was saying, but all this talk about the subconscious tired me out. He was looking at his watch, pushing it up and down on his wrist. He seemed to have run out of questions, and I hoped he might release me soon. "By the way," he said, "some

time ago you mentioned Mr. Williams's funeral."
"Yes, I did," I said, somewhat surprised. These guys
were organized, they did read the material in the file.
"Well, I don't mean to contradict you, but Mrs.
Williams says you did not attend the funeral." "Then
Mrs. Williams," I said in a guarded voice, "is mistaken. I was there, but it's possible she didn't see me,
or maybe she forgot. She was the grieving widow,
surrounded by hundreds of well-wishers. I was nothing to her, I came with Elsbeth, I didn't count." "But
you stayed in her house, how could she forget?" "We
didn't stay in her house, we stayed in a hotel. Elsbeth
wouldn't go into the house, not with her mother
there." "Why not?" "I don't know," I said, suddenly drained. I was tired, I wanted to go home. "Which
hotel did you stay at?" "I don't remember." "Don't
you keep records? Receipts?" "Elsbeth paid for the
hotel, and for the flight," I added, saving him a question. "She insisted on paying for everything." "And
you let her," Mr. Maddox said. "Yes. I didn't want
to argue." "I see," he said, and for a while we sat
there, he looking over his notes, and I looking over
his head at the dusty, nearly opaque, window. To
combat my mental fatigue, I began to think about
my dinner and what I would make. A salad, for sure,
and maybe spaghetti with garlic and olive oil. I tried

to remember what day of the week it was, and what I had had for dinner the night before. Then Maddox sprang to his feet and mumbled, "I'll be right back," and before I could say anything, he was gone. A man in Indian garb walked past, and I recalled that Indian sage who had said that one of the wonders of the world was that people, seeing how others dropped dead all around them, still didn't believe in their own demise. For me, of course, these were just words; the fact of my own demise had already been programmed in the hard wiring of my brain. One of the caretakers greeted the homeless man and asked him how things were. Things were all right, said the homeless man. He wore sandals today, not his usual brown leather shoes, and a white, short-sleeved shirt. He took care of his appearance and sported a trimmed little beard, but most of his teeth were missing and the two front ones had a large gap between them and were crooked. When he noticed me he waved and said good morning. I waved back and said good morning. He arrived with a brown paperbag and sat down to his breakfast of coffee and a roll. I hoped he had money for eggs on a roll, when and if he felt like having eggs on his roll. He wasn't a drunk, I never saw him drink beer or liquor, only coffee, or Coke, and I never saw him beg. He was black, in his fifties, I thought, though it was hard to tell. He seemed warm, gentle, and except for his missing teeth had a pleasant, handsome face. When he smiled his face lit up, even as the smile itself remained sad and resigned. He had a cart full of stuff, and he collected cans. I figured that if he earned ten dollars a day selling his cans he didn't have to go hungry. He even had cigarettes: a pack of Marlboro Lights; so he was a smoker after all. I opened my book and watched the people come and go. For a long time I watched a girl with a blond ponytail, sitting cross-legged on a bench. She wore maroon pants and a blue, buttoned-down shirt, and something in her sweet limbs reminded me of Elsbeth. She had earphones in her ears and a bottle of Diet Coke in her hand. She smoked a cigarette, her elbows resting on her knees as she slouched over a magazine, spread open before her. Once in a while she moved her head to the music she was listening to and sipped her Coke. She would be perfect in a Coke commercial—she seemed so carefree, so American. Maybe it's her breakfast, I thought, a Coke and a cigarette. I never wore earphones and never drank Coke. I smoked cigarettes and only occasionally read a magazine. I sneezed, then shivered with abandon. Then the girl sneezed, and I recalled what Tom had said about sneezing. When you sneezed, he said, your heart stopped, and that was why people, even strangers, responded with, "God bless you." The history professor and I appreciated the information. I had slept very deeply during the night, the best sleep I had had in a very long time, and I couldn't remember having dreamt at all. I was particularly tired last night, and the deep sleep was an unexpected boon. The girl shifted on the bench and I noticed that she was wearing tennis shoes, sock-less, just like Elsbeth. I felt a sudden pull in my gut; I wanted to lie down next to someone and open my mouth. Such sudden longings frightened and saddened me. I envied the girl who had all her senses engaged and seemed so thoroughly and deeply content in the moment. Before Maddox and Daley switched on me, Daley's phone rang and he took the call, importantly feigning indifference. As he listened, he doodled on his pad. "She won't talk," he said into the receiver. "Just the usual bits and pieces." He listened a moment, then laughed and hung up the phone. "What do you mean, I won't talk?" I said, enraged. "You won't listen, that's the problem." Daley eyed me coldly. "Calm down, I wasn't referring to you," he said, and then Mr. Maddox walked in. It now occurred to me that it was Maddox who had called, and that the two detectives had planned the call in advance, for Mr. Maddox, after he left the room, never returned, and it was Daley all over again. Mr. Maddox, in fact, had spent so little time with me, I began to worry that my reputation in the precinct was such, that Maddox, to amuse himself, begged to get a crack at me. "Sally," Mr. Daley spoke softly, and I winced at the sound of my name in his mouth. It was the first time he addressed me directly, almost like a friend, using my name. "You'll have to do better than that. I can see in your eyes that you're a decent person. I know that eventually you'll do the right thing and talk to us, so you might as well start now and save us all a lot of time." I bit my lip. "But I am talking to you," I said, wanting to point out that he had lied to me, that he did discuss me earlier on the telephone. "I don't understand why, or what game you're playing," I added cautiously. "Yeah, right," Mr. Daley said, and the renewed contempt in his voice made me ill. He had the authority and power to insult me and there was nothing I could do short of hiring a lawyer. But even a lawyer wouldn't help me, I thought. Often, lawyers and cops schemed and made deals behind your back. "Did you go upstairs with her that night?" the detective asked, looking straight at me. "No, I didn't," I said. "Are you sure?" "Positive." "I don't get it," he said. "How is it that you're so positively clear about this one particular detail, whereas, by your own admission, everything else is a jumble in your head? You were dead drunk, weren't you? You said to me, right here in this room, that everything was fuzzy in your head, these were your own words." Mr. Daley tapped his index finger on the papers before him. "Some things I remember." I tried not to flinch. "Some things I'm sure about." "Why?" he demanded, then continued, not allowing me time to reply. "I'll tell you why. You're smart enough to know which details would incriminate you, so you came here, all prepared, with a little story full of holes. Like, you can't remember this and you can't remember that, but you clearly remember that you didn't go upstairs with her. Oh, boy, I tell you. We made one big mistake with you. We should have grabbed you right from the start and never let go. And that's a fact." By now Mr. Daley was shouting, and I felt myself go pale and numb with fear. I was trying to think of ways to escape, but, of course, I couldn't escape. As he continued to shout I stopped listening and a miraculous calm overtook me. Plainly, his facts were different from mine. He was shouting, which, in a way, was a good sign, a sign of weakness. Also, I remembered, he was a moron, far beneath me on the intellect scale, and I despised him. "I don't know why you're so upset," I said when it was quiet in the room. "Scientists tell us that human memory is failing because we've come to rely on machines to do the remembering for us. But, they also say, our brains are cluttered and overworked. They're working on memory-chip implants to facilitate ever faster access to data." Mr. Daley clenched his fists on the desk. "Implants," he said, nodding his head and keeping his gaze on me. A muscle twitched in his cheek and for a long moment it seemed that he was trying hard not to burst out in a hysterical laugh. I could see far into his eyes, I could see the wheel of his thoughts spinning out of control. Ours was not so much a battle of egos as a battle of two psyches, foreign and far apart. "I thought you said you were drunk," he said. "I was, I did, I said I was drunk, but in addition to that...." I let my voice trail. "Don't play mind games with me, young lady," Mr. Daley said, and I gloated inside. He's a primitive, I thought and made a show of glancing at my watch. "Are you going to keep me here much longer?" I asked. "I have an appointment." "What kind of appointment?" "My hairdresser," I lied. "Your hairdresser," Mr. Daley snorted. "You must be joking."

IT WAS WINDY. Out my windows the river looked murky, agitated, as if a storm were churning right below the surface. I, too, felt murky, agitated, and as soon as I arrived in the park and sat on my bench I contrived to induce a sense of purpose, a sense of self-worth, but to no avail. The coffee tasted salty— the taste, I thought, was in my mouth and the joy I normally felt at being out was not there. I wondered what had gone wrong and changed; it must be, I brooded, the detectives and their insidious, insulting ways. They had insinuated themselves into my life, they had polluted me. Or maybe, I hoped, it wasn't the detectives, but simply the onset of autumn. A homeless man, not the one I knew, came over and began rummaging in the trash can. He wore a heavy-duty glove on the hand that was doing the rummaging; the other glove he held in his free hand. He found three cans and put them in his cart. He went to the other trash can and fished in there. He worked quickly, furtively, because, I suspected, this wasn't his territory. He put two more cans in his cart and walked off hurriedly. A man in a suit, carrying his shirts to be laundered, walked past. Two sparrows chirped and hopped on their tiny feet. Once in a while I heard the engine of a truck. The weather was changing. I was wearing a sweater on top of my T-shirt, and still felt a little chilly. My eyes hurt, as though I didn't get enough sleep. A brazen mosquito landed on my knee and I slapped it away, then wondered what mosquitoes subsisted on—did they feed solely on blood? The homeless man I knew came and looked in the trash can. I wanted to tell him not to bother, that this other man had come and taken the cans, but I didn't know how. The homeless man looked up; he seemed a little puzzled. He greeted me and went to the other trash can. Again, I said nothing. I calculated he must collect at least two hundred cans a day to have enough cash for more or less decent meals. I wondered if he had friends. The matchbook he had given me had two telephone numbers on it; I still had the matchbook in a small bowl in my miscellany drawer in the kitchen. He too, I thought, must dread winter. People didn't sit as much outdoors, drinking soda. Not to mention the cold, the short gray days, the wet sky. Migration, of course, was an option, but the homeless, like everyone else, got attached to a place. Last night I went out for a walk, but had to turn back for it began to rain. I sat and looked out my living-room window as sheets of rain drifted in the wind. Even now, in the park, the sky seemed to darken as if preparing for a downpour. In the night my aunt and cousin came to me in a dream. I didn't like them, in my waking life I never gave them a thought, and yet, every now and then they made an appearance in my dreams as if adamant that I remember they existed. In my dreams I liked them all right and was quite happy, if a bit apprehensive, when spending time with them. We were traveling together in some Moslem country, and while my cousin and I waited outside, my aunt went into a hotel to book a room for us. I knew the hotel—I had stayed there in the past with my cousin—and it was quite dingy. I didn't think my aunt would like it, but then I remembered the hotel had a few rooms which were nicer and more expensive than the others. In the dream my aunt looked a little like Mrs. Williams, but in real life she had grown fat and old and was no longer attractive. Throughout my childhood I often heard her brag that strangers on the street stopped to tell her she looked exactly like Marilyn Monroe, a claim that I, even as a child, found ludicrous. When my father died and most of his assets went to me and to his new wife, my aunt tried to get her hands on some of the money that was to be mine. After all, she was his only sister, she said, shedding her crocodile tears. She took care of him, like a mother, when they were growing up. "You stole enough from him when he was alive," my mother said, and I cried. After all, I was grieving for him, my only father, while these two women, one of whom was my mother, fought over his money. I woke from the dream with a phrase that had the word "salvation" in it, something like: "The salvation of ____." The wind picked up and a strange light filled the sky. It started to rain but I stubbornly remained on the bench, wondering about this obsession of mine to sit in the rain. My spirits lifted. I got wet, my book got wet. I stood up in a hurry and sought shelter in the entrance to one of the buildings. I hugged myself and watched as the rain pounded the pavement. The sky got darker and it felt like an evening in winter. There was nothing to do but wait for it to stop; I smiled. It amused me that the rain was coming down so hard. Across the street, a group of tourists wheeled their luggage into a Hertz office, and I wished I could walk into that office with them and go away in a car. Pack my life into a suitcase, eat and sleep on the road. Then the sky cleared, the rain stopped, and I went back to my bench. Three sparrows fought over a wet piece of bread. One of them grabbed it and flew away, victorious. Soon, more sparrows arrived and I watched them hop, taking turns pecking at a piece of pretzel. Tomorrow, I thought, I'd bring bread and feed them. "Correct me if I'm wrong," Mr. Daley said, "but you don't seem to take this business very seriously, do you? You think this is just a little game we play." I looked at him, quite calm. Let him talk, I thought. It no longer irked me that I was at the mercy of a moron; briefly, inexplicably, I felt sorry for him. "I asked you a question," he said and I shook my head. "No," I offered, "I don't think it's a game." "So, what do you think this is?" Daley tapped his pen against his chin. "I don't know. Do you think I should get a lawyer?" I asked with sudden inspiration and Daley looked at me, and then at his watch. "Go to your hairdresser," he said, releasing me from the nightmare of his presence. I sneezed. God bless, said one of the caretakers and I thanked him. Cars honked. Traffic was blocked and men stood in the street, calling instructions to one another. I sat and enjoyed the warm, wet air. The homeless man who had given me the matches sat with his coffee and donut and his morning paper. I couldn't tell which paper it was, but I could tell it wasn't *The New York Times*. A strong wind blew and it felt as though it might start raining again. The homeless man finished his breakfast and picked his two crooked teeth with a toothpick, cleaning his gums. He sat and looked straight ahead: he seemed to be contemplating something. The paper lay folded at his side. He wasn't ready yet, I thought, to immerse himself in world affairs. He led a calm and quite an orderly life. People in the neighborhood knew him, I saw them wave at him, give him things. A few mornings ago I gave him a comforter I kept in my closet for the occasional friend who might stay over on the living-room couch. I shook his hand and introduced myself, then handed him the bag with the comforter in it. His face brightened and he uttered a small surprised laugh as if welcoming me into the exclusive club of his benefactors. He took the package from my hand and thanked me, simply but warmly, and said his name was Franklin. His firm and confident handshake, the handshake of an equal, humbled me and brought color to my cheeks. I went to my bench, and Franklin put the bag in his large canvas cart which, so said the bold lettering on it, was the property of the U.S. Postal Office. A woman in white pants and a flowery shirt hobbled past on her very high heels. Her long frizzy hair was bleached and looked damaged, and I thought about what women did to themselves, about the many ways women hindered themselves. The Baby-Doll Syndrome, I mused, wondering if Franklin had noticed the woman and if he found her attractive. I wondered if he had any thoughts about me, now that

I had given him the comforter, and if he remembered that he had given me the matches. Me and Franklin together. We were both sitting on our respective benches, watching the world go by. I was watching the world. Franklin, still staring straight ahead, seemed to have his mind on something else. Maybe he was dreaming with his eyes open. The sparrows had left. I lay down on the bench and looked at the blue sky beyond the canopy of green leaves. I watched a bird or two fly overhead and listened to the steady splash of the fountains. I felt peaceful, even blessed. How lucky, I thought, to live outside the manic pace of the world. Only when alone I felt complete and one with myself, so why did I hunger for the existential noise of others? Was it merely social conditioning, or was there more at stake? Like my sanity, for instance. Through the veil of my reveries, I noticed a woman heading toward me and I sat up, bracing myself. She wore large black glasses which covered half her face and big curlers sat on her head under a flimsy blue cloth pinned to her hair with safety pins. As she approached, I noticed the heavy makeup, the exaggerated lipsticked lips. "Can you tell me how close it is to ten o'clock? I have an appointment." She pointed at her naked wrist. "Of course," I said, remembering I had used the same exact words with the detective, "it's nine-fifteen." "Nine-fifteen," she repeated. She stood for a moment, making up her mind, then sat down on the next bench and lit a very long cigarette. She took out a square makeup case and looked in the mirror, smearing more foundation on her cheeks and nose. Franklin stood up, said goodbye, and wheeled his cart away. "What paper are you reading?" I called after him, aware of the woman smiling at my side. "It's today's paper," he said. "Yes, but which?" I asked. "*USA Today* and *The New York Times*." Now it was just me and the woman with her make-up case. She had a large asymmetrical face and, smiling, she whispered and nodded her head, and I reminded myself there was always a human brain at work. When she finished the cigarette, she stood up and adjusted the cloth on her head. For a moment she seemed undecided as to where she wanted to go, if at all. She took a few steps, stopped, then contin-ued on, taking deliberate, coquettish steps, swinging her hand from side to side as if walking on stage. "It used to be," Elsbeth said, "that a woman could get whatever she wanted from a man, but not anymore. Now we have to compete and fight for everything. Some of us go crazy with the pressure." "You have nothing to complain about," Drew said. His mouth was full and he stabbed the plate with his fork, already working on the next mouthful. He ate voraciously, as if it were his last meal. "I'm not complaining," Elsbeth said, "I'm just explaining something to Sally." Normally, I loved shrimp scampi, but that night I was struggling with the food before me. I put down my fork and lit a cigarette. "Are you done?" Elsbeth looked at me quizzically. "No," I said lightly, "just taking a break." "Good idea," Elsbeth said and pulled a cigarette from the pack. I waited for Drew to say something about us lighting up while he ate, but he didn't. His eyes were heavy-lidded and cloudy, and I sometimes thought he had cataracts. Sometimes I thought he was retarded. He took classes at New York University, Elsbeth told me. "What kind of classes?" I asked, but Elsbeth was evasive. "All kinds," she said. "He has an eclectic bent."

A SOFT WIND BLEW. Across from the fountains, near the vending machines, Franklin lay asleep. I had given him a comforter, and yet he slept wrapped in his cardboard. I hoped he was saving the comforter for winter, yet it occurred to me that he might have sold or traded it away. As I watched, he sat up from his slumber, noticed me and waved. I smiled and waved back. The sky was evenly gray and it felt like rain. Still, I was alert and fully awake, even though I had had a hard time getting out of bed; the fresh air and coffee helped. Franklin stood up and put his night things away. The sparrows were quiet, and I wondered if birds slept late, and I rose before they did. Franklin left to get his coffee and newspapers. Reading the papers, he was probably better informed than I was. He had slept in a short-sleeved shirt and now pulled on a sweater and went to get his coffee. I was tempted to peek into his cart and see if the comforter was there. On the bushes near the cart one of his shirts was spread out to dry, and my heart warmed to this small token of domesticity. The other day Lydia said that now that she had renovated her apartment, she fired her maid. She said she fell in love with her apartment all over again and wanted to clean it herself. "You can't love something if you don't clean it yourself," she said, and I was impressed, yet I doubted it would last, this love affair. "Did you give her notice?" It occurred to me to ask, and Lydia looked at me. "The things you worry about," she said. "Do you think I should have?" "Yes," I said, and Lydia said she would send her maid a check. I thought of Jean, dead at forty of a heart attack. It wasn't just the coffee and cigarettes, maybe drugs, too, Rebecca had said. On her two Visa cards, Jean's debts totaled $10,000. Each card had an additional authorized user, two different males. "Both black," Rebecca said, a certain insinuation in her eyes and tone of voice, and I remembered that Rebecca and her family had emigrated from Romania a few years ago. "How do you know they're black?" I asked. "Their names," Rebecca said. She was a heavyset woman with a calm face and deep blue eyes. She reported her sad news without emotion, and I wondered if she had cried at the funeral. "Were they her boyfriends?" I asked. "I don't know," Rebecca said. "You weren't close? Didn't you discuss these things?" I pressed on. "We were close," Rebecca said, "she lived near me. But people, you know, they have secrets." I nodded and stared as I always did when people came out with such clear, knowing statements. I wondered if I had what could be considered real secrets, and if Rebecca had secrets. It was windy, but the sun appeared from behind the clouds. I missed the sparrows; usually at this hour they'd be here already. Maybe, I thought, they had left town. Tiny drops fell from the trees on my arms and face. Franklin, too, was late coming back with his breakfast. The first time I saw him rummage in the trash cans, I averted my eyes, as if his dignity didn't allow me to watch. By now, I had gotten used to it and thought of it as just another part of his day. Every time I saw an empty can on the ground I carried it to the trash can for Franklin to find later. Two sparrows arrived, twittering and chirping as usual. I remembered Nili and Ethan, and imagined them in their spacious home in Westchester. Nili, a high-school friend, had married and moved to the suburbs. We were still close and spoke on the telephone at least once a month. Every July I went to a barbecue they hosted in their back-yard and usually stayed for the weekend. I swam in the pool and played with their two little kids, a boy and a girl. The girl, five years old, was named after me, and the boy, seven years old, was named Andrew, after Nili's father. I loved Andrew and Sally, I loved to press their small amazing bodies close to me and hold them in my arms for as long as they let me. At such moments the world felt like a safe, immutable place. Over the years, I got to know Ethan and like and appreciate him, but when Nili first began to date him, I had to overcome and conceal my bewilderment. He was short and roundish, cross-eyed, and had an awkward way of walking and carrying his body. Then Nili went ahead and married him, and only years later I saw why. They had two great children, a beautiful home, and a good marriage. They were both accountants, they made good money, they worked together for the future of their family. Nili had wanted a solid life and she made one for herself, and Ethan, I discovered, was fun to be with. He could laugh and giggle like a boy, and when I came to visit I felt completely at home. Ethan, it was obvious, would never sleep around, his wife and kids were his whole life. He helped me with my computer, and there was something endearingly inept in the manner he held his hands over the keyboard, typing with two or three fingers. This past July I went to their barbecue and spent a nice, quiet weekend with them. At lunch, their neighbors came over with their pots, pans and children, and I sat at the long picnic table and ate their food and listened to their stories. They were cheerful and noisy, they laughed a lot, they seemed to have no worries, no doubts about the choices they had made in life. Once in a while they glanced over at their kids playing in the yard. This was the way of the world: people got married, they had children. It was a good life, I thought, orderly and secure, and I wondered why what was so clear and obvious to others wasn't to me. What worked for them, I mused, wouldn't necessarily work for me, and yet I coveted their presumed wholeness. I had hoped to discuss this with Nili sometime during the weekend, but when I finally got around to it I couldn't formulate my thoughts into a simple, coherent question, so I said instead: "You have such wonderful neighbors, you're so fortunate to have them near you," and Nili stopped what she was doing and turned to me. "You're idealizing," she said. "They're okay, they're nice, so-called normal people, but you're much more special to me than they." I felt myself blush, thinking I didn't deserve such loyalty, and then something broke in me and I cried in her arms. "What's the matter, sweetness?" Nili asked, and I told her about the detectives. I wanted to get a lawyer, I said, but resented having to pay for one. "Then don't get a lawyer, at least for now," Nili said. "Just answer their questions, and if they keep up the pressure, maybe you should consider hiring one. But remember, don't volunteer anything, keep your answers short," she added after a pause, and we didn't discuss it further. Later in the afternoon, the men kicked a ball around the yard, the women sat in the shade and talked. Then we took a nap under a tree on the lawn. And then it was time to eat again. I ate and drank, feeling no remorse. Franklin arrived with his breakfast and papers. For a while he sat and stared, as if resting from the effort of starting a new day. What do I have to complain about? I thought. At least I have a home, a bed to sleep in. Franklin reached for the brown paperbag and brought out his coffee. "I'll tell you the truth," Mr. Daley said in a light, friendly tone, "we have some problems with your story." He was scratching his head as if truly in a bind and waiting for me to help him out. "My story," I said, "I didn't give you a story." "I stand corrected." Daley looked at me. He hadn't shaved, and I almost found him attractive, or could see why other women would find his beastly, scarred face attractive. "What did you give us, then?" "I told you what I remember," I stressed. "Fine, that's exactly what I meant," Mr. Daley said, and I didn't contradict him. "About them holes," he continued, studying his notes. "In your story. You said you went upstairs with her—" "I never said I went upstairs with her." My heart was pounding. Mr. Daley, again, pretended to study his worthless notes. "Are you sure?" He frowned, and I shook with indignation. They were trying to trip me, they thought I was a fool. And maybe I was, for talking to them. My

Chilean neighbor, who said he knew about such things, was right, I must get a lawyer, even if it cost me a bundle. "No need to get so riled up, we're here to work together," Mr. Daley said affably, and my throat stung with the acrid memory of nausea. "You're putting words in my mouth," I said, almost in a shout, "I won't stand for it, that's criminal." "Look who's talking." He sounded offended. "I'll decide what's criminal around here, if you don't mind?" I gave out a wild laugh, and Mr. Daley regarded me as if I had flipped. "Did I say something funny?" he asked, his lips curling into a smile. "No," I said, "I'm sorry, I just remembered something." "Well, what is it?" he asked, trying to mask his curiosity. "It's not relevant to your case," I said, knowing that now that I had him hooked, he'd insist for me to go on. "Tell me anyway," he said, and so I told him. "Earlier, when I was walking over here, a car alarm went off and this robotic sort of voice began to whine: 'I was tampered with, I was tampered with.'" I impersonated the metallic voice. "It sounded very aggrieved. It must be a new device, no? Against car thieves?" "I wouldn't know." Mr. Daley drew circles on his pad. "What was I saying?" he asked, and I waited for him to get there on his own. "Oh yes, let's go back a little," he resumed, and the word *tango* popped into my head. Yes, Mr. Daley and I were doing the tango, one step forward, two steps sideways. He was a good partner, I thought, if dim-witted. An old couple I had seen before walked past; the man, I realized, must have gone blind since I last saw them. He had a cane in one hand and held onto his wife with the other. The wife pushed a walker laden with plastic bags hanging from its hooks. I always saw them together, inseparable into old age and absolutely devoted to one another. Once in a while they stopped for a short rest and talked in hushed voices. Every day they got themselves out of the house and went somewhere, maybe to a center for the elderly where a cheap, or free, meal was served. At the beginning of summer, I thought the man was the hardier of the two, but now he was the one who seemed the weaker. They both looked gaunt and were shabbily dressed, yet the woman always wore red lipstick and white beads around her neck, and the man's long white hair was stylishly brushed back. They had strong, dramatic features, and I thought they must have been actors at one time, now dying in a city that failed to fulfill their dreams. "All right." Mr. Daley snapped to. "I have a feeling we'll get somewhere today." Really? I wanted to say, but swallowed my attempt at sarcasm. "So, you didn't go upstairs." "No, I didn't," I confirmed. "Then tell me what happened." "I went home, I went to bed." "You took off your clothes." Mr. Daley nodded his head encouragingly. "Yes, I did," I said, wondering if Daley was trying to picture me in my bedroom, taking off my clothes. "And then?" "And then?" I repeated. "I'm not sure I understand." "Your clothes, what did you do with the clothes?" "Nothing. I probably threw them in the wash." "Were they soiled?" "No, I don't think so, not more so than usual, or maybe, you know, just sweat." "Was it a warm night?" Mr. Daley asked, and I shrugged. "I don't remember, but I always throw my clothes in the wash." "So, you're a person of habits," Mr. Daley said, and I nodded. "What time do you normally go to bed?" he asked and I thought a moment. "Usually around midnight." "And what time did you get to bed the night your best friend was murdered?" "I don't remember, I mean, I can't be sure, but it must have been late." "How late?" "Maybe one, maybe two in the morning, I think." "Did you have a hangover the next day?" "I don't remember," I said, my voice rising with the crescendo of his questions. "Predictably," he said, and so, to rebut him, I added, "I normally don't have hangovers." "Oh, alcohol agrees with you," he said, and

I smiled. "I guess it does." Yesterday, as I walked to the park, it began to rain. At first it was just a light drizzle, and I told myself that as long as my cap kept my head and sunglasses dry, the rain wasn't such a terrible nuisance. As a matter of fact, the drops falling on my bare arms and back cooled my skin; it was going to be a steamy, muggy day. The rain began to fall a little harder, yet I continued on my way, hoping it would soon taper off. I went into the coffee shop and the Hispanic man at the counter gave me paper towels to dry myself. I saved them, semi-wet, and put them in my bag to wipe the bench with when I got to the park, but soon after I had left the coffee shop, it began to pour. I found shelter under the awning of a *Blockbuster* and waited for the rain to stop. I watched as kids and adults jumped out of SUVs and dropped their videos in the drop-box. A steady rain continued to fall. I crouched under the awning and drank my coffee and ate my grapes right there on the sidewalk, feeling very bohemian. The coffee, I noted with satisfaction, was delicious. I smoked my cigarette. When the rain let up a little I decided to brave it and walk back home, but then, just as I expected, the rain stopped as soon as I reached my building. I considered turning back and going to the park, but I had already drunk my coffee and eaten my grapes, so I went upstairs and hung my clothes to dry. I took a shower and sat by the window with a book. The guillotine, I read, was named after a Dr. Guillotin, yet another man who had become a noun and who was very proud of his invention, extolling and promoting its excellence; I wondered how much money the good doctor and his offspring made off his killing machine. I rested the book in my lap and gazed up at the still, overcast sky. There was a progression to my life, I thought, even though I couldn't know precisely what that progression was and where it led. Things weighed on my mind, not important things, just things, or the notion of things weighing on my mind. Lately, I was aware, I suffered mood swings. Not from day to day, which was normal, but from moment to moment. Some deep unrest gnawed at me, interspersed here and there with inexplicable bouts of exhilarating joy, or stretches of neutral calm. I thought I liked best the stretches of neutral calm because at such times I lost sense of myself. Like when I stood in Nili's kitchen and watched Jane, one of Nili's neighbors, wash lettuce. Jane filled a pot with water, sprinkled in a pinch of salt, then let the leaves soak. "I never saw anyone wash lettuce like this," I commented. "My mother does." Jane smiled bashfully. "Oh," I said, remembering Elsbeth whose mother never taught her practical, everyday things, like, how to put a doll in the wash. My mother didn't teach me much either. She believed that I would marry money and would be spared the onus of practical things. I had yet to realize my mother's dream but in the meantime I, the orphan, had managed to pick up a fair amount of mundane, necessary survival knowledge on my own. "Maybe I'll try it some day," I said. I helped prepare the salad and the women, once they heard I loved garlic, trusted me enough with the dressing. Through the window we watched the men congregate near the grill, marinating the meats. "It's so much better," one of the women said, "to be a woman. If only because we get to be in airconditioning, while they roast in the sun with the smoke and grill." The women laughed. Nili, I thought, laughed the loudest. "I can think of a couple more reasons," Nili said, and it suddenly hit me that Nili and Ethan, for all their reticent and quiet demeanor, had good, perhaps wild, sex.

IT WAS CHILLY. This morning I did have a sweater with me, and I wore it. A gardener was sweeping leaves off the ground. A drop of rain landed heavily on my head and I, all set to have my little outdoor breakfast, exclaimed with dismay: "I don't believe this! Rain again?" The gardener looked at me. "Yes, rain," he said laconically. A sudden wind blew, then subsided. No rain, I thought with relief, just a drop from yesterday, left over in the tree. A lone bird shrieked. I drank my coffee and ate a pecan and raisin roll I had bought on a whim in the new bread store. "Only one? They're tiny," the young, chirpy vendor said and I, intimidated by the implication that I should buy more, hesitated a moment. It was one of those modern, rustic-looking stores where the vendors seemed poised to sell not merely bread but a way of life. "Just one, yes," I said. The roll wasn't so tiny and not as good as the look of the store suggested. It was actually stale but I ate it anyway, together with the grapes. A man walked by, sorting out the sections of the paper. I smoked my cigarette. Two elderly men strolled by, one of them saying something about symptoms and doctors. The other one listened, looking down at the ground. I wished for the sun to come out and warm me a bit. The two men came around again. The same man was still talking, I heard "medicare." I sat up and stretched out my arms and neck. "My mother," Nili told me, "was depressed all her life. Now, at seventy, she gets to do what she always wanted to do: lie in bed all day and be left alone. They say that people have children to protect against the death of their parents, that if you have children it dulls the pain. Maybe it's true." Nili's mother had moved in with them a couple of months before, and when I went upstairs to say hello, Nili's mother didn't seem depressed. She smiled at me and we talked about the last time we had seen each other. "Her mind," I said, "is as sharp as ever." "Yes," Nili agreed, "her mind is sharp. And she loves the kids, maybe more than I do. Maybe more than she ever loved me." Nili smiled ruefully. "And they love her back. They're upset when she leaves the house to see her doctor. They think grandma belongs in bed." The wind picked up. I was cold, even though I had the sweater. The air felt damp, my hands felt clammy. And then, as if by magic, it began to clear. The sun, although not visible, gave off a pale light. Two caretakers went past, one of them skinny, the other supporting a pot belly. The skinny one patted the belly of his colleague. "And what's that?" He laughed. "Beer?" "A little bit of everything," said the other, and I smiled. I knew the one with the belly. His name was Tony and he was as strong as a horse, he told me once. He was a gardener by day and a singer by night, singing Italian oldies at weddings and at a local radio station in Queens. The other caretakers seemed to fear and respect him, he was the foreman, I guessed, even if he worked as hard as the rest of them. Some time ago he gave me his business card; when I was ready, he said, I must come out to Queens to hear him sing. Eyes mellowing, I watched a couple walk past. They embraced, the woman resting her head on the man's shoulder with grateful lassitude; everything, it seemed, was right with the world. Canyons of nostalgia, I thought. It was a phrase I had recently encountered in a book, and it stuck. I recalled my first visit with a gynecologist, I was young and pregnant, I wanted an abortion. The gynecologist, an older man, spoke casually while examining me: "Take a good look at your breasts. They'll never be as beautiful again." I found it odd and unbecoming that a doctor would compliment me on my breasts, but I was too nervous and dazed to say anything. He performed the abortion in a private clinic, and when I woke from the anesthesia there was blood on the sheets. Nili, who came to the clinic to take me home, later said that when she arrived I was asleep and so very still, she feared that

I had died. So the doctor tweaked me and my body twitched all over. Like my mother on the hospice bed. My eyes hurt. Many times I woke in the night, speaking or mumbling, then dozed off again. In a dream I go to visit my mother with a childhood friend. Through the open window we see her prepare for bed. She is wearing a purple nightgown and looks beautiful, much younger than her years. "She looks great," I say, overwhelmed with joy. When we go in, my mother asks if we have cigarettes, and my friend says she has some. I tell my mother she looks great, and my mother smiles her coquettish, yet diffident, smile. Four pigeons approached and stood waiting, looking at me sideways. Franklin and his bed were missing, and I wondered where he had spent the night. Maybe he had a date, I thought. Maybe someone took him into their home. The sun came out, and I opened my eyes wide and stretched my facial muscles. I let out an audible yawn, lowered my chin into my palm and shut my eyes. Last night in the elevator a woman reeked of perfume, and I remembered Elsbeth saying she stunk down there, as if "down there" weren't a part of her anatomy. I wondered if men referred to their genitals as "down there." When I finished the coffee I walked to the river. As I went past the dog run, an old bulldog on the other side of the fence took a fancy to me, looking up at me and plodding at my side, his long tongue dangling from his mouth. The woman with the gray poodle sat and talked with the woman with the white baseball cap. The woman with the cap wore cut-off jeans that came up to her hipbone, and I thought I could glimpse her crotch. More people arrived, others left, there was constant movement at the dog-run gate. Some of the dogs barked, in spite of the signs. The woman with the gray poodle and the woman with the white cap came out together through the gate and walked away. The woman with the cap had a German shepherd on a leash and, next to the woman with the gray poodle, looked a little common. Gray poodles, I mused, especially when coiffed, looked fierce and suave. I watched the people in the dog run, surprised and gratified to see so many smokers among them. I was equally amazed that so many city people took it upon themselves to care for dogs. A city reputed to be so heartless and cold. A city of glass towers and cell phones. A new dog arrived, probably a female and much in demand, for at once all the dogs were on top of her; the owners had to get involved and pull them apart. Up the road, high on a crane, a man sawed the side branches off trees along the FDR Drive. Another man fed the fallen branches into a machine that crushed and diced them with great noise. The sun reached my bench and warmed my back. The woman with the German shepherd reappeared, this time with a second dog in tow, and I wondered if she was a professional dog walker. She still wore the same cut-offs and again I glimpsed her crotch when she sat down. Dog walkers, I thought, were in fact modern-day nannies, and possibly better paid. Walking home, I felt a sudden uplift. The mere fact of walking, of moving, made me look forward to what would come next. Nothing was final, things were always in flux. Nothing endures but change, my good Heraclitus had said. In the bedroom, as I was changing into my house clothes, I heard a strange sound coming from outside, so I went to the window to have a look. On the roof of the next building, a guy in bathing trunks lay on a low lounge chair, drumming his hands on his thighs. Like an insect, making a noise to attract the female, I thought, but as soon as he noticed me in the window he stopped, so I turned away and continued to undress. "Them holes," said Daley, and I got furious. They were insatiable, the detectives, I gave them nothing, they said, only bits and pieces, and they were disappointed. "What were you wearing that night?" the detective asked. "I don't remember," I said for what seemed like the umpteenth time. "Are any of your clothes missing?" he asked. "I don't think so," I said, and Elsbeth's missing cardigan became an entity in my mind. "You don't think so?" he sounded incredulous, as if such a reply were an outrage. "Don't you know what you have in your closet?" "I know what I have in my closet." I struggled to maintain my calm. "Nothing is missing, I don't lose things." "You don't lose things." He made a notation on his pad, or pretended to, and I began to doubt he wrote down real words, sentences. I hated how he repeated my words back to me, like a ping-pong meant to hit me in the face. More disturbingly, what I thought important, the detective dismissed, and what I thought trivial, he noted in his book. "No, I don't, I'm very careful with things." "What things?" "Things, my things, stuff, you know," I said, hoping he'd grumble, "I *don't* know," but he didn't. Instead he said, "Would you destroy a garment, let's say, a shirt, bloody perhaps, or a pair of pants, or a skirt? You wear skirts, I assume." "Very seldom," I said. I was dying to throw in his face: "What do you mean, bloody?" but had the sense that he was setting a trap for me, and the less I dwelled on the mention of blood, the better. "Very seldom, what? Destroy a garment?" "Wear a skirt,"

I clarified, "and I *never* destroy a garment." "I see." The detective paused. "What you're telling me is that you never destroy a garment, or discard it." "I'd rather give it away," I said, "to a friend, or the Salvation Army." "Not if it's stained, you don't, or if it's bloody?" said the detective. "I take good care of my clothes," I said slowly. "They're not stained, and they're not bloody." "Let's say then, for argument's sake, that you had a nose-bleed and you bled all over your shirt. Let's say you had to destroy such a garment and throw it away. The blood, you know, it could be evidence." "Of a nose-bleed?" Now it was my turn to sound incredulous, and Mr. Daley gave me a look. "A nose-bleed, or whatever. What would you do with the shirt?" "I'd probably try to get the stain out, and if I couldn't then yes, I would discard it." "So, you would discard an item of clothing." "Yes," I said, "if I had to. If I had no use for it and couldn't give it away." "So, it's possible that the morning after, after your friend was stabbed, you tried to get the stain out, and since you couldn't, you destroyed the shirt, or threw it away." "But I didn't," I said, keeping my cool. "I threw it in the wash."

I PATTED MY STOMACH. I'm full of vitamins, I thought. I felt cheerful, nearly happy. In my dream Elsbeth lifts me up in the air, four or five times, and I, amazed at how strong she is, can't stop laughing, yet beg her to put me down on the ground. Unbeknownst to Elsbeth, I have just extracted a piece of dried snot from my nose and I'm very careful not to drop it on her shoulder. In the end, she lets me down, the snot safely hidden in my palm. Remembering the dream, I picked my nose, anticipating the illicit pleasure of pulling the crust off the wall of my nostril. Near the playground mothers fed their babies from small, pastel-labeled jars. Maybe that's why, I reflected, tranquility reigned in the park. High above, the top branches majestically swayed in the breeze. The day was overcast, the sun emerged in spurts, then hid again. Pigeons flew low and gathered around a very fat, ponytailed man who fed them out of a plastic bag. A gardener groomed the hedge. The wind picked up, and I held on to my things on the table. A woman on roller blades zoomed by, tossing something into the trash can while in full speed, and I admired the precision and skill. I yawned. I was a little late this morning and my body felt stiff. A woman in a white suit walked her large brown dog who bore the enigmatic face of a lion. Yesterday in the gym a woman and her personal trainer discussed the woman's career. The woman said she was switching back to estate law because estates, she said, were more fun than litigation. Her trainer, pert and chipper, kept praising the lawyer, modulating her voice into various emphases of "good," and "excellent," which annoyed me, for the lawyer wasn't good, nor excellent. Absent from her own workout, she stood inert, like a spoiled child, while the trainer got weights from the rack and put them in her hands. Pensively, I scratched my back, then noticed Franklin a few benches away; he, too, seemed dazed, like he needed more sleep. I wondered at what time he went to bed and what his dreams were about. He sat, resting his head in his palm, dozing off; his coffee and a can of Coca Cola sat next to him. On top of his things in the cart lay a long, black umbrella with a beautiful wood handle. One afternoon, coming out of Yankee Stadium after a day game and Elsbeth and I pushed through the crowds, I heard her emit little sounds of anguish, sounds that came out with her breath and which, I knew, she was unaware of. She must have panicked, I now thought, but kept it to herself, gathering the necessary grit and willpower to combat it. I remembered a story she once told about her childhood when her father took her to see a dentist for the very first time. While the dentist pulled out her front tooth she was very brave, determined not to cry. But as soon as they were out on the street and her father congratulated her on being so brave, she began to cry. She was five or six years old, she said, and it was the first time she could remember feeling sorry for herself. It was an interesting thing to remember, I thought, and tried to remember when was the first time I felt sorry for myself. I remembered feeling sorry for my mother, feeling sorry for my father, but I couldn't remember feeling sorry for myself. Maybe, I thought, I was filled with so much sorrow for my parents, there was no room left for me. Only after they died I felt free to turn inward. Dying, I thought, they liberated me—the ultimate parental sacrifice, even if involuntary. I could feel the sting of tears behind my eyes, but then Tom arrived on his bike and we chatted for a while. He chatted, chewing hard on a piece of gum, I listened. He couldn't decide what he wanted to do. He had a doctor's appointment at noon and he wondered if he should ride to Chinatown and do his shopping before his appointment. "I don't want to rush," he said. "You have plenty of time," I said, looking at my watch. He didn't run this morning, he said. He was going to, but then conked out. He figured he'd go swimming, but it was too cold. In the afternoon, he said, he was going to the Turkish bath; it was his new love. "What do you buy in Chinatown?" I asked. "Fish," he said. "Ocean bass and salmon." "You cook for yourself?" I asked with admiration. "Oh, yeah, I'm a bachelor. I have a girlfriend, but I'm a bachelor." I knew about the girlfriend. She was Chinese, Tom had said, and very wealthy. "She's a trust fund person, you know. She does nothing so well, you know she's been practicing for years. Thank God she sleeps till one, so I get to do all my outdoor shit before she wakes up." "Are you a good cook?" I asked. "Fair," he said. "I cook to my own taste. You name it, I have it. Every kitchen utensil you can think of." I watched him take off on his bike. A few days ago, the history professor told me in confidence that Tom had been diagnosed with colon cancer. "Colon cancer," I said, "is curable." "If they catch it in time," said the professor. Friends of his, he continued, went to a wedding a couple of weeks ago. As they were about to leave, the wife said she had to go to the bathroom, so her husband went with her and sat down on a couch in the lobby to wait for her. When the wife came out, the man was dead. "A massive heart attack," said the professor. "Terrible," I said, and we both shook our heads. Men, too, I thought, were dropping like flies. "Lately," said the professor, "it's nothing but funerals for me. And I'm only fifty-three." Again, I shook my head in sympathy. "How old is Tom?" I asked. "Older. Maybe fifty-seven," said the professor. Earlier, when I arrived in the park, a large man I never saw before was sitting on my bench, having his breakfast. I couldn't believe my eyes. Annoyed, I went to another bench and wiped it with the paper towels I still had in my bag. I ate my apple and drank my coffee. I had had a restless night, and was still restless. And the large man was coughing, he didn't stop. I picked up my things and went looking for another bench. I spotted Franklin, still asleep, near the vending machines. As I approached I recognized my comforter, nestling him. His cart stood at his side, shielding him from the world. His sleep, I thought, was as deep as anyone's. Over his head he had put together a new cardboard construction which protected him from the cold and gave him, I thought, a sense of privacy, of being in a room and not out in the open. I knew he had a pillow in there, for I saw it one morning when he folded his things. Pleased that he was putting my comforter to good use, I sat down nearby and resumed eating my apple and sipping my coffee. Franklin had washed his socks and hung them to dry on hooks on his cart. It occurred to me now that he washed his face and things in the public bathrooms nearby. The large man, I noticed, had left my bench, so I got up again and went back and settled down like one returning home after a long absence. I felt a little better, not as restless as before, but I knew it to be a short respite. I lit a cigarette and stretched out my legs, hoping to trigger emotional peace. Two women sat down with their groceries and said that something—I didn't hear what—was very painful. A special light, kind of pale, illumined the trees and calmed my heart. "Stupid," one of the women said in a loud, contentious voice. "I'm sitting there, ready to laugh, and nothing, not even a smile." "It got good reviews," said the other. "Stupid, I'm telling you," the woman barked. She was the older of the two and I tried to imagine what life would be for someone living with her. The younger one spoke in a soft voice, trying to please and placate her. Mother and daughter, I thought, feeling sorry for the daughter, no longer young and still emotionally chained to her mother. "Isn't it a wonderful breeze?" A man called to me as he walked past, giving out a small, awkward laugh. "Yeah." I smiled, surprised that he had addressed me. He was young and handsome; the people who talked to me in the park were usually older. I wished he had stopped to talk some more, but if he had, I knew, I would have acted reserved, suspicious of his motives. Why couldn't I be normal and flirt with guys? A white plastic bag rolled on the ground like tumble-weed, and I considered running after it and throwing it in the trash. I felt my nipples harden. I was wear-ing a sweater and short white socks with my yellow sandals. The air felt crisp and the sky was blue, strewn with small puffs of baby clouds. I gazed at the flowerbed, my head full with last night's dreams. Franklin went to get his breakfast and the thought crossed my mind that I should let him sleep in my liv-ing room—no one used it in the night anyway. It was a crazy idea and yet, in some respects, sensible. People would say I was nuts but when I felt right about something, people's opinions merely amused me. Elsbeth once gave shelter to a woman she met in a bar, and then had a hard time getting rid of her. The woman, Elsbeth said, began to abuse her. "Abuse you how?" I asked. "Oh," Elsbeth said, "making fun of me, of my clothes, the stuff in my fridge." On the way home I stopped at the vendor on the corner and bought strawberries, blueberries, grapes and peaches, immensely grateful for summer and the abundance of fruit. In my kitchen I made fruit salad and topped it with yogurt and cinnamon and shaved almonds. I called my broker and sold a stock I worried about and bought another. When evening came I sat next to Frenchie and watched him lose a few games in rapid succession. "How come you're losing tonight?" I asked, and Frenchie shrugged. "Losing is an illusion," he said in his wonderful accent, and I laughed merrily. "Come back tomorrow and I win, I promise you." On the street, a guy "pssst" at me to get my attention and when he did he flexed the muscles of his upper arm, pointed to his biceps and said: "I'm the man." I didn't know how to respond to such a declaration, so I looked at him a moment then crossed the street, turning around to make sure he wasn't following behind. Maybe a new type of artist, I thought, needing to express himself. Upstairs, I worked on my dissertation for four straight hours and later, in my kitchen, listening to the news and trying to decide what I felt like having for dinner, I realized I had had a full day without, for once, hearing the detectives talking in my head.

I SIPPED MY COFFEE AND MUNCHED on my grapes. It was cloudy again and a pleasant breeze stirred the leaves. The same handsome man went past my bench again. "Another breezy day," he called, smiling happily and continuing to walk. "I'm leaving for Lake George in two days, I can't wait." "Good for you," I called after his back just as cheerfully as if I were leaving for Lake George with him. Still, I felt a little resentful, wondering why he was giving me this information. Tom arrived on his bike. He was on his way to buy fruit, he said. He had already gone to the gym but couldn't lift weights because he had injured himself; he held up his bandaged finger. "In the last two years, I've hurt myself more than I ever did my entire life." "Why is that?" I asked. "I'm not as quick as I used to be, and I misjudge," Tom said, and again I felt a rush of affection for him. "I take things for granted," he said, "and I shouldn't." He drove away to get his fruit. A black woman wearing a green turban and green and red sandals tiptoed toward me. She leaned over and whispered, "Every time I see you sitting here with your books, I'm reminded of my niece. She was studying in Albuquerque for her exams and she found a spot in the wilderness, near a little brook, and that's where she did all her studies. It's so peace-

ful here." The woman sighed. "And beautiful," I
added, smiling brightly at her. "And healthy," the
woman said, walking away, "like a health camp."
Tom came back and offered me a banana, while peel-
ing one for himself. "I must take care of myself," he
said. "I have what they call an arrested cancer." Tom
laughed. "I'm a cop, remember? I arrested the bug-
ger." I laughed with relief. "So you don't have it? The
cancer?" "I still have it," Tom said, "but it's in
remission." He was wearing his usual red shorts and
white T-shirt and sat on the crossbar of his bike. I
lowered my gaze and contemplated the contour of
his penis and balls; they seemed soft and vulnerable,
resting on the frame. He was talking about the sev-
enties when he lived on the Upper East Side and went
hunting every night. "It was all women over there.
You didn't have to date, you didn't have to get married. If you had a bullshit line and confidence, you
did all right. I went for the less attractive ones, and
you know what? Once you got used to them not
being pretty, you suddenly discovered they had a
beautiful profile or something. With a beautiful one,
if she got on your nerves, you suddenly saw she was
ugly. It was all I did in those days, especially in the
summer. After work I went out to look for girls. I
learned body language. I didn't know I was learning

it, but I did. I'd go up to a woman and start talking, and if she curled her toes or touched her hair, that was it. Or I saw it in her eyes." I wondered what Tom saw in my eyes. A woman whistled to a squirrel who rushed to her side while she fished in her pocket and threw him a peanut. I noticed Franklin in the distance, collecting cans. The park, I realized, was my small haven and social club. But women always touched their hair, it occurred to me to say, but Tom had already left. I wondered if I was being gullible, listening to and believing every word he said. Briefly, the sun appeared then drew behind the clouds, and I thought I might go home soon and take a little nap; this kind of cloudy, grayish weather made me sleepy and undecided. "How often would you see your father?" Elsbeth asked. "I mean, after the divorce." "Not often." I said. "For one thing, he remarried, and he traveled a lot." "You must have missed him," Elsbeth said, and I gave it some thought. "I don't know," I said. "Even when he lived at home, we didn't see him much." "But it was different," Elsbeth said, "when he lived at home." Elsbeth, knowing that I didn't like to discuss my parents, usually broached the subject gingerly. "Yes," I agreed, "it was different, but not better. When he did come home, they fought. My mother accused him of having a mistress in every port. Her words." I laughed. "Did he?" Elsbeth asked. "I don't know," I said. "Anyway, I was glad they finally divorced, it was a good thing." "How brave of you," Elsbeth said. "How old were you?" "Twelve," I said. "When I think about my father," Elsbeth said, "I wonder if he would still be alive had he had the courage to divorce my mother. Maybe it's genetic." "What is?" I asked. "Suicide. And guilt. You carry the genes of the parent you feel close to." "Maybe," I said, hedging, "but I don't think that suicide is necessarily genetic." "Sometimes," Elsbeth said, "I look in the mirror and see a huge dollar sign run down my face. That's what I'm good at, making money and spending it. I don't even *make* it, I get paid for a certain look they happen to want at the moment. Is it my Jewish side, I wonder? I feel guilty making so much and giving so little." "Give it away, then, or at least some of it," I said. I had heard it before, about Elsbeth wanting to give her money away, but nothing ever came of it. I listened and offered my input because I knew that she needed to hear her thoughts echo in me. "I can't give it away. I want to, but I worry about the day when they'd stop paying for the way I look. I've become a ghost in my own body, I don't know how to have fun anymore." "But what about Drew?" I asked. "What about Drew?" she repeated, and I had to think. "The two of you together," I said. "You must be happy, no?" Elsbeth looked at me and burst out laughing. "You're a sweetheart," she said, and I, even though I was pleased that I had made her laugh, also felt a little snubbed, like I was missing something very basic about her and Drew, or about life in general. "What do you mean?" I asked, and Elsbeth said, "Oh, Sally, you're so inquisitive." "But I want to know," I insisted. "Do you mean I'm naive?" "Something like that," Elsbeth said.

UNDER THE AWNING of a Korean grocer, I sat at a wobbly table and slowly sipped the hot hazelnut coffee I had bought inside. Near the door a gray cat wearing a pink collar sat in a crate. After I left the house a light drizzle began to fall and I, deciding not to risk it, stopped at this Korean deli that had a couple of tables under a green awning. I went inside for my coffee, then sat, facing the avenue, and watched the traffic. It was cold and wet. It had been cold and wet for two days straight. I was wearing long cotton pants and a white T-shirt under a pale blue sweater with a V-opening, which revealed the white shirt underneath. I thought I looked smart, maybe even angelic, with the pale blue and the white playing off each other. The rain was coming down hard. A man in shorts, clutching two small poodles under each arm, ran past. The night we went out to eat, Lydia kept bitching and whining about the rain and, once again, I lost my patience with her. If I were out with a man, I thought bitterly, he wouldn't be bitching and whining about the rain. I wished I could turn around and walk away from her, but, of course, I couldn't. I wanted to say, "Oh, stop whining already," but that, too, was out of the question. When we reached the restaurant I pointed to a table near the open glass doors where, I told Lydia, smoking was allowed and where we could look out to the street, but as soon as she heard that, she shook and shivered and said she was cold and wanted to sit away from the doors. I stood there a moment, unwilling to budge: it was her will against mine and I was determined to have my way. I tried to come up with a good argument why we should stay near the doors, but was distracted by the irritated maitre d' who had kept a cold and blank expression on his face while waiting for us females to make up our minds. I looked at myself and saw a forlorn, grumpy child. The longer I stood there, the uglier I felt, and so, in the end, I let myself be led to the back, to a small table near the kitchen where I couldn't smoke and where I felt hemmed in. At that moment I hated Lydia, and right on the spot decided I was not going to enjoy my meal. Women, I thought, were difficult and rigid. "You can go to the bar when you want a cigarette," Lydia said. "Not that it would kill you not to smoke for a couple of hours." "I feel like I'm in the ghetto," I grumbled. "The ghetto." Lydia stared with her big, almond eyes. Upset as I was, I couldn't suppress the thought that she had beautiful, soulful eyes. "What are you talking about?" she asked, but I didn't bother to explain. I was surprised at the term I chose, yet it must have been on my mind if it came so readily out of my mouth. "It's time you quit anyway," Lydia continued in her high, preachy voice. Lydia knew everything about nutrition and health and used statistics to back up her claims. She knew what was good or bad for me, what was proper or improper behavior. When I brought food to my mouth, using a knife rather than a fork, her whole being inflated with shocked indignation. "You will cut your tongue," she warned. Once, when I bummed a cigarette from a guy in a bar, she said in a voice loud enough for him to hear: "Never go up to a man and ask for a cigarette. Men always assume you're asking for more." It was obvious, I thought, that it was Lydia, in fact, who was asking "for more," but the guy ignored her, smiling at me and lighting my cigarette; for once, I felt victorious over her. I watched the rain. This morning for some reason I stuck a bottle of water in my bag, so I took it out and drank some. Still, I felt aimless, maybe a little sad. A woman with a bed sheet, or something that looked like a bed sheet wrapped around her neck, cleaned up after her dog. She held up the plastic bag in her hand as the dog barked and jumped, wanting to sniff his excrement, but the woman, cruelly depriving him of this primal right, told him to be quiet. One of the boys who worked in the store, Mexican I thought, called, Good morning, when he saw me sitting there, under the awning in the rain. I smiled, nodding my head in greeting. I began to think that I liked this place. Maybe this Korean store would be an adequate alternative on rainy days, and also in winter. It would rob me of a walk, and I would miss the regulars in the park, but at least I'd be sitting outdoors, watching the activities around me. I wished I had another apple with me, when I realized I was surrounded by crates of produce. I got up and scrutinized the fruit, then picked a green plum and poured myself another coffee, French Vanilla this time, and went back to my table. This wasn't so bad, it was actually pleasant to sit in the rain, and feel protected and dry. When we left the restaurant it had stopped raining and Lydia insisted that I come and see her newly renovated apartment. So we went to her place, and as I observed the freshly painted rooms, especially the pale cucumber bedroom, I thought it all looked a little sterile, but to Lydia I said, "It's very nice." "It feels a little sterile, don't you think? Come on, you can be honest with me." Lydia laughed, as if to lend credence to her words. "I'm honest," I said. I was taken aback, surprised that Lydia saw it as I did. "Yes, maybe it is," I admitted. "But I'm sure that after a while...." "That's what I'm hoping." Lydia sighed with contentment. "Once it's lived in a little, it will look better." "Yeah," I agreed. Later, when I walked home, it began to rain and thunder. I opened my umbrella and counted the blocks and so the minutes it would take before I got home. Two women, slightly drunk and unsteady on their heels, came toward me. They were leaning against one another under their one umbrella and laughing hysterically. "I don't want to know from anybody," one of them shouted, and her friend shrieked with laughter. "I don't want—" the first one continued, but I couldn't hear the rest of the sentence. I felt warm all over, thinking how wonderful it was that women could walk the city streets late at night and feel safe. Even when drunk. For the most part, so said the statistics, women were safe from strangers, but not from the men they knew. I saw myself and Elsbeth, laughing and hugging against the rain and wind under one umbrella, wallowing in our sense of freedom and independence. There were magical moments, I thought, when women shared a special bond, a primeval connection they couldn't and needn't express in words. We were all mothers to each other, I thought, breathing in the night air. I looked up at windows, mostly dark at this hour, but some were softly lit, intimating a tranquil life within. At home I turned on the TV and lay on the couch, watching programs about forensic science; it had become a morbid habit with me, watching programs about forensic science and reenactments of true crimes. I told myself I mustn't pollute my mind with this type of show, but every night I found myself caught up, yet again, in the gruesome details of a crime and its resolution. People, it seemed, killed for the flimsiest reasons, and as the cases unfolded I kept asking: How did they ever expect to get away with it? In the programs, the cops and detectives were very competent and knowledgeable and always solved their crimes. They seemed kind and caring, never cruel and conniving like I knew they had to be. On TV I was on their side and rooted for them against the killer, even if sometimes I felt sorry for the accused when they looked especially pathetic and faced the death penalty. I looked at my watch. The rain had stopped and I thought I might go to the pool, yet remained seated a while longer. I still felt a little sad, and my heart, or what I thought was my heart, ached. The wind blew, water dripped from the awning. The world was gray and wet and so were my thoughts. Finally, I got myself to the pool and swam a long hour. I was sheathed in silence, my strokes swift and furious. My mood swings, I reflected, were not violent, but they were mood swings all the same, and they unsettled me. If the day clears, I resolved, I will go to the park; only there, peace was restored and random encounters cheered me. I lingered under the hot shower then slumped in the sauna, wrapped in a towel. Leaving the gym, I heard the Hispanic receptionist behind the desk say into the phone, "Don't mess with me." Her tone was teasing and seductive when she said it, and

I wished I had someone I could say this to without sounding ridiculously out of character. All day it rained on and off, and I didn't go to the park. I tried to do some work, I tried to avoid my dreary face, but every so often I found myself in the bathroom, scrutinizing the mirror, trying to look into my eyes. I couldn't abide my face, I couldn't abide my state of mind. How futile it all is, I thought. Who cares if I finish or don't finish my dissertation? Who cares if I live or die? Even the detectives, it seemed, had forgotten about me, even if my Chilean neighbor believed otherwise. "Now that they've got you in their computers, they'll come after you," he said, and I wondered why I bothered to talk to him. He was smirking, and I thought he must be one of those oddballs who relished delivering bad news. "Are you always this gleeful?" I asked, and he gave me a pained look. "I know about these things, I just tell you what I know. Take it or leave it," he said, and I decided to leave it. The following morning I sat on my bench and sipped my coffee and ate my peach. Franklin went past, not seeing me, busy with the buttons of his raincoat. He looked good, almost dashing, in his raincoat that came down to his knees. He has quite a wardrobe, I thought. I sneezed. The day was gray and chilly, but so far dry. A woman carrying a large *Strawberry* shopping bag sat down on a bench. The bag looked old and battered, yet solid enough to hold her things. She pulled a croissant out of a brown paperbag and proceeded to eat it. A couple of napkins fell to the ground, but she didn't bother to pick them up. Her white shirt was soiled and her blondish hair, under a blue cap, looked stringy and unwashed. She ate mechanically, without pleasure, chunk after chunk, as if impatient with the necessity to feed herself. When she finished the one, she pulled another from the bag, which now flew to the ground. Between bites she put the croissant down on the bench. A couple of pigeons approached and she kicked the air with her foot and howled then picked up the unfinished croissant and the *Strawberry* shopping bag and went away. I sneezed again. I bit off a piece of cuticle and chewed it then spit it out. Two women, back from grocery shopping, took the bench the bag lady had vacated. One of them lit a cigarette and they talked softly; watching them, I felt peaceful. It was strange, I thought, how at times I felt peaceful and at others restless. Maybe the thing to do was to remember the peaceful moments when restlessness came. "I'm fifty years old," the smoker said, "I'm tired. I don't want to be nice anymore." The woman's voice trembled and I thought she was going to cry. The other woman nodded. "You have to play the game," she said. "I know," said the smoker, "but I can't, I won't." A man arrived with a three-legged dog and stopped for a chat with the two women on the bench. They were neighbors and now discussed the work being done in their building. They had over a million dollars in the reserve fund and because of this useless renovation job a quarter of it would be squandered. Their board, they said, was corrupt. The sun came out and surprised everyone. The women sighed and petted the dog, and I wondered if the dog was born like this or if he had had an operation. When they left I stood up and went to the river and watched the dark gray water. The streets were empty, the city felt deserted. It was the weekend again, and people were away in their summer homes. A small boat bobbed in the wind and three men stood on deck with their long, expensive-looking fishing rods. Three guys on a weekend outing, I thought, feeling a twinge of envy. I needed to pee. The light changed in the sky; soon, I thought, it would start to rain. Last night on the news the weatherman said something about a torna-do, but I didn't pay enough attention to know where and when the tornado would strike. Heading back I saw the woman with the *Strawberry* bag going toward the river. She and I, I thought, roaming the empty streets like ghosts. She was tall and possibly beautiful at one time and possibly still beautiful if someone had bothered to give her a bath and some clean clothes. When evening came I went to the park and sat with the chess players, chatting a while with the history professor who said it was time that I played a game or two; he offered to lend me a book so I could learn a couple of openings and moves. No, I said, I wouldn't have the time to read the book, there were things on my mind. "What things?" the professor asked, and I was tempted to tell him about the detectives. I watched the games for a while, then went home and watched a mindless TV drama. I hated myself for watching such drivel, and yet watched it through to the end, shedding bitter tears on cue. "Remember," Elsbeth said, "how we used to vow never to cry in the presence of our boyfriends and we did anyway? How silly we were, feeling so feminine and *weak*. Why do you think women cry?" "Maybe," I said, "because we never get what we want?" "Do gay women cry when they have a fight?" "I'm sure they do," I said. "Do both of them cry?" Elsbeth asked. "Possibly," I said. "I don't cry anymore, and I miss it," Elsbeth said. "I haven't cried in ages, and it worries me." "I don't miss it," I said, "I cry too much. I cry in the movies, even the silly ones." "But that's good," Elsbeth said, "you're crying for yourself, the movie is only the trigger, the excuse you need to let yourself go." "What do you mean I cry for myself?" I asked. "I mean," Elsbeth said, "you cry for things that haven't happened yet, which aren't and could never be whole. You cry for beauty, ideal beauty." "Really?" I said, overwhelmed. "Yes," Elsbeth said. "Crying is good, it brings you closer to who you are."

DREAMILY, I WATCHED AN OLD MAN and his dog. The old man pushed a walker, and the dog, a small, white poodle on a leash, tottered at his side. It was a new day, the sun shone brilliantly. As soon as it rose, it shone brilliantly. I sat on my bench, sipping my coffee and eating my grapes. The fountains were relentless, aiming for the sky. A bird, at regular intervals, gave a short cry. A couple of joggers trotted by, the mothers emerged with their toddlers and strollers, making their slow way to the playground.

The poodle, a little old-looking himself, took small steps, adjusting his pace to the man's. Every so often, like a fastidious nurse, he glanced up anxiously at the man, making sure his old master was all right. My heart went out to the man and his dog: they weren't long for this world. A man I saw last night at the chess tables arrived with his newspaper. He had earphones plugged in his ears, and he now took out his reading glasses and fit them on his nose. Last night Tom was there too, and he told me that this man was a Master, rated at 2200, the highest-ranking player among them. He's a loner, Tom said. Unlike the other players who would play until they got "chess eyes," this man, Tom said, would play just one game and promptly leave. Last night I saw him lose a game to Frenchie then briskly walk away, his head sunk low between his shoulder blades. Now I sat and watched him read the paper. There are quite a few of us, I thought, quietly existing, like posts, like phantoms, at the fringes. The image pleased me and yet I had to wonder when and how I became a loner. Even so, in becoming a loner I seemed to belong in a growing global trend, and this according to a study I read which noted the rise in solitude in the world. This phenomenon was attributed to city life, the life of the Window through which people looked but didn't touch. Last night, I sat next to Frenchie and watched him closely. Frenchie who, to believe Lydia, was crazy. True, once in a while before making a move he would push his right index finger into his mouth and bite down on it, but his blue eyes gleamed with a lively intelligence. I watched him beat player after player, and his often-repeated warning to all opponents, streaked with a light, French accent— "Whatever you do, remember that I exist"—made my laugh. "He is French," I had said to Lydia, "he's a big importer of French cheeses," but Lydia wasn't impressed. "I don't care what he does," she said, "he is crazy." Franklin was slowly waking up, rising from his cardboard bed. Yesterday, I got down my photo albums and looked at Elsbeth. When she modeled she was only half there and that was the quality top photographers and designers liked about her, the cool, vacuous look on her face; hers was a quality they could glamorize as an ideal for generations of growing girls. But in my photos, the photos I took of her, Elsbeth was fully present, smiling, or putting on a mock-serious face for the camera. Yes, Elsbeth bursting with life, seemingly more alive in photographs than in real life. She looked three-dimensional, because, I believed, she was aware of angles and knew what a direct, unfaltering gaze can do to the observer. Real life, I thought. Real life was where Elsbeth carried a life in her womb then got herself killed. No foreign DNA under her fingernails, only her own, wouldn't even lift a finger to defend herself from the knife. So drunk and so full of life, real life. "She didn't put up a struggle," Mr. Daley, or Mr. Maddox, had told Mrs. Williams who told me while waiting for her order of soft shell crabs. She was back in town for Elsbeth's memorial service. The killer had the audacity to take a shower while Elsbeth bled to death, Mrs. Williams said, and I remembered the detective's questions about me taking showers at Elsbeth's. I wondered how they would know such a thing, about the killer taking a shower, but didn't want to ask. When the food came Mrs. Williams ceased all conversation and ate. Mrs. Williams, I knew from Elsbeth, didn't believe in small chit-chat during a meal. "No marks on her hands. She was probably asleep when the attack occurred. Maybe it's a good thing," Mrs. Williams said later and bit her lip. "It's too bad you can't remember anything. We were counting on you." "Who's we?" I asked. "All of us. Me, and the police, of course." All at once, it felt warm, the air stood still. I felt empty, jittery, maybe a little like a mad person looking for a dark hole to hide in. I put my feet up on the stone table and took a deep Yoga breath. Even the coffee, hot and bitter, annoyed me. Some type of insect hovered near my face, and I shooed it away. Maybe I'm losing it, I thought, and in a strange way it pleased me that I might be losing it. There was a certain appealing logic to madness, to utter submission. Madness could be pure, sobering. Two elderly women walked past, talking about nursing homes. "Too bad you can't remember anything," Mrs. Williams said, echoing the detectives and seemingly just as cold and unforgiving. God knows I tried to recapture my last moments with Elsbeth. We must have taken a cab, we were both very drunk, much more so than the two women I saw on the street late one night. Elsbeth had ordered another bottle of wine, the third of the night, after Drew left in a huff. "You shouldn't drink so much," I chastised and Elsbeth laughed. "You're my conscience, aren't you? Tomorrow, I promise, I'll be a good girl and stop everything," Elsbeth said, or something to that effect, I now thought. Like the detective said, I was useless. I couldn't hold on to the important details and report them to him. "Never talk to cops," said my Chilean neighbor. "If they call you again, go with your lawyer." "Then they'll think I have something to hide," I said, feeling stupid and insecure. "Do you? Do you have something to hide?" the Chilean asked and I stiffened, taking offense. "Of course not," I said. "So, what do you care? Get a lawyer," said the Chilean. "I'm innocent," I said. "I refuse to spend my money on lawyers, they only complicate matters. Besides, I don't think they'll call me again." And that was when the Chilean said that once they had someone in their clutches they never let go. A sudden light breeze brought relief. I have to be strong, I thought, and listen to no one. "All the comforts of home," a woman, laughing, called out to me, and I smiled and nodded. People spoke to me, and I still had it in me to respond. I still cared, which reassured me. On my way to the river, I saw an old man with a metal cane run toward the bus stop, yelling and waving his cane for the bus-driver to wait. A woman, his wife I assumed, walked calmly behind, not assisting in his efforts to catch the driver's attention. She must hate him, I thought. She must hate him and mock him in her heart, seeing him as an old, pitiful man, an invalid. Maybe they had a fight, or maybe she was paying him back for years of abuse. Still, I felt sorry for the man, and angry at the wife. "These are the last summer days of the century," Lydia said when we sat and watched the river. "Of the millennium," I added, and Lydia looked at me.

"You're right, it didn't occur to me." We sat and watched the river for a while. "I respect rivers, I respect all bodies of water," Lydia said and I nodded. "New York," Lydia said, "is a powerful place because two rivers converge in it." "True," I said. I liked the idea of power and two rivers converging. We were experiencing, I thought, a rare moment of mutual serenity. "When I think of some of the men I slept with, especially in the last year or so. I must have been desperate—God!" Lydia suddenly exclaimed, and there was so much self-reproach in that short invocation, I felt something tighten inside of me. Sometimes I did appreciate Lydia's candor and openness. "What was wrong with them?" I asked. "They were awful, just awful and selfish," Lydia said, her jaw dropping with the vowels, giving her face even a longer, more haunted look. "How were they awful?" I asked. "I don't want to talk about it." Lydia looked away. "All right," I said, even though I didn't like it when people started to say something and then stopped. "What did they ask you at the station?" Lydia asked. "Same as you," I said lightly, "generalities." "That's odd," Lydia said. "I hardly knew Elsbeth, but you were with her on the night of the murder." I could strangle her, I thought. "I don't like the way you put it," I said. "Well, it's the truth.

You saw her on the night of the murder." "Will you stop," I shouted, "using that word? It gives me the creeps." "I'm not one to badmouth the dead," Lydia said, "but you know what I think. She took advantage of you." Lydia pursed her adamant lips. "She did not," I said hotly. "She was different with me when we were alone." "If you say so," Lydia said. When I got home I made myself a cheese sandwich and watched TV. Then, still hungry, I threw a few leaves of lettuce into a pot of water, deciding to forgo the salt. Years ago I had learned how to make a genuine French salad dressing, and while the lettuce soaked I took a small bowl and mixed in a spoonful of extra sharp Dijon mustard, chopped garlic, lemon juice, vinegar, a pinch of black pepper, and a tablespoon of olive oil. I drained the lettuce and chopped it into fine, long strips, then saturated the salad with the rich, yellow dressing I had so lovingly prepared. While I was eating the telephone rang. The investigation was going nowhere, Mrs. Williams said. Drew was a suspect, and so was I. Was I aware of it? Numb with incredulity, I said, No, I had no idea. Mrs. Williams asked if there was something I wished to tell her, something I wouldn't tell the detectives? No, I said, there wasn't. They're very diligent, Mrs. Williams said of the detectives, they're doing their best, what else could she do but put her trust in their judgment? It was a tragedy, Mrs. Williams said, for all concerned, and I thanked her for calling. I recalled a case I saw on TV where a mother, not relying on the police, hung posters and placed ads everywhere for seven years until the man who had killed her daughter was captured and tried and sentenced to death. Mrs. Williams, I thought, was not the type to devote seven years to find a killer. Besides, she had two other daughters; the mother on TV had had only one. I thought that I might have gone on a crusade if someone had only pointed the way. Some things must remain a mystery forever, Mrs. Williams said. A cul de sac, I thought. "You were after her money, weren't you?" The detective asked, and I shook my head with consternation. "Of course not, I have my own money." "Mrs. Williams told us you asked about Elsbeth's will." "I was curious, that's all," I said. "Curious about what?" "About if she had written a will." "Why do you care if she did or didn't?" "I don't care," I cried, "I just asked a question." "An innocent question," he said. "Yes," I said, "an innocent question." Poems were read when a few of us assembled in a hall to commemorate Elsbeth's life. Surreptitiously, I looked for Drew among the faces but he wasn't there. When the speeches began I sat there and sobbed. I hadn't meant to, but as soon as the first person went up to speak, a dam inside me broke and the tears began to flow. People expected me to take the podium, still I couldn't bring myself to go up there and expose myself so nakedly. Elsbeth's sisters sat on either side of their mother. Like Mrs. Williams, they sat blank-faced and dry-eyed. I wanted them to cry, but they didn't. One after the other they went up to the podium and read a few words from prepared statements. About how they loved their sister and missed her every day. The statements were beautifully written, maybe by a professional, and were beautifully delivered. I sobbed into my tissues. I felt ridiculous, exhibiting my grief, while the family, Elsbeth's blood relatives, remained elegant and composed; I was an embarrassment they did their best to ignore. I was too emotional, which was synonymous with poor taste. I went to the coffee shop and got another coffee, then went back to the park. I felt a little sad and pensive, yet peaceful, like a monk, I imagined, in the quiet of the monastery. The street, though, was alive with sounds, Con Edison men drilled a hole in the ground. These were the last summer days of the millennium, a whole century was lumbering to a close. In the last millennium people worried about the sins they might have committed which would bring about the end of the world. Now they worried about how computers would cope with a couple of zeros. Elsbeth was born to outlast the millennium but some other force intervened, and I worried it was now my turn to be caught in the quicksilver spin of fate. Last night I heard a man shout to his friends: "I love this city." His face was wild with joy. "This is a jay-walker's paradise." I smiled, agreeing with him whole-heartedly even though I now crossed the street only at the crosswalk and only when I had the light. At the bus stop two men hugged. They stood very close, facing each other, and talked. They were lovers, I thought, or were about to become lovers, and I wondered if they practiced safe sex. I had recently read about the papilloma virus that could cause penile or anal cancer and against which even condoms were no help. I watched the men and wished I were a fly, perched on the shoulder of the taller one who was blond and smoked a cigarette; his physique and demeanor suggested daring, danger. The other man, older and with a deep tan, had perfect teeth, perhaps too perfect, perhaps fake. In his pleasant, smiling face I read decadence and a real potential for cunning and cruelty. The two men, I thought, probably saw each other for what they were and took it as a challenge. "He ripped me apart," Lydia said of her first lover, and I was impressed with the strong, emphatic language. I watched her mouth. My periodontist, I thought, would love the healthy pink of her gums. Lydia, I mused, looked especially stylish when she told me her stories of woe. Her first lover, she said, gave her herpes. He was married now, had a couple of kids, and lived in Indonesia. Listening to her, I thought about the first boy I let kiss me. He was my boyfriend, we were going steady, but when he pushed his tongue into my mouth, all I felt was revulsion and a touch of wonder at why I was letting him do this. He must have had a stubble, for when I ran home my face was on fire: he'd given me a rash. I didn't love him, there were other, more adventurous boys I had my eye on, but they ignored me. Already then I understood, or vaguely sensed, that certain boys would forever remain beyond my grasp. I was pretty but not stunning, intelligent but not clever, and always, always, too uncertain. There are no enemies, only the self, the yoga instructor said. She told us to close our eyes and concentrate on the third eye between the brows. "Were you ever pregnant?" I asked, thinking about my own abortion. "No," Lydia said. A group of children arrived and filled the playground with wild cries and running feet. They swung and crawled and shrieked, except for one boy who sat on a bench and watched the ground. Then he stood and stomped his feet on a passing beetle or ant. He told the coach he wanted to eat and she told him it wasn't time yet. I watched the boy and saw future problems; I ached for him a little, so apart and unwelcome and not fitting in. An Asian woman with a takeout salad and a bottle of water sat down on the next bench. She was painfully skinny and I wondered how her internal organs all managed to squeeze together inside her frame. Last night in my sleep I made lions dance. They were about to attack me so I began to dance and soon they were dancing too. One of the lions had a round face and looked a little like Tom. He seemed friendly, and he told me: Take a simple event and transform it. A few feet away, a cute little toddler kept running from her father. She had on a long white dress dotted with orange blossoms, and her fine blond hair fell to her bony shoulders. A feisty little Elsbeth, I thought, instantly charmed. The father pushed the stroller, the toddler walked at his side for a couple of steps, then veered off in another direction. "Lili, Lili," the father called after her, and Lili pressed on even faster, her arms up in the air, her small feet in tiny sandals. She ran, I thought, like an old lady, leaning forward in her haste to get away. I feared that she would lose her balance and fall, but she didn't. Daddy, giving in, let go of the stroller and ran after her; he wasn't amused. They resumed walking and for a moment it seemed Lili had understood that she must go where Daddy wanted to go, but all at once she took off again, and again he had to run after her. "The only thing that's free in this country is disease," Tom said, straddling the crossbar of his red bike. I smiled, then remembered Tom's cancer. "And air," I offered. "No," Tom said. "Not in New York. Maybe in Canada it still is, in some remote area. If they came here and stood near the Holland Tunnel they'd be dead in an hour. Look behind you." Tom pointed and I turned. A fire engine, very red against the trees, slowly drove by, with the handsome firemen poking their heads in the windows, just like Elsbeth said. "What are they doing here?" I wondered aloud. "They're coming for you," Tom said with a smile, "they heard you were hot." I laughed. It was the first time he said something that directly involved me. "They have the best job, they hang out all day," Tom said. "Sometimes," I said, "they die in a fire." "Nah," Tom said, "not so much anymore. They go out on inspections, then they go back and eat and take a nap. I was a cop, I know. Food was the highlight of our day. You forget all the police shit and sit down and be normal." Tom took off. I could go to my hairdresser, I thought. I didn't have an appointment, but I would sit there and watch him work until he could fit me in. That was the only way I ever got a haircut, on impulse, I never called for an appointment. People sat at tables in outdoor cafés, and I thought it would be nice to sit in an outdoor café and have lunch with someone. But when I used to sit with friends in cafés and restaurants, I felt a little empty and absent from the scene, unless Elsbeth was around. But even with Elsbeth, I now thought, I was not entirely at ease when we went out. I much preferred it when it was the two of us alone, in her place or mine; only then was perfect communion possible. It was strange, I thought, how my feelings for Elsbeth hadn't changed, I still felt so very close to her, even though I couldn't hear or smell or touch her as before. Again I remembered that awful movie from years ago about a guy who goes looking for his lost girlfriend and for all his troubles gets buried alive. Curiosity killed the cat, people said, laughing, as they walked out of the movie theater, a remark that I thought was cruel and crass. It wasn't curiosity that killed the cat, it was the compulsion to come clean and do penance. "You're my real sister," Elsbeth said, and I tried, in vain, to remember her very last words. I had a vague notion of the two of us huddling in a cab. I must have dropped Elsbeth off and then continued on. Unless, like the cops insisted, I went upstairs to help her into bed. We were both drunk, but Elsbeth even more so. She gave up control when she drank; that was the whole point, she said, and after Drew left, we felt happy and free. Like two puppies, I thought. We babbled incoherently into each other's ear and laughed helplessly for no reason at all. We were drunk but pure in our hearts. Lili and father reappeared, Lili this time strapped in the stroller, kicking and screaming, banging her head with both tiny fists. Daddy, obviously, had had enough: he was taking Lili home.

I GAZED AT THE TREES. A couple of early joggers jogged by. Tom drove past on his way to the gym. I asked if his girlfriend, too, worked out. "Only when she frowns," Tom said, and I laughed. It was quiet. Franklin was still asleep, the leaves rustled in the breeze. Last night Lydia and I went to a party but it was so boring we left early. Some guy sat down next to me, commenting on my hair, on how short it was. "I got it cut today," I told him. I said I wanted to get rid of the blond and go back to brown. The guy nodded, and we sat for a while and watched the others. I wanted to say more but felt frozen inside. People stood in groups and shouted above the music. "Nobody dances anymore," I remarked, and the guy looked at me. "They talk," he said gruffly. "They all talk, empty talk. That's why I like TV. I can shut them up with a click." Thinking it was a joke I giggled but the guy didn't even smile. After a moment he stood up and showed me his beer. "I need a refill," he said and left me sitting on the couch. For a while I thought he might come back, but he didn't. Lately, I seemed to have forgotten why men would be attracted to women, and this realization alarmed me. The detectives came to my mind and I remembered my constant, inexplicable fear that they'd suspect me of lying. They put so much weight on each question, questions that I for the most part thought irrelevant. "Just routine questioning," Lydia had said. "They have to fill out forms." They think aloud, one question leads to another and then, almost by default, they hit on something. Sometimes, on the real killer. "You'd be surprised," said the detective, "how many people get away with murder." He looked straight at me when he said that, and I took his words as a warning. Walking home from the party I told Lydia about the guy who had talked to me, I said I thought he was weird. "He went for a beer and didn't come back," Lydia said, "what's so weird about that?" She was implying, of course, that the guy had lost interest in me, and that my pride was injured, which wasn't the case, not entirely. "I'm talking about him saying that he likes TV because he can click people off. I thought he meant it as a joke and I laughed but then I realized he was totally serious." "Maybe it's his style, deadpan," Lydia said and I dropped it. At the next bench a man was reading the paper. Maybe it was time for me to start reading the paper, I considered. That way I would know what everybody else knew with such certitude. The sun went behind the clouds and a sudden wind blew. I ate my peach and drank my coffee. It was a little chilly, some people wore jackets. I wore my khaki shorts and my small black sweater on top of a green T-shirt. I sipped the coffee, imagining nutrients and warmth coursing through my veins. In a dream a round blue globe rolled toward me and I thought I might pick myself up and go traveling. "She talked about buying a house in the country," I told Mr. Maddox, or was it Mr. Daley? "She wanted to buy a Tahiti swing." The detective looked at me. "What's a Tahiti swing?" he asked. "I'm not sure," I said. I could see he was wondering why I was telling him this. I was wasting his time, but he did invite me, didn't he? He wanted to see me and I made time for him, sitting in his office, compliant and sweet, talking to him as I would to a shrink. "Some type of swing you'd put in your backyard or garden," I said. "Why are you telling me this?" the detective asked, and I shrugged. "Just something that came to my mind, I thought it might be helpful." "How?" "Maybe it shows that she had plans. She was making more and more money, and she was making plans." "We know she had plans," said the detective with malice in his voice. "Someone put a stop to those plans. Out of mercy, according to you. She was unhappy you said." "She was," I confirmed with animation, "and that's why she bought things." "What things?" "Things. Dishes, towels. She wanted a big house, a house in the country." "So," Mr. Daley said. "She wanted a house in the country, then got someone to kill her. Now, which is it?" "Maybe both?" I offered miserably. Too often, something that was clear in my mind became muddled when I tried to explain it to others. I was disconnected, I thought, yet still very much alive with wants and desires of my own. Franklin was asleep, wrapped in my comforter. A forlorn pigeon patrolled the grounds. Elsbeth dead, consecrated to God, stabbed numerous times. I imagined that once you began stabbing, you couldn't stop, you went into a frenzy, like when you were furious with someone and you listened to your voice rise in the heat of argument. You told yourself to stop, but you couldn't stop, you shouted louder and louder, trapped in a spiral of madness, incited and emboldened by the sound of your shouting voice. I shivered. Every time I thought about the knife, a tremor went through me, the knife penetrating Elsbeth's smooth skin, making this peculiar swishing sound as it broke through tissue, decimating the perfection that Elsbeth was. I saw the horror in Elsbeth's eyes as Elsbeth, even through her stupor, realized what was happening to her. I saw the blood, Elsbeth's thick, rich blood, ooze over the bed, the walls, all over the white-bleached floors. I tried to remember the last, drunken words she and I exchanged. Did Elsbeth, perhaps, try to say good-bye? Was it why she insisted that I join them for dinner? Did Drew leave early so that Elsbeth and I could be together one last time? My thoughts, I knew, made no sense. My thoughts implied it had all been planned. "We were drunk," I told the detective who all at once featured large and ominous in my life. Mr. Frank Daley snorted through his nose. Obviously, he didn't approve of women drinking. Women were women, they should be womanly. Unless, of course, they were drinking with him. "You realize, I'm sure, that you were the last person to see her alive," he pointed out, a smug, oddly content expression on his face. "Except for the murderer," I remembered to add. The detective looked at me; he hadn't expected me to be so quick on my feet, alert to his maneuverings. Again, as during our first interview, something in his eyes told me that he loathed me and loathed Elsbeth, two slatternly drunks, one of them butchered. This was the inevitable outcome when women took liberties and ventured into man's sacred territory. "Except for the murderer," he repeated as if he had just thought of it himself, then let his tongue roam in his mouth. I began to feel tense under his frown. I yearned for Mr. Maddox who seemed to have vanished. He was nice, I thought, or so I remembered him. Just another detective, and yet, more humane than Daley. "Murder has a language, and I'm the interpreter," Mr. Daley said, and I regarded him with what I had hoped was silent scorn. A soft wind blew. Franklin, in the shelter of his cardboard, stirred as if deep in a dream. He had his sandals and white socks on, which surprised me; normally, he'd take off his shoes before going to bed. His white socks, I noted with pain, were soiled. I worried that perhaps he was slipping, giving up. Just then he sneezed, a loud hard sneeze, then another, and another. He stood up and stretched and, noticing me, waved and called, Good morning. I waved and called back. He turned and began to put his things away. A half moon stood high in the morning sky and I felt a little groggy. Last night I got stoned and lay on the oak floor and listened to Patsy Cline sing "Crazy" over and over again. At one point, I got my mother's jewelry box and put on her diamond ring on my middle finger. I had no inkling as to what brought the ring to my mind, or what impulse got me to my feet—it was the first time I ever put it on. When I was a child she used to laugh and point at the ring. "When I die, this ring will be yours," she would say, and I, almost against my will, looked forward to the time when I could wear it. But last night, as soon as I put it on, it felt so foreign, so bulky on my finger, I took it off and put it back in the box. A sudden rush of wind rustled in the leaves. Franklin went to get his breakfast and the morning papers. We were almost a couple, I mused. He rising a little later than me. "Aren't you chilly?" he asked when he saw me in my little shorts, my little T-shirt, my little black sweater and white socks. "No," I said, "are you?" He had his jacket wrapped around him as he hugged himself. "A little." He smiled his sad smile. If he had all his teeth, I thought, he'd be a handsome man. "It was cold yesterday," I said. "It's going to be nice today." Yesterday, in yoga class, the instructor played one of her mantra CDs, and now that same melodic loop kept repeating in my head. Franklin arrived with his coffee, but without the paper. He blew his nose. Maybe he has a cold, I thought. The wind tousled my short hair and I took pleasure in the silhouette of my head on the chess table. Last night, with a sudden burst of hope and a need to immerse myself in beauty, I leaned out the window to breathe in the entire sky. The windowsill reached below my waistline, right at my hipbones, and it occurred to me that I could easily slip or lose my footing and fall out. Especially when stoned. Architects, I thought, overestimated the will and control people exercised over their bodies. If I fell, people would assume I had jumped. I killed my cigarette. A woman in black leotards walked past with her white poodle. She smiled, I smiled back. Last night, a bear in my dream got up on his hind legs and took a clumsy step toward me.

I remembered I must make noise to scare him away, and I woke up just as I opened my mouth to scream. Franklin drank his coffee. No roll, no donut, no paper. He didn't have enough money this morning, I thought. In the sauna, I lay naked on a towel and covered my face with my hand against the heat. Shapes formed under my closed lids, and they were so vivid, I thought for a moment that my eyes were open. Round cups opened, revealing shifting cushions of bright colors. "Bikinis," Elsbeth said, "are a state of mind." The two of us were lying on the beach, sunning ourselves. Elsbeth said she didn't like my one-piece suits, she wanted me to get a bikini. I said I didn't want a bikini, a bikini would cut me in half, and Elsbeth said it was ridiculous, that I would look good in a bikini. I said I would think about it, but the truth was that next to her flawless body, a one-piece suit was the only option for me. No matter how hard I looked, I never found even the tinniest blemish on her amazing skin. I had dubbed her body: The Land of Surprises, because every time she bared a little flesh, new discoveries were to be made: a little ring here, a tattoo there. In the steam room, she rubbed her skin with lemon peels and spread warm honey all over her body, luxuriating in her warm softness. "I'm as soft as a baby's heinie," she'd say. I didn't rub my skin with lemon peels, I didn't have tattoos, and wore no rings on my nipples. I would have loved a small diamond stud on my bellybutton, but my bellybutton was invisible, hidden in a deep tunnel—a dark and primitive slit in my flesh. "If, like you, I had a ring on my bellybutton, maybe I would wear a bikini," I said. "Why don't you get one, then?" Elsbeth yawned. "I'm thirsty," she said, "aren't you?" "Not really," I said. "I can go get you a Coke, if you like." "Oh, would you? Please?" Elsbeth smiled. "You're so good to me, I don't deserve you." "Of course you do," I said and went to get the Coke.

BITS AND PIECES OF ELSBETH created a mosaic in my head, a mosaic I tried to recreate for the detectives. I had placed my future on her shoulders, I wanted to tell them, and now my future was cut down. The park was deserted; I listened to the hum emanating from the buildings. Soon, the street would wake and people would hurry on their way. This morning I had bought a buttered roll with my coffee, and the Hispanic man behind the counter seemed very pleased. At last, his expression said, or so I imagined. I sat and chewed, a little disappointed, for I had looked forward to enjoying it much more than I actually did. But I was hungry, and it was good. Tom arrived on his bike and, lowering himself to the crossbar, continued his unremitting monologue about his unfortunate, third ex-wife. She was great fun when they lived together, he said, and then she went and changed on him. As soon as they got married, she showed him her true nature. "What happened?" I asked, fully engaged in his story. "She opened the rulebook." Tom shifted on the crossbar. "She became stupid. We lived together for two years and never a bad word between us. I walked into church with a woman I loved, and God switched her. She began to fight me right there, in church, and we weren't even married five minutes. She was a good-looking woman, too." Tom shook his head. "Not anymore?" I asked. "Yes, she still is, when she pays attention. When she thinks you're not looking, she makes funny faces and this bitter expression sits on her face." I nodded. Tom's foot was on the pedal and every once in a while he brought the pedal up as if ready to take off. Watching his massive, muscular thigh, I felt a sudden jolt of deep sadness. Lately, I'd been catching myself looking at men on the street, all types of men, short, tall, heavy, skinny, and even though I told myself that on some level mine was a purely scientific quest, it still made me feel needy and lonely. "She doesn't care about our daughter. She only cares about fucking me over. She's crazy." Tom brought the pedal up and took off, and I went to the coffee shop and got another coffee. I bought a plum from a street vendor and went back to my bench. The air smelled of bacon and eggs, an aroma that usually sated me, almost as if I had eaten the bacon and eggs myself, but this morning it was overbearing. Overnight, it seemed, the leaves had lost their luster. A cloud of foreboding hung over me, so I put a finger to my nostril and practiced a way of breathing I had learned in yoga. Breathing through the left nostril, the instructor said, cooled the system and calmed you. Breathing through the right, gave you energy. Sometimes these deep breathing techniques worked for me, sometimes they only made me more anxious. When women committed suicide, I learned on TV, they shot themselves in the chest. Men, said the forensic scientist, did it the macho way, shooting themselves in the head. I watched them work on cadavers in the morgue. They stripped a woman of her black pantyhose, revealing her white legs and the red nail polish on her toes. She was young, and the nail polish looked freshly painted. On the day she was killed, or the day before, she went to the nail salon and got herself a pedicure. A Jane Doe, said the detective matter-of-factly. The thought that Elsbeth's body was handled this way made me sick to my stomach. I wondered if the morticians bothered to remove the diamond from her bellybutton and the nipple-rings from her nipples to give to Mrs. Williams who anyway hated the rings. The day was gorgeous, sunny and mild, and a pleasant breeze coursed through the park. I lit a cigarette, the first of the day. Across the street people waited for the Hamptons jitney to come and take them away for the long weekend. They were an orderly bunch, patiently standing on line, a vacant expression on their faces. Some of them talked into their cell phones, also vacantly. I kind of pitied them, thinking of the trouble they put themselves through to get away from the city. Three hours going, three hours coming back, the packing, the unpacking, the schlepping, just to escape the stigma of not having been included, and to be able to say in a studied, nonchalant voice: "I went to the Hamptons for the weekend." One less worry for me, I thought, congratulating myself. A very handsome man in a white shirt came into the park and sat down on a bench. I had my book open on the chess table, but I sat and watched his back. He lit a cigarette and offered me his profile when he blew smoke to the sky. In my dream, one of Elsbeth's old boyfriends came around the house. He flirted with me and I laughed, flattered yet nervous that Elsbeth would be upset if she found out. We kissed a little, then I said, "Let me go get her," and I ran out of the house to find her. I ran as fast as I could, realizing how piteous and inadequate I was. I found Elsbeth and told her to come home, but she wouldn't listen. She wore a light summer dress and frolicked in the yard, waving her arms. Last night, Lydia and I sat in a restaurant near the U.N. and silently watched a man and a woman at the bar. It was late and, except for a couple of people, the bar section was empty. The man, Lydia said, was probably a U.N. technocrat. He was tall, maybe Scandinavian, and looked uncomfortable on the bar stool, very rigid and stiff in his dark-blue suit. The woman, in her plain print dress and cheap eyeglasses, lacked any definite style and looked young and naive. She seemed to be in awe of the man, he was possibly her boss, and it was obvious they were out on their first date. They downed their drinks fast, seemingly in a hurry to get drunk and shed their inhibitions before succumbing to the frivolity of romance. The woman, her face flushed, stood up and went to the bathroom. "She's probably a temp, or a secretary," Lydia said, and I nodded. The man meanwhile fidgeted on the stool as if trying to strike just the right pose. The woman came back and they began kissing at once. The man splayed his fingers across her back and bent his head, pushing his face into her mouth. I wondered if they made noises as they kissed. I wondered what the bartender was thinking, having to stand there and watch. "I never saw anyone kiss like that," I said to Lydia. "Look how he cranes his neck, it looks like he's assaulting her." "It's not his neck I'm thinking about." Lydia cackled. "He may be a great kisser. He certainly seems to give her his all." A couple of days ago, when I went to see the detective, he embarked on a new line of questioning that had nothing to do with Elsbeth. He wanted to know about my parents, my money situation, my cousin and aunt in Michigan. At one point I said, "I know it's a cliché, but am I suspect?" and the detective laughed; I smiled at his simple gullibility. When he was done asking about my family, he rose and offered me a cup of coffee. He left the room and as I sat there waiting for him I suddenly got the distinct impression that the air around me had turned dense and that I was being watched. I wanted to swivel around toward the door, but didn't. I began to fidget, just like this U.N. guy on the bar stool, and I told myself to breathe and be calm: If I was a suspect, like Mrs. Williams had said, I'd better show them a rational and sincere face. It was curious, though, how only a short while ago they dismissed me, I was useless to them, and now, all at once, they were eager to talk to me. Things changed and shifted behind my back, without my knowledge or control. I must pay attention, I thought. The detectives could and would corner me into a passivity of will and mind. If they applied pressure and pushed me against the wall, if they intimidated me and called me a liar, I'd be numbed into submission, unable to proclaim my innocence in a full, strong voice. In fact, I would resent having to protest my innocence. In my mind I was innocent, in my whole being I felt innocent, but the detectives, the agents of the State, had a job to do, their egos and professional pride were on the line. If they kept up their unified assault, they could, by power of suggestion and sheer persistence, bring me around to adopting their point of view. They were skilled, they were trained, it wouldn't take much to break me. If they couldn't find the knife with my fingerprints on it, it didn't make me innocent, it made me clever, and they had to break me. It would be their conviction against mine, and they had a whole power structure backing them. Maybe they did find the knife. Maybe Drew's fingerprints weren't on it. Maybe he had a strong alibi. And witnesses. My only witnesses were the walls of my apartment and my fuzzy drunken memory. My judgment, which adequately served me on a daily basis, wouldn't serve me in criminal court. I was a specimen, Elsbeth liked to say, a bit off, a bit slanted, and people, especially in courtroom situations, tended to veer toward the normal, only too eager to point a finger. My heart was beating away in my chest; I saw myself addressing a jury of my peers and failing to convince them. I was in trouble, I knew. I would stumble, trip on my own words, and not even realize it. I'd been too careless in my responses and the detective, when he wanted to, could easily trick me and use my own words against me. Every careless word, every slip of the tongue, could be given a sinister meaning. And, if it came to that, I had no allies I could turn to, no character witnesses. I couldn't rely on Lydia and her peculiar perceptions, her ambiguous statements. Ethan and Nili had two kids in the house, I couldn't ask them to get involved. I took a deep breath, reminding myself I panicked too easily, often for no good reason at all. "What about Drew?" I could say. "Why don't you talk to him?" But I was getting ahead of myself. The detective returned with two cups of coffee. "We both drink it black," I said, hoping to suggest an alliance, an alignment of a sort. I was tempted to tell him that at one time I seriously considered joining the police force because I wanted to be in a position to help people. I liked to help people, I'd say, being truthful, but just then, as we sat and sipped our coffees like old acquaintances, another detective came in and sat himself on a chair against the wall, directly behind me. I began to turn my chair to half-face both of them, but Mr. Daley stopped me, as I knew he would, and I resented his right to control my movements. I sat still and waited while he opened a file and pretended to be looking over some documents. The other man breathed behind me, and I became conscious of my own breathing, rising and falling with his. "We need to go over a few points," Mr. Daley said, and I nodded. Should I ask to speak to a lawyer, or was it too late? "Could you tell me what we're doing?" I asked. "Legally speaking?" "We're having an informal chat," said the detective. "I understand that," I said, proud of my grownup, confident manner. "But if it comes to trial, whatever I say will be held against me, won't it?" "Against you?" Mr. Daley sounded surprised. "We have nothing against you." I watched him. "Still," I said, "should I get a lawyer?" "With or without a lawyer present, you'd have to talk to us," said the man behind me. "With whom do I have the honor?" I turned to face him, and this time Daley didn't stop me. The new detective had kind, brown eyes, and he looked familiar in a comforting way. I liked his mouth. "My name is Larry," he said. "Larry Maddox." Oh yes, I thought, I remembered now. He was the nice detective I yearned for earlier. Somehow, he looked different today. His face, like Mr. Daley's, was mapped with scars, and I couldn't recall why I thought I liked him. He did seem more sympathetic, though, scars and all. Maybe he was Daley's superior, someone I could talk to more openly and without fear. "But what am I supposed to be doing here?" I asked, putting desperation into my voice. "I already told you everything." I didn't mean to, but I began to cry. Mr. Maddox handed me a tissue and went to get me a glass of water. Mr. Daley seemed upset. He kept his silence while I sat across from him in the small, airless office, ridiculous tears streaming down my cheeks. Then Maddox came back, and Daley left the room. "Why are you crying?" Mr. Maddox asked in a soft, concerned voice, and for a moment I thought he was my doctor. "I don't know," I whimpered, wiping my tears. "I don't know what's happening to me. My thoughts, they're all confused. I don't know what you want from me, I don't know why you're doing this to me." "Doing what to you?" Mr. Maddox asked, still sounding like my doctor. "You're trying to break me," I howled, "but even if you succeed you'll find nothing there, it won't work, you're wasting your time." It was a crisp morning. The very handsome man who smoked a cigarette before now ate a roll and drank coffee from a tall *Starbucks* cup. I bit into my apple. The detectives, I thought, had nothing to go on, they were shooting in the dark. Yesterday evening I came to watch the chess players and for a couple of hours found comfort in their company. I had hoped that Tom would show up so I could tell him about Daley and Maddox, maybe he knew them, maybe he could say a word in my behalf, but Tom wasn't there. The handsome man stood up and left. It was a beautiful day, glorious in fact, but my mind was overcast. I couldn't concentrate, and when I attempted to focus on one thought the fog in my head only grew denser. I sat, waiting for Tom to arrive on his bike and divert me with a story. I cleaned the dirt from under my nails; I hadn't showered in two days, I realized, and I smelled; maybe I was slipping, like Franklin. The blue sky shimmered, the gardeners sawed dead branches off the trees. The sycamores, a gardener had told me, were dying and would eventually be replaced with maples. I saw Franklin fold his things and put them in his cart. He was slow and methodical, taking time to care for his possessions, and I considered taking my fate in my hands and committing a vanishing act. I could share his life, I thought. I'd help him collect cans—better four hands than two—and he, with his street-life experience, would protect me from potential hazards. Stripped of everything, we would be free, living from moment to moment, and we wouldn't be alone. I saw them everywhere, homeless couples, kissing and laughing on the street, always engaged in spirited conversations. Most often they seemed fuller, happier human beings than the harried citizens around them. An owl, or something that sounded like an owl, hooted. An old couple arrived with their breakfast and the morning paper. "She had a very bad operation," the wife told the husband. They brought out their bagels and coffees and I was seized by a sudden hunger. Yesterday afternoon Daley and Maddox ceremoniously took their respective seats and went over my relationship with

Drew. "We didn't have a relationship," I said. "He didn't like me." "Why not?" Maddox asked. His voice was soft and solicitous. Again, he was sitting behind me, but somehow I didn't mind it anymore. It was better this way, I thought, talking into the void. I shrugged. "I don't know," I said. "Elsbeth and I were best friends." "And he was jealous," Maddox stated and I nodded. "I guess," I said. "Why would he be jealous of you and Elsbeth? You weren't lovers, were you? What do they call it?" Mr. Maddox's voice brimmed with conviviality. "Ménage à trois?" He mangled the foreign words, and they came out sounding like rocks. "I don't know," I said, panic rising in my chest. Now the questions came one after the other and I began to lose track. They were cunning, these detectives, they came at me like cats, and I, the mouse in the middle, had nowhere to turn. "Maybe he wanted her all to himself," I offered. "I told you, he was the jealous type." "How do you know he was the jealous type? Did he say something to you?" "No, but you could tell from the way he reacted when Elsbeth mentioned other men, even just friends." "What would he do?" came the question from behind. "Nothing," I said. "He'd just sit there and glower, not saying a word." "But you too," Mr. Daley said. "You wanted to keep her all to yourself."

"That's absolute nonsense," I said. "So, you think he killed her?" the detectives said again and again. "Why would he want to kill her?" "I don't know, I don't know," I kept repeating like the loop of Indian music in yoga class, a mantra, the instructor called it. Was it too late to mention the baby? But maybe there was never a baby, the autopsy would have revealed it. Maybe Elsbeth lied to me that night, or maybe she was joking. My head, I thought, was about to explode. "I want to go home," I said, "I'm tired." "In a few minutes," they said. The sun warmed my back. The old couple finished their breakfast. They read the paper and once in a while they looked up and smiled at each other, and this comforted me: old people with a smile on their faces filled me with hope. At the chess tables the highest-ranking player, the loner, came back for a match against Frenchie. "It looks ugly already," one of the spectators said and the men nodded and hmmmed. "Ooooo, penetration," the men crooned when the loner made a bold move into Frenchie's territory. "Is it deep?" Frenchie asked. "We shall see," said the loner. Frenchie didn't seem worried. His eyes darted over the board, lovingly caressing the pieces, and I imagined the flashes zooming across his brain. I knew that Frenchie's pieces, somehow, were always arranged in a configuration that allowed him free movement, invariably surprising his opponent, practically paralyzing him into momentary inaction, and causing the men on the sidelines to gape with awe. Intimidating your opponent was a critical part of your strategy, the history professor told me, and I thought about the cops. Frenchie made his move. "Ah, that's a move," the men on the sidelines sighed collectively, "that's a killer move." "I haven't done my homework," the loner mumbled a few times. Tonight, I noted, he was talkative, he didn't stop talking, as a matter of fact. "I'll be a very bitter man if I lose this game," he said. "You'll play another game," the men echoed philosophically. "I'll be bitter," the loner said. "They're only pieces," the men murmured as Frenchie and the loner gobbled up each other's queens and bishops in quick succession. I watched raptly. I loved how the two of them pointed at a square before going there. "A man's got to do what a man's got to do," the men intoned. "We have a liquidation sale going on," said the loner. "Give me good sound effects when you think I made a good move." A man named The Killer from Manila arrived and the sidelines grew rowdier. As the pieces dwindled on the board, the men got very excited. "Ohohoh," they chanted, "open fire, open fire."

Then they quieted down. "It looks dangerous," a man said. "It won't go far," said another. "He's a tough petunia," the loner now muttered under his breath, and I began to wish for him to win this one game, even though I was in the habit of rooting for Frenchie. "Call time, call time," the men shouted, and the clock ended the game in the loner's favor; everybody sighed. "What is it called," I asked, "when the clock wins?" "A cheap win," they said and laughed in unison. I sipped my coffee. Every day, things were getting tighter, denser, and I felt myself adjust to the pressure, I was becoming adept at playing the detectives' game. In flashes, I viewed my life as a movie where the heroine, innocent of the fate that awaits her, sets out in the morning from her home. It's a morning like any other morning but the spectators, already in the know, fearfully watch. "Were you perhaps jealous of him?" Maddox asked with sincere interest, his tone suggesting we were having an amicable, gossipy exchange. "Why would I be jealous of him?" I asked cautiously. He was cagey this Maddox. "She was your best friend, and they were getting married." "Who told you that?" I turned to face him. "Just answer the question, please," said Mr. Maddox. "What was the question?" I asked. "Were you jealous of him?" Patiently,

Mr. Maddox repeated the question. "No, I wasn't, I had no reason to be. Nothing could come between Elsbeth and me." I was tired, I sought sympathy. "All these questions," I said, almost to myself. "They exhaust me." "I have to tell you," Mr. Maddox said. "We met Drew a few times and he didn't strike us as the jealous type." "You never saw them together," I pointed out. "True, but others did. You're the only one, it should interest you to know, who claims he was, as you put it, the jealous type. Is it possible that your perception of him is somewhat distorted?" Mr. Maddox smiled, waiting, and I took a moment to think about this. "Maybe," I admitted. "So, he wasn't the jealous type," Mr. Maddox said. "In my mind he was," I answered calmly. "I see." Mr. Maddox nodded his head, still smiling and, I thought, reappraising me. "So, that night, what did they fight about?" he asked. "I don't know, I don't remember, it happened so fast and unexpectedly, he just got up and left, like he couldn't stand being with us. One minute he was there, and then he was gone." "Why?" Mr. Maddox asked. "I just told you, he was upset. He took a marble out of his pocket and rolled it across the table. It was very strange, to say the least, and I remember thinking he was trying to threaten us." "With a marble?" Mr. Daley sounded dubious. "Yes, with a marble. It was all in the gesture. He was a control freak." "Funny how you construe such an innocent act," Mr. Maddox said, and I thought that maybe I was talking too much. I'd better remember what I was telling them, or they would find ways to twist everything and put words in my mouth. I thought I remembered most of what I had told them, but not always in the right order. There was too much noise in my head, much of it garbage. At a nearby bench an Asian man, talking very loudly, sternly scolded his wife who had obviously displeased him. He spoke Chinese, I thought, and the wife, small and thin, sat with her head bowed, silently taking the harangue. I wanted to tell the man to shut up, he was disturbing the peace, but didn't have the nerve. Leaves rustled in the breeze. At night, I had fantasies about him, about Mr. Maddox, and it unnerved me that he had taken hold of my subconscious. "It must have been hard," Elsbeth said, "practically having to raise yourself. It's one of the things I admire you for." I basked in Elsbeth's words. "What else do you admire me for?" I asked. "Let's see," Elsbeth said. It was a mild summer afternoon and we were sitting side by side in an outdoor café, watching the passersby and having a late lunch; both of us, I remembered, felt peaceful and leisurely.

"You're always on time," Elsbeth said, laughing. "That's all?" I said, a little disappointed, and Elsbeth gazed at me, puckering her lips. "You have a good heart," she said at last, and I smiled. I thought this was something I might offer the detectives, but they'd probably dismiss it as irrelevant, maybe even as untrue. I sat and found solace in the trees. The world was full of horrors, full of misdeeds and misguided souls. People flared up, consumed with rage and uncontrollable demons. Mr. Maddox knew that, it was his trade. Maybe they were good detectives, Maddox and Daley; one way or another they caught their prey. "You and Elsbeth," said Mr. Daley. "After Drew left, you stayed in the restaurant, right?" "Right," I said. "You stayed there for quite a long time, right?" "I don't remember very clearly," I said. "You don't remember?" Mr. Daley raised his brows. "I don't remember specifically how long we stayed." "Well, let's try and figure it out together." Mr. Daley paused. "How long would you say?" I shrugged. "Maybe an hour. Maybe two." Mr. Daley consulted his notes. "More like three or four, isn't it? Our records show—" he said importantly, laying both hands on the open file before him. "We have information that suggests that at midnight you were still there, drinking. Drew left around nine, didn't he?"

"It's possible," I agreed. Why were they so insistent about how long we stayed in the restaurant? "And then what?" asked Mr. Daley. "Where did he go?" "Who?" "Drew," the detective said. "I don't know," I said. "Home, I suppose," I added, and all at once Mr. Daley seemed charged with revitalized zeal. Evidently, it was the answer he'd been waiting for, although I couldn't imagine why. "You know he didn't go to Elsbeth's, and you also know—" he pointed his finger and jabbed the air not far from my face, which I found insulting and aggressive in the extreme—"why you know it. You know it because you went upstairs with her and you finished her off, your best friend. Mercy killing you called it." "I didn't call it anything," I shrieked, but the detective continued. "Again and again you plunged a knife into her, mercilessly, and left her to die in a pool of her own blood. You didn't know there'd be so much blood, did you? And then, very cleverly, you took a shower so there would be no blood traces in your home. Isn't that a fact?" I felt my stomach contract. I stared with horror at the grotesque spectacle of Mr. Daley's face. His lips were moving, but I didn't hear a sound. I knew it would come to that, and now it did. "You don't know what you're saying." The words left my mouth in a hiss. Like at the chess tables, it was open fire, but I was losing my voice and, with it, my ability to defend myself. "I didn't go upstairs with her." "You're shaking," said Mr. Daley. "Why are you shaking? You went home with her and helped her upstairs." I'm a caged animal, I thought. I wondered if Maddox was still in the room with us, he'd been so quiet, but I didn't have the strength to turn around to check. "I didn't," I whispered. Indeed, I was shaking, and I couldn't stop. "So this you remember, conclusively, but the rest, somehow, is in a fog," Mr. Daley was shouting. His eyes, I thought, looked crazy. A little like Tom's. Maybe that was what Tom meant when he said that detectives had evil eyes. And yet, the louder and more abusive Mr. Daley got, the calmer I became. "I remember what I remember," I said, plotting my next move. I saw it so clearly, I wanted to laugh. At last, I thought, I had a game plan. "If I had gone upstairs with her, I'd be dead too," I said in a quiet, measured voice. "Whoever killed Elsbeth, would have killed me too." "Very clever," Mr. Daley said, then he, too, reverted to a normal, conversational tone. "Drew called the restaurant, he wanted to speak to Elsbeth. The waiter came to your table, but Elsbeth wouldn't talk to him because she was busy fondling you, or vice versa." "I wonder," I said, "where you get your information." "You will soon find out." Mr. Daley shut his eyes for a moment as if he had tired of looking at me. "I asked you about the waiter." "The waiter didn't come to our table," I said. "No one said anything about a telephone call." "How can you be so sure? Maybe you went to the bathroom when the waiter came over?" "It's possible," I said, "but Elsbeth would have said something." "What would she have said?" Mr. Maddox asked from behind me. So, he was still in the room, boring holes in my back. "She would have told me that Drew had called." "And you have no doubt that she didn't tell you such a thing," Mr. Daley said. I breathed deeply. "So, you found him? Drew?" I asked. "Found him?" Mr. Daley seemed perplexed. "Didn't he vanish? Wasn't he your prime suspect?" I asked, playing for time. "Who told you that?" The detective tapped the table with his pen. "Mrs. Williams, I think." "Mrs. Williams, I assure you, never said such a thing." Mr. Daley leaned back in his chair and a slow, gleeful smile spread on his face. "He had gone on a scuba-diving trip, I think I told you, and initially, for a day or two, we had the wrong idea about what had taken place, but everything he told us checked out so far. He's been very helpful all along, which, sadly, I can't say for you. And, he has a strong alibi, which, again,

I can't say for you." "What alibi?" I asked. "Well, if you must know." Mr. Daley straightened up in his seat. "After he left you, he met a couple of friends in a bar. They confirm his story." "They're lying," I said. "I see." Mr. Daley looked past me, communicating with his colleague. "So, we're all liars, and you're the one truth-teller among us, right?" I said nothing. "I asked you a question," Mr. Daley said, and my mouth went dry. I licked my lips. "I lost it," I said. "What was the question?" "Do you tell lies?" Mr. Daley asked, and I looked at him. His question, of course, was insidious and silly at the same time. "No," I said, eliciting the response I expected. "Wow," he said. "Never?" Again he looked past me, and I imagined Mr. Maddox gesturing behind my back. "I know what you're doing," I said, "stop torturing me." "You call *this* torture?" Mr. Daley pushed himself forward across the desk, his elbows jutting out at his sides. "I'm asking you a simple question." "It's simple for you but not for me," I said. "Okay, fair enough." Mr. Daley shifted gears. "Just so that we're clear. You said yourself that Drew did not go to Elsbeth's, and you were right, he didn't. But *you* did." "He didn't have her keys," I said. "Maybe he went later when he knew she'd be home." "How would he know she was home?" "I don't know," my voice grew louder, "maybe he called. Maybe he waited for her downstairs." "You mean, he stalked her. Now, he's a stalker." Mr. Daley let out a short, unpleasant laugh. "I didn't say he was a stalker. You're putting words in my mouth." "But you had them, didn't you? Her keys. Do you still have them?" Mr. Daley pressed on. I shook my head. "I may have them somewhere, she gave me a spare in case she got locked out." "That's what close friends do, they exchange keys. I'm sure she had yours." "Yes, I think she did." "All right." Mr. Daley seemed pleased. "I need you to focus, will you do this for me?" he asked, and I nodded that yes, I would do this for him. "Good, good. Now, did you have occasion to use her keys?" he prodded gently, and I wanted to cry. "Maybe once or twice, when she was out of town and I went to water her plants or get something that she needed." "Like what?" Mr. Daley casually jotted down a note. "I don't remember," I said, watching him scribble away. "Maybe a number from her rolodex, or maybe look up something in her diary." "Her diary." Both Mr. Daley and Mr. Maddox jumped. "What diary?" "Her address book," I said, startled. "I meant her address book, her day book. Sometimes she forgot it behind." "You said diary." Mr. Maddox came forward and stood leaning against the desk, his arms folded across his chest. "She didn't keep a diary," I said, looking up at him. "How do you know?" "Because she would have told me," I said. "How can we be sure you're not lying?" "Because I'm not," I cried. The detectives sighed. Mr. Maddox pushed from the desk and went back to his corner. Mr. Daley rose to his feet and started pacing the room. Every so often he went over to Maddox, and I wondered what the two of them were doing behind my back. I hit the heel of my hand against my forehead, like someone who had just remembered something. "Wait a minute!" Excited, I turned to face them. "The security cameras! You must have looked at the tapes?" The two detectives smiled and shook their heads. "Didn't I tell you?" Daley said to Maddox. "Cute, isn't she?" He turned to me. "You're good, very good, but not good enough. You know as well as we do there are no security cameras in that building." I sighed. "No, I didn't know." "Well, I don't believe you, but we'll let it pass, for now." Mr. Daley came around the desk to face me. "So, let me tell you how it all happened. You went upstairs with her because she was drunk. She didn't feel well and you went upstairs with her because she was your best friend and she needed your help. You loved her," Mr. Daley droned on. "You loved her, no one is denying the fact. You loved her, so you went upstairs and helped her into bed, and then something happened, she hurt you, you were drunk and confused, you were both drunk and confused, you exchanged some words, and you went to the kitchen and got a knife." "I want a lawyer," I said and Mr. Daley laughed. "Lawyers, lawyers, with you people it's always lawyers, as if a lawyer could save you. Go ahead, get yourself a lawyer. Sweet Jesus, how I hate these people." Mr. Daley made a gesture as if wiping sweat off his forehead and again went over to his colleague, Mr. Maddox. The two detectives now huddled in the corner and whispered; they seemed to have forgotten that I existed. Then Mr. Daley said something, loud enough for me to hear, about the criminally insane. "You can't hold me here," I said feebly, and Mr. Maddox turned to me. "Who's holding you?" he said, and the cold indifference in his voice stunned me. I wasn't human to them, I was sub-human at best. I sat a moment longer, then stood up and left, and all the way home shook like the mouse I felt I had become. I couldn't handle it any longer. I had to make my move, or I'd go crazy. I had to save myself, save my sanity, or what was left of it. I booked my ticket, packed a few things, and left the following night. On the plane I slept and when I woke up all was dark around me and hushed. We were cruising the night sky, crossing time zones, and I felt detached and calm, on my way to freedom. I exist at the surface of things, I thought. I can see, I can hear, but nothing can touch me. As soon as I arrived at the hotel I unpacked my valise and walked to the beach where I lay in the sun for a long hour. Next to me, four women lay on lounge chairs, offering their breasts to the brilliant sun. The nipples on one of them looked like rubber, good quality rubber, hard and brown, nearly dark, and I admired her robust European skin. A green fly floated in my green bottle of *Mythos* beer, and for a slow moment I watched him, thinking I would let him die, but then had a change of heart and decided to save him since the beer, anyhow, was no longer drinkable. I poured him out onto the sand and watched as he struggled up on his tiny feet. Soon, his wings would dry and he'd be as before, I thought, wondering if he was aware of, and grateful for, this miraculous rescue. Nostalgically, and with some regret, I remembered my life in New York, how I sat in the park and sipped my coffee, how I talked to Tom or the history professor, how I watched the men play chess. I wondered if they realized I was missing, and if they asked themselves what had happened to me. On the island I went for walks along the beach, cracking roasted pumpkin seeds between my teeth, expertly fishing out the meat with my tongue and spitting out the hull. I saw a stone in the shape of a heart, I yearned for it, but didn't bend to pick it up. My cheeks were flushed from the sun, and I thought about what I would have for dinner. A naked boy ran ahead of his parents and I watched his small button of a penis, wondering at what age penises really took off and began to grow. Nili once told me that when Andrew was a baby and she washed and diapered him, he sported tiny erections that always made her laugh. Sometimes, she said, Andrew would pee and the piss shot up and sprinkled her face. The naked boy's mother was an attractive blonde, a fertility goddess, tall on her wide, solid loins. She shouted something to her son, waving her hand, and the boy turned and ran to her. Women bear the children, the thought forcefully became concrete in my mind. All around, distant hills turned lavender as the sun began its descent toward the water. It was getting dark, a furious wind blew, and I put on the small black sweater, similar to the one Elsbeth had lost in a restaurant. Elsbeth was so upset for having lost it. "It's only a sweater," I said, trying to comfort her.

"But I *loved* it," she said, her voice full of emotion. On the terrace at the hotel at a table next to mine a young German couple, maybe on their honeymoon, sat and drank. At first he read the paper and she stared. Then she read the paper and he stared. People lived in pairs, I mused. Even gays and lesbians neatly paired off. The German woman sneezed, I sneezed. The man stood up and went into the bar. Another couple walked out to the terrace and I asked myself if I felt alone, or if I felt self-conscious about being alone. I went inside and ordered another *Singapore Sling*, then walked over to the basil plant in the garden and tore a few leaves and put them in my drink. In the morning it was still dark when I arrived at the beach. With the sun rising behind them, the hills burnt red. The fisherman I had seen the day before was already there with his line and hooks and chunks of stale bread he used for bait. Like old neighbors we waved hello. I walked along the beach until I reached the edge of the cliff where the water below had smoothed out small caves in the rock, an ideal spot for young village couples to fool around and proliferate. When I walked back, a red sun rose from behind the hills. Two elderly Germans called to each other as they ambled into the water. A man walked his dog. It was early Saturday morning and the village was waking up. Back at the hotel the breakfast table was laid out and people filled their stomachs. After breakfast I checked out, then drove to the port where I sat in a café and watched the ferries come and go. Young and old everybody smoked, and I thought about how life in Europe was more easy-going and civilized. I boarded a ferry and arrived on another island, even more beautiful than the one I had just left. I sat on the balcony outside my room and cooled off in the breeze, drinking a beer. This time my hotel was practically on the beach, and the door to my room was painted a brilliant red. I washed my socks and underwear and hung them on the makeshift clothesline on the balcony, thinking of Franklin, of his socks drying on the bushes. On the beach I walked toward a small church that stood alone up on a hill; wherever I looked, I saw water and cliffs. Descending on the other side of the hill I came upon a nudist beach where I openly stared at the men's hanging genitals. The men were mostly middle-aged, and yet I looked. Most of them were fleshy and well-hung, which surprised me. A woman rose from her chair and spread herself on top of a man who was reading a journal. Reluctantly, he put down the journal as the woman began to move her hips, rubbing against his pelvis, trying to rouse his desire if not his affections. I lingered a moment to see if he got an erection, then continued on. A few men glanced my way, perhaps because I was fully clothed, and I considered stripping off my shirt and shorts. Farther up in an isolated spot I changed into my bathing suit and went in for a long, refreshing swim. Now I understood why people flocked to these islands. I sat in a café facing the water and drank a glass of *kitro*, the local liquor. A haze fell on the hills and a soft light caressed the water; I felt quiet and safe. The owner of the café offered to marry me and take me back to America. The wind picked up and blew sand into my face and mouth. What if, I thought, it all ended in some disaster, right before the end of the millennium? I sat down to dinner, while my husband-to-be labored in the kitchen to satisfy the hunger of his only guest. Two cats patiently sat on the floor on either side of my chair, keeping me company, and when my dinner came I gave them each a piece of grilled lamb. A few fishermen set out on a boat. They shimmered against the horizon as the sun sank behind the hills, leaving in its wake a faint golden hue. More fishermen set out in their boats. I felt mellow and content and a little sad. Elsbeth would have loved the island. She would have loved the wine and the setting sun. Now that she was dead, it no longer mattered, really, for Elsbeth couldn't know what she was missing, and she couldn't care, she was free of cares. It was the one good thing about being dead: you didn't know what you were missing. I tried to think more deeply about this, about Death, about caring so much about this life on our small and insignificant earth, getting all worked up over one petty matter or another. This we understood and tried to accept. And then came this other thing, this thing we called Death, and nothing, you simply ceased to exist. Maybe it wasn't so bad to cease to exist. My husband-to-be interrupted, offering me a glass of the local brandy, and I thanked him. It was good, I thought, being married to him, even though he'd charge me in the end. Elsbeth danced in the club and everybody watched. I saw the look in the men's eyes, I saw them fantasize about how Elsbeth's lithe frame, sitting on top of them, worked them up and down in slow, deliberate motions. You could not not watch Elsbeth when she deigned to dance, or even when she just stood idle against the wall. I remembered that particular night very clearly. It was the beginning of June, the month of her death, and Elsbeth wore a white halter top and white Capri pants that hugged her hips and bared her bellybutton and her long, elegant calves.

The small diamond in her bellybutton gleamed and my eyes fastened on it. I imagined a tongue, Drew's tongue, flicking it, and so, through direct channels, sending waves of acutely localized pleasure to Elsbeth's cunt, to her clitoris, to that bundle of eight thousand nerve fibers. When I went over to Elsbeth and tried to get her attention, she said, "Oh, Sally, leave me alone," so I left, and when I got home it was Elsbeth's voice on my answering machine, crying, begging me to forgive her, and I remember thinking that women were a tiresome bundle of aches and confusions. But it was Elsbeth, my revered Elsbeth, what choice did I have but to say that I understood and forgave? Back in my room, on the balcony, I gazed up at the stars in the sky and flossed my teeth. My cotton blanket and sheets were stark white and this thrilled me; I felt pure and clean, like a newborn. The pillows were soft, and a sweet breeze came in through the slats of the wood shutters, cooling the room. I could stay here forever, I thought, caressing my smooth knee. A fat brilliant moon hung low in the sky, and I went out for a walk along the harbor. The wind was warm but fierce. The boats rocked upon the water, the water flapped against the rock. I walked on the beach, moaning with the beauty of it all. What a perfect night for lovers, I thought. What a perfect night to be alone. Like Rousseau in his *Rêveries du promeneur solitaire*, I felt myself sufficient unto myself, like God. Small lights shone in the distance, different strains of music wafted from the outdoor cafés. I wished I could drop on the sand and continue moaning. I wished I could drop in the water and let myself float away. I walked back to the hotel. It was perfectly situated, right at the center of things, and only a few steps from the water. I could have my whims and my safety, too. I was proud of myself, of the choices I had made. I peered into the windows of the low houses and saw an old couple watch TV. The next day I called Lydia, and she shouted, "Where are you? I've been calling you." The police, she said, wanted to get a hold of me. "What for?" I asked and Lydia, in her studied, infuriating manner, replied, "How should I know?" "Don't tell them that I called," I said. "I won't volunteer it," she said after a pause, "but if they ask...." I hung up and went in for a swim. In truth, I didn't care one way or the other, if she told or didn't tell. The water was cool and refreshing and when I came out I brushed a lizard off my shirt and put it on. More tourists arrived, the small square was crammed with slick, colorful coaches. It was lunchtime, the tourists ate. One of them thoughtfully picked his nose. I was hungry. I got a gyro in the corner café and sat on the hotel's terrace and ate it. I traveled from island to island, always dreading disappointment, always happily reassured that I had chosen wisely. I hated packing, but loved unpacking, leisurely setting up my new territory, deciding what would go where for maximum functionality and a provisional feeling of home. I had gone swimming immediately upon arrival and felt very small, yet secure, against the massive black rock that loomed above the water. It was late afternoon and I looked forward to going to bed, to reading, then falling asleep. I existed at the surface of things where my needs and expectations were minimal, a state of affairs that suited me just fine. Once in a while Lydia, as was her way, sneaked into my thoughts. "You don't seem to understand," she said, "it's the police." "I know it's the police," I said. "Well, are you coming back?" "Eventually," I said. Elsbeth never liked or trusted Lydia, but I let Lydia hang at the periphery of my need. Walking along the beach I stopped at a café and indulged my whim for a banana crêpe. A fart escaped from a middle-aged woman sitting next to me and I froze, pretending not to have heard it. On the night we had our silly argument, Lydia announced with contained excitement in her voice, "By the way, they interrogated me about you." "Interrogated you," I said with disgust. Leave it to Lydia to dramatize her role in this. "What about?" "The obvious," Lydia said. "You and Elsbeth. I told them what I think. I said that Elsbeth used you." "Used me?" I was appalled. "How did she use me?" "She only had to say it and you would do it." Lydia sounded triumphant. "You did whatever she told you to do. I'm sure you don't like to hear it, but it's the truth." A cold sore appeared on my upper lip and I wondered if it had to do with stress. Maybe I was tense and didn't even know it and yet anxiety, it occurred to me, was the other face of stimulation. Alone, I felt romantic. I stood on my balcony and listened to the crickets and the voices from the street and thought about routine and how I had left it behind. I was a tourist and therefore, just like Elsbeth, free of cares. I took my vitamins and poured more whiskey into my glass. I was reading an article about endocrine disrupters, keeping up with what went for news in the rest of the world. Mr. Daley occupied a corner in my mind; at moments he grew in size, at others he shrank or disappeared altogether. "Let's start from the beginning," he said. "Drew tells us that on the night of the murder you wore a white shirt and white slacks. We need you to bring those items to us or we'll subpoena your whole wardrobe." "My wardrobe." I wanted to laugh. "I have an assortment of white shirts and white pants in my wardrobe. Besides, why do you believe every word he says?" "Because," said the detective, "all his facts check out, and his memory isn't as fuzzy as yours." "He is making it all up, don't you see? He is very shrewd, Elsbeth told me. He'd lie through his teeth and you wouldn't even know it." "You don't say." The detective snorted. "Now you propose to do our work for us, telling us who's lying and who's telling the truth?" I'd better shut up, I thought. Let them subpoena my clothes, they won't find what they're looking for. Evil eyes. Now it came to me, the day Tom said that detectives had evil eyes. He had arrived on his bike, and as he stood near my bench, talking to me, this other man, in a suit and tie, walked by. The two men shook hands. "He was my boss," Tom said, "in the vice squad." "He is telling you stories?" the man asked me, and I smiled, nodding. "How come I don't have so many stories as you?" the man asked Tom. "I was at my sister's the other day and I'm sitting there thinking: I had a life, but I don't know where it went, I don't remember much, like there was nothing there." "That's because," Tom said, "you used to drink in those days, you were heavy on the oil." I watched the two men and tried to imagine them as heartless detectives who routinely got drunk on the job. I wondered if Daley and Maddox were drunks, and that was when Tom said, seemingly out of the blue, that detectives had evil eyes because they looked at people. It was an interesting observation, I thought, it made perfect sense. Tom's eyes weren't evil, I didn't think, but he did have a crazy look. "He stopped drinking ten years ago," Tom told me after the man left. "And you?" I asked, wondering if he'd lie to me. "I still drink," he said, "but I don't get sloppy." At sunrise I walked along the beach. The water quivered—the distant half was blue, the near half was golden. A couple of locals at the café were setting up for the day. A dog barked as I passed, and I did my best to ignore him. It's only a dog, I told myself, trying to contain my anger. It was silly to take it personally and yet I did, I took it personally when a dog barked at me; it made me feel vulnerable and helpless, especially in foreign places. There was nothing I could do to shut him up, except perhaps bark back, which I was inclined to do. People harbored pain and impotent rage, and I now realized I might be one of them. It was Sunday morning. Church bells rang out and a man on the beach, getting into his wet suit, stopped hopping on his feet and crossed himself rapidly two or three times. Birds twittered. The sun rose, round and red through the haze. The village seemed deserted and it felt as though everybody had gone away, leaving their trash behind—empty beer cans and rotting fruit lay strewn in the gutter. A cat walked at my side, adopting me. In the night I had a series of strange dreams, or maybe it was just one long dream with many scenes. I had helped catch a serial killer and became very popular. People sought my company, even friends I hadn't seen or heard from in years. It was going to be a hot, hazy day. A woman drove by, her poodle installed in a basket on her moped. The type of music I heard everywhere, especially on the public buses, reminded me of the loop of Indian music in yoga class. On the beach, corpulent women sat in their narrow bikini bottoms, baring their breasts without a hint of self-consciousness. On some, the breasts disappeared among the folds of flesh, distinguishable only by a nipple. Women, I thought, were the mystery of creation. I considered buying a bikini and going native, maybe even bare my breasts like all the others. Like Elsbeth said, a bikini was a state of mind. I called Lydia again but got her machine, so I hung up without leaving a message. I sipped my *Mythos* and smoked a cigarette. I went up the hill, following a handwritten sign to

"Anthony Quinn Beach." A Doberman chained to a tree welcomed me with frenzied barks. The more frenzied he got, the angrier I became. I watched the iron chain tighten around his thin neck. It was just the two of us and I hissed my hatred, telling him to shut up. He didn't, so I picked up a rock and, furious, threw it, not at him exactly, but close enough. To my astonishment the dog got my meaning and stopped barking at once. Breathing hard I continued to the beach. I swam in the warm, soft water and felt restored. Beautiful schools of fish nibbled at the rocks and I held my breath and hovered, observing them through my goggles. How still the world of fish! Mr. Daley tried to penetrate through the stillness but I didn't let him. Last night, upon arriving on this island and waiting for my luggage, I met Abdul who offered to come to my hotel when his shift at the airport ended. He would drive me around, he said, and show me the island by night. Normally I would have said, No, thank you, but this time for some reason I said yes. Maybe I was hoping for something, I thought later. He arrived at ten and drove me around in his small fast car. The streets were dark and empty, there wasn't much to see, but I kept my side of the bargain and pointed at buildings and asked questions. He bought me a semi-cold pizza at a stand, then took me to the beach where he promptly stripped off his clothes and lay back on a lounge chair. He tried very hard to appear relaxed, but I knew he wasn't. I tried very hard not to look at his nakedness, but every so often, when he asked me a question, I would glance at him and glimpse what I thought was a small, pale erection. I wondered if, surreptitiously, he was touching himself, hoping to showcase his splendor and so entice me to nibble. I felt a little sorry for him but didn't nibble. At breakfast, I sat on the patio with the smokers and faced the sea; the non-smokers ate inside in the dining hall. Why anyone would choose to stay indoors on such a glorious day was beyond me. On the patio, though, men and women coughed the discreet cough of smokers after a wild night. It was a bit sickening, and embarrassing, for it was clear to everyone what was coming up the neighbor's gullet and then swallowed. On the beach tourists lay on chairs in various degrees of nudity. A very large man stood up and, bending over, offered me a view of his elephantine behind. After dinner I stood on my balcony and drank wine the woman in the small supermarket at the corner poured into plastic bottles and sold by the weight. I had chosen a small bottle and when it was my turn to pay she refused to charge me. She smiled and waved her hand to let me understand it was her gift to me. I thanked her in her language and was so touched, I almost burst into tears. Someone likes me, I thought. Someone, a stranger, looked into my heart and saw that it was pure. The night was warm and humid, so I took off my T-shirt to welcome the breeze and stood on my balcony, blowing smoke into the air and watching the men in the kiosk down below. I couldn't see what they were doing, but safely guessed that they were drinking and playing backgammon. Except for the lights in the harbor and the few stars in the sky, all was dark. A movement in a window in the villa across caught my eye. A tree half-covered the window yet I could see into the room. A man, I realized, was leaning forward in an armchair, smoking. Every time he drew on it, the tip of his cigarette glowed in the dark. His TV was on and once in a while he drank from a glass. He too, I gathered, must be naked, for I saw no clothes, only skin. I couldn't see his features but his bulk suggested a large muscular man in his thirties or forties. The thought that I was spying on him titillated me. We were both naked, we both smoked and drank. I was riveted on the tip of his cigarette when it suddenly occurred to me that he was watching me. I killed my cigarette and went into the room. When I came out again, the man was still there. He had turned off his TV and I sensed that he had been waiting for me. As I watched, he left the room and reappeared in a window directly facing my balcony and where no tree obstructed his view. This overt move annoyed me. I went back inside, plugged the mosquito repeller in the socket and got into bed. The following night I stood on the balcony in my T-shirt and lit a cigarette. The man was sitting in his chair, also smoking a cigarette. Innocently, I leaned against the railing and looked toward the harbor where the men played backgammon in the kiosk. The man in the villa stood up, filling the window frame with his bulk; I stubbed out my cigarette and went inside. At the sink I washed the grapes I had bought at the grocer's and went down to the lobby to watch CNN News. When I came back upstairs, his rooms and windows were empty and dark. A plane took off from the nearby airport. Naked, I stood on the balcony and lit a cigarette. Still, the windows of the villa remained empty and dark. The next day I got on a bus to tour the island, but, feeling drowsy, I dozed off most of the time and saw nothing. Maybe I was tired of seeing, tired of looking. Night came and it was morning again. After breakfast I went back to bed. I was exhausted. I thought I was coming down with something, I thought the room smelled. I lay on my back, my hands in the pockets of my khaki shorts. I told myself to get up and go outside and be the tourist again, but I couldn't move. It felt so good to just lie still and listen to the occasional noise from the street. With sudden resolve I jumped out of bed, took off my clothes and got under the covers. The next morning I flew home. We left on time and landed on time, which, I thought, was a good omen. The guy in the seat next to me had his ears plugged throughout the flight. He watched the movie, then listened to music and, when preparing for sleep, removed the earphones and stuck bright orange plugs in his ears—I was ready to puke. Back to techno-land, I thought. When I opened the door to my apartment, despite my fears to the contrary, I felt instantly at home. The walls weren't threatening, they seemed to welcome me in their quiet, serene way. I called Lydia who was leaving the house but was willing to talk for a minute or so. I thought I would be happy to speak to her, to hear a familiar voice, and I was, initially, but then the old ennui set in. "What did you do every day?" she asked, almost accusingly. "I walked," I said. "And?" she probed. "That's it," I said, defensively. "That's how I do a new place. I walk it." "Well," Lydia said. "Not exactly my idea of fun. By the way, did you call the police?" "Yes," I said, "I'm going to see them tomorrow." There was a long pause, then Lydia said, "I don't know if I should tell you this, but they talk as if you did it." "Did what?" I asked. "You know," Lydia said in her clear unwavering voice, "killed Elsbeth." I took a deep, audible breath. "Did they say so?" I asked. "Not in so many words, but yes, that was the general drift of the conversation." "What did you say?" I asked. "I said I didn't believe it," Lydia said. "Didn't believe that I did it, or didn't believe that I was capable of such a thing?" I asked. "Both," Lydia said. "My exact words were: I don't believe it for one minute." "Thanks, Lydia," I said, with some hesitancy, for I still wasn't sure if she truly believed in my innocence, or if her dislike for Elsbeth stood behind this statement of trust. "You're welcome," she said with a chuckle, and we hung up. In the morning, I put on some clothes and went to see Mr. Daley. "Welcome back," he said cheerfully. "Pleasure or business?" he asked. "Pleasure," I said, recalling the disapproval in Lydia's voice when she said that walking wasn't her idea of fun. I laughed. "What's so funny?" asked the detective. "Questions," I said. "Questions are funny. If you think about it." Mr. Daley gave me a look, evidently formulating a new question in his mind. I thought I might tell him about the naked man in the villa, or about my missed opportunity with Abdul. "I have to tell you that we were very displeased when we heard that you had split," Mr. Daley said. "I came back." I smiled at him. "I was only gone ten days." "A previous commitment?" he asked, and I nodded. He was growing a mustache, I noticed, and once in a while he moved his thumb across it, as if remembering he had a new thing on his face. Mr. Daley sighed. "A few things turned up," he said, "that's why we tried to reach you." He pushed back his chair and walked up and down the small office. I looked at him, saying nothing. "You went to college, right?" Mr. Daley stopped pacing and turned to face me. "You know what consciousness of guilt is, don't you?" They had regrouped, I thought, and were now coming at me from a different angle. "I think so," I said, assuming a tentative tone, "but I'm not sure." "It means," Mr. Daley indulged me, "that a person, when she knows she is guilty, even if she tries to suppress it and goes on pretending that she is innocent, still has this thing, this burden, she still carries with her a consciousness of guilt until she comes clean. You really need to put this behind you." I watched him as he pulled his chair and sat down. "That's why you came back so soon," he concluded his little speech. "It can also mean," I said, newly invigorated and ready for combat, "that when someone is falsely accused, they begin to believe it, even if they know, in their heart of hearts, that they're innocent." "I think that this whole affair is weighing on you," Mr. Daley said. "It's like a stain on your conscience, and it will remain so until you tell us everything you know. I wish you believed me." He sighed. "I know from experience that you'll feel a lot better once you talk to us." "I'm okay," I said, even as my heart, as if to contradict me, was pounding hard. Were they getting ready to arrest me? Formally accuse me? The brain is a frightening thing, I thought last night when I lay on the wood bench in the sauna room. I had gone to the gym to relax, but a vague sense of apprehension soon turned to dread. "Do you want to know what else he says? Drew?" the detective asked, and I shrugged. "He says that now, in retrospect, he understands everything, he knows exactly what you were up to." "Does he?" I gave a short laugh. "How fortuitous for him." "And for us as well," said the detective without missing a beat. "If I were you, I wouldn't be so sarcastic." I have a life, too, I thought with lightening clarity. A single life, but I'm entitled to it. The detective, deep in his tunnel vision, had to be shown the way. "You think my life is empty, don't you?" I said, and Mr. Daley flinched; I had caught him off guard. "You would hate it, wouldn't you, if you had to put him behind bars? Such a young man, such a promising future. He can breed and reproduce, whereas I, I'm just a womb, one womb, and an empty one at that." "What are you talking about?" Mr. Daley blew air through his mouth, and for a moment I thought he was a fish, not a beautiful fish like I saw in the water only a couple of days ago, but hostile and portentous-looking. Some fish, like people, bore their malevolence like a badge. "I'm talking about Drew, naturally. You'd hate to put him away, one of your own kind." "You're hallucinating," Mr. Daley said, recovering from his momentary stupor; we were back on familiar turf, with him at the controls. "We put away those who deserve to be put away. And, since you insist." He paused for effect. "Talking about wombs. That night, Drew tells us, you deliberately talked about how certain men were great in bed, providing, I might add, very graphic details. So graphic, in fact, and *pornographic*, he felt nauseous and had to leave the table. He didn't have a fight with Elsbeth, he had a problem with you, he couldn't stand having you around. He says you corrupted Elsbeth, that you encouraged her to drink. He says you wanted to be alone with her, and so you got rid of him. He says he never had a marble in his pocket, and that you made up the whole thing." I gaped at the detective with mounting agitation. "What a cockamamie story," I finally said, "and you, a so-called seasoned detective, swallowed every vile word." "It makes sense," Mr. Daley said, disregarding my comment about seasoned detectives. "It fits our theory of the case." "Your theory!" I sneered. "Go ahead and arrest me if you dare." "All in good time," said Mr. Daley, flashing a smile. "Let me tell you the rest of it before you get all riled up." He shut the file, leaned across the desk and said in a confiding whisper, "You're guilty as sin. You know it, and we know it. We know you did it, we know why you did it, we know how you did it, we just need to find the link." "The what?" I was trying to make sense of what I had just heard. "What do you mean, you know I did it?" I pushed up, my chair falling behind me, and then I was shouting, watching myself through a third, cold eye, the third eye from yoga class, the eye that sees all. "I don't have to take this from you, you moron! I came here of my own good will, I wanted to help, but clearly that's not what you're after, is it? For whatever sick reason, you take pleasure in harassing me, but your time is up, you understand? It's over! I want a lawyer.

Now!" I shrieked. I put my hands up as if to shield my ears from my own voice. That's it, I'd crossed over to the other side—would I ever recover and be normal again? Like a madwoman, I paced my corner of the room, unable to stop. Mr. Daley, I noticed, stood up, too. He looked pale, which satisfied my desire for vengeance. As with the Doberman I threw a rock at, not knowing it would achieve the desired result. "Sit down," he said and I screamed right back at him. "You will not tell me what to do, I'm done listening to you, I'm not afraid of you, you dimwit, I won't let you order me around. What gives you the right to insult me? Your uniform? You don't even wear a uniform, you, you—" Tears ran down my cheeks and I wanted to swear at him some more but couldn't find just the right words. "I've taken enough abuse from you, and I'm done, you hear me, I'm done, I'm through." I screamed with an abandon I hadn't felt in years and, strangely, was nearly jubilant. "You're mad with authority. You think you're important? You're not important, you're a civil servant, and you would do well not to forget it. Consciousness of guilt! Ha! Big words they teach you at the academy, but you're a little man behind a small desk in a filthy room in the police department, assigning guilt. I'll sue you and the whole frigging system, I'll make you regret you ever dealt with me, let alone threatened me, you mother-fucker," I shouted, stunned by my own vulgarity. The door flew open, and a few men burst in. I retreated, still foaming at the mouth. "Stay away from me, stay away." I could smell their collective force, their animosity. The detectives and I, we were one step away from total mayhem, I could picture them coming at me, hooking my arms behind my back and cuffing me. I raised my hand as if in self-defense. "I want a lawyer, NOW. I won't say another word, and don't you dare lay a hand on me." I pressed against the wall to catch my breath. They must think I'm mentally deranged, I thought, which was good, very good. As long as they stayed away. "Calm down." One of the men stepped forward and picked up my chair. The fact registered in my mind that he was tall and handsome, but I quickly remembered he was the enemy. "We don't want to hurt you, take it easy," he said, reaching his arm toward me. "Stay where you are, don't come near me! Where's Maddox? I want Maddox," I said hoarsely and the men looked at each other. "Get Larry," the man told one of the officers, and signaled the others to leave. "Now, calm down," he said to me. "I'm calm," I said, "just don't come near me." "What happened?" he asked. "What got you so upset?" "Ask Mr. Detective," I said with vehemence, motioning Daley. "I'm asking you," said the man. Like the rest of them, he wore nondescript pants and a dark shirt and tie, but something in his shoulders, in his manner, suggested authority. Maybe he was just as good as Maddox, I thought, maybe I could talk to him. I liked it that he asked me, in a calm voice, to calm down. I liked it that he swiftly took control of the situation. Indeed, I felt calm. "I want a lawyer," I said. "I thought you said you wanted Larry Maddox." He smiled at me, as if genuinely intent on fulfilling my wishes. "I want a lawyer," I said, but less forcefully. "I'll talk to Maddox, but not to this nut." I pointed at Daley. "I'll talk to anyone but him. Who are you?" I asked, softening my tone. "The name is Brian," he said. "Brian Conn." "Are you a detective?" I asked, and he laughed. "Yes, I'm a detective." "Are you this creature's boss?" I asked, hoping he'd laugh again, but he didn't. "No," he said, "I'm not his boss." The door opened and Maddox entered, but now I wasn't so sure I wanted to talk to him. "Actually," I said to Conn, "I'd just as soon talk to you. Just get him out of here." Again, I pointed at Daley. "All right," Conn said, "it'll be just you and me." "That's fine with me," I said, trying very hard not to smile. "Do you want to sit down?" Conn asked when we were alone in the room. "No," I said, regaining composure, "you sit, I'll stand." "All right." He took a chair and turned it to face me. "Now. I want you to tell me exactly what happened. Actually, before we start, would you like some coffee, or water?" I considered. "Yes, in fact, a glass of water, and black coffee. And I'd like to smoke." "No problem." Smoothly, he got to his feet, and I admired his fluid agility. "You just stay here, nice and calm, and I'll be back in a flash." The perfect host, I thought as Conn gently shut the door behind him. I stood and watched the door, trying to think. They tossed me between them, putting into play the old ruse: good cop, bad cop. I already knew who the bad cop was, now I was invited to find out who the good one was. "The people at the top," Elsbeth said, "know it's a dirty game, and they play it. It is only the little people who are continuously shocked." "And where are you? At the top, or bottom?" Drew asked. "Naturally at the top," Elsbeth said, but only to annoy him. All at once, I felt exhausted, emotionally depleted. I went to the window and looked out to the street. Police cars were lined on both sides of the road, taking up precious parking space. Some precincts, Tom said, had their own parking lots and that's where the cops got drunk at the end of their shifts. Cops, I now thought, had all the power. Their authority was a given, they were trained to use it. They were trained to break me, to treat someone like me—a suspect—as if they had proof I had committed the crime. My Chilean neighbor knew what he was talking about. Conn entered the room with a small tray, carrying my coffee and water. He went around the desk, taking Daley's chair and inviting me to sit. I sat opposite him and lit a cigarette without offering him one. He watched me a moment, then said, "Now, let's start from the beginning." "The very beginning?" I asked. "Well," he said, picking up the exasperation in my voice. "Start wherever you want." I looked at his hands clasped on the desk and noticed his wedding band. He had good hands, reliable; if only he were my ally. I wished I were his wife and had his kids. "I want a lawyer," I said, gently, as if seeking advice. "I know, we'll get to that." Conn rubbed his chin as if he had just realized he needed a shave. "But, first tell me what happened in this room, with Daley." I took a long drag on the cigarette "Nothing happened with Daley," I finally said. "Then why did you scream? Were you scared?" "Yes, I was scared. He attacked me. Verbally," I added for clarification. Conn nodded his head, waiting for more. "He said you guys knew that I did it, you just needed to find proof." "Are you sure he said that?" Conn seemed surprised, but I didn't buy it. "I want a lawyer," I said. "All my friends say I should get one." "Wait a minute." He leaned forward, and again I fixated on his hands. I thought about the true-crime programs I saw on TV where real cops pushed real criminals and convicts into cars, into prison cells, how mesmerized I was and newly amazed at how physical the cops were with their victims, at how they would readily lay their hands on the bare skin of their catch, indifferent to sweat and other bodily discharges. "I must know," Conn said. "Are you sure he said that?" "Are you implying that I'm lying, that I'm crazy?" "Not at all, I just want to be sure I know all the facts." "He said it. I tell you he said it." "All right, stay calm, I believe you." Conn slumped back in his seat. "He was out of line, that's all, he shouldn't have said it, he should know better." "You must think I'm a fool," I countered. "I know this is standard procedure around here, the kind of tactics you love to use. It makes you feel you're in control." "You've seen too many movies." Conn's eyes turned cold, and I wondered whether I had gone too far. "I'll say it again, he was out of line. Maybe he was desperate,

trying to get somewhere. You've been one tough cus-
tomer, let me tell you." He gave me a big smile.
"Really?" Somehow, it pleased me to hear that. I was
a tough petunia, after all. "You're a smart cookie,"
Conn continued and I thanked him with a nod, even
though I knew it wasn't meant as a compliment.
"Still," I said, "what exactly are we talking about? I
don't suppose you expected me to waltz in here and
sign a confession just to make your life a little easier." Conn laughed. He seemed warm and gentle
again and, for a moment, I was tempted to walk into
his trap. "Let's talk a little about Elsbeth," he said.
"Tell me about the two of you." "What do you want
to know?" I asked. I remembered Lydia's remark
about routine questioning, about how detectives
sometimes hit, by default, on the real killer. "We
were good friends," I said, measuring my words.
"We were close." "How did you meet?" Conn
asked. "We were next-door neighbors," I said, "ten
years ago. Then Elsbeth moved, but we stayed in
touch. She moved a couple of times, in fact, she
would get restless if she stayed in one place for too
long." "The other day," Conn said, "you mentioned
her diary. What happened to it?" "She never had a
diary," I said, raising my voice. "They misunderstood me. I meant an appointment book." "Who

misunderstood you?" "Daley and Maddox." "So did she or didn't she keep a diary?" Conn asked. "She didn't. I *knew* her, she wasn't the type to bother with the small minutiae of her daily life." "And you?" Conn asked. "Do you bother with the small minutiae of your daily life?" He smiled at me, so I smiled back. "No, I don't," I said. "You were orphaned very young," Conn said, his voice deep with felt sympathy. "Yes," I said. "And you have family in Michigan," Conn continued and I nodded, surprised yet not surprised that he was familiar with my file. "How often do you see them? Your family?" "Never," I said, "we're not in touch." "How come?" "Just because," I said. "They're not nice people." "Were they mean to you?" Conn asked, and I sighed with forbearance. "They were mean to my mother, they tried to get their hands on my father's money." "I see," Conn said, leafing through the folder on the desk. "And there was something said about a bloody shirt." "That's just another figment of Daley's imagination," I said. "He claims I destroyed the shirt and pants I wore that night to conceal the evidence." "Did you?" Conn asked calmly. "Of course I didn't. I could never kill Elsbeth, or anyone else for that matter." "How do you know?" Again Conn smiled and I felt drawn to him. "I just know," I said. "And even if I could, if someone assaulted me and I had to, in self-defense, even then I couldn't use a knife. A gun maybe, but not a knife." "Well, you can't always choose the weapon. Most often you're too enraged and circumstances dictate the type of weapon." "Maybe," I said, "you're the expert, but I tell you, I could never kill someone, not up-close." "All right, I believe you." Like a kid, Conn swiveled in his chair from side to side. "Thank God somebody around here does." I drained my coffee and dropped the cigarette in the cup. I was beginning to relax, thinking that soon I would walk out of the stuffy stinking office and go to the park and watch the chess games. Conn was all right for a cop but I wanted out, out. He was still swiveling in the chair and seemed to be in a deep meditative state which I began to find amusing when he, perhaps sensing this, stopped swiveling and leaned forward. "Of course, we're always the villains," he said in a soft, plaintive voice. "You think we want this job? This job is nothing but misery, day in and day out, nothing but misery, but someone's got to do it. All kinds of human scum come in through these doors. All we ask is that you help us out. From what I read in the file, it might very well be a case of self-defense. You do the right thing, and we'll work with you, it's time we put this behind us. She was your best friend, you know, all we're trying to do is solve a murder case." I listened, dutifully nodding my head. The words 'self-defense' caught my attention, but I let go of them; he was trying to enlist me to their cause, trying to seduce me into paying the price. I, too, employed a soft tone. "I wish you did," I said, "solve it. Unfortunately, you got it all wrong, barking up the wrong tree, so to speak. I can't help you, and yet you keep badgering me. Not you personally, you've been very decent I have to say, but your colleagues. Like you said, they were out of line to speak to me the way they did. That's why I demanded to see a lawyer." I waited for Conn to say something but he just sat there, looking handsome and thoughtful. I felt a stab in my gut— handsome men made me think of chivalry and love. If only I could let down my guard and relax in his arms. "Believe me," I continued, "I'd rather not waste my money on lawyers, but if I have to I will. As I'm sure you're aware, there are many horror stories about the stuff you guys do here. Right from the start of this ordeal, my friends urged me to get a lawyer, and I said, No, they'll be fair with me, they're professionals, but now it looks as though my friends were right and I was wrong. They say that once you've got someone in your clutches you never let go. Is that true, by the way?" I asked, and Conn squinted, apparently unprepared. "Nonsense," he said, "we're too busy to play such games. Once we know you're innocent we wish you all the best and send you on your way. We're human beings too." "Well, are you done with me? Because, if not, I think I should get a lawyer." I reached for another cigarette, this time offering him the pack, which he declined. "Do you have one?" he asked, and I drew on the cigarette and blew smoke to the ceiling. "I'll have to make a few phone calls. I have a friend who is a retired detective, he'll help me." "Oh." Conn didn't seem too impressed. "What's his name?" "Never mind. I don't want to get him involved unless I absolutely have to." For a long moment Conn watched me, then continued in the same silky tone. "We deal with blood all the time and let me tell you, it smells. And it's sticky, you know. Someone else's blood is not a pleasant sight, it turns your stomach. You understand what I'm talking about, don't you?" "I think so," I said, tensing a little. I thought I knew what he was talking about, but maybe I didn't. "How do you react to blood?" Conn asked. "How do I react to blood?" I repeated, uncomprehending. "Yes, your instinctual reaction, like when you cut your finger, do you suck on it or rinse it off?" "I'm not sure," I said, trying to remember. "If there's a lot of it, I rinse it off. If it's only a drop, I'd probably suck it." "That's very normal," Conn said. "That's how most people deal with their own blood." I nodded, pleased to hear I was normal. "How do you react to other people's blood?" Conn continued. "I can't look at it," I said, and again Conn assured me it was normal. "At any rate." He sighed. "As I was saying before, our work is nothing but misery. Blood sweat and tears, like the song goes. We see plenty of those. But then, you women, you have a special relationship with blood, don't you?" Conn observed me, waiting. "What do you mean?" I asked, trying to keep my gaze steady. Sweat gathered above my lip but I didn't wipe it off. "I mean, very simply, menstrual blood. She had her period, you know?" "Who?" I shivered. "Elsbeth. On the night of the murder. She was menstruating. You seem shocked." Conn smiled at me. "I'm not shocked, I'm just....picturing it." "Picturing what?" "The blood. I didn't know she had her period." "Would it have made a difference? If you knew?" "What do you mean?" The sweat had dried and now felt cold and itchy on my skin. "I think you know what I mean," Conn said. "I mean, this is intimate stuff we're talking about here. Let's assume, for argument's sake, that you're the killer, just like Daley claims. Would it have made a difference? If you knew she was bleeding?" "Why would it make a difference?" I asked boldly. If I was the killer, as they claimed, I was a cold-blooded one. "You're right." Conn smiled, nodding his head. "It shouldn't. Not to a woman. But men, you know, they freak out when a woman menstruates. That's one of the reasons why Daley, and a few of the others, point the finger at you. You can't blame them, can you?" "That's why I want to see a lawyer. He would know how to deal with you guys. I am just a normal, everyday citizen. I was never questioned by the police." "There's always a first time," Conn said distractedly as a decision seemed to form in his mind. "You know," he started again. "You people, truly, never cease to amaze me. I mean it, I'm truly at a loss. You just love beating the system, don't you? You cheat a little on your taxes, you deceive your friends and neighbors, you shoplift a little on the side, and when the system catches on to you, you scream bloody murder." He shook his head and muttered, "Bloody murder. Who do you think you're kidding?" Horrified, I felt my insides freeze up. I thought I was home free, and now it was starting all over again. "Now, let's get serious," Conn said, still speaking in that soft, hypnotic voice. "Just like

Daley said, it's all in here." He pushed a typed form across the desk. "I want to be absolutely frank with you. We know you did it. All we need you to do is sign this. If you don't, you're only going to make things harder for yourself and for us, and you won't find us as supportive as we've been up to this point. It won't be pleasant, I assure you, I'd advise you to consider." I stared at him, aware on some removed level that I was being transformed into a flat, placid, one-dimensional plaything. Not one of us is innocent, we're all guilty of something, I thought, sinking deeper and deeper into the chair, drifting into surrender mode, masochistically giving myself over to my executioners. What better way to make them stop? If I let them do with me as they pleased, this nightmarish rigmarole would play itself out and I would have peace. I would confess and so end the battle. Conn observed me intently and I, bewitched, looked into his blue eyes. He didn't blink, and neither did I. We were both still, immobile, touring our own brain. Yes, submit and give them what they were waiting for. They would know what to do, they were in charge, and Elsbeth and I would be joined forever, at least on paper. I opened my mouth to speak, I said, "I...." and something stirred in me, my survival instincts kicked in, and I began to tremble.

"Please stop, you're playing with my head, you can't do that," I pleaded. "See?" Conn leaped forward in his seat, a look of concern and exasperation on his face. "That's what we've been trying to tell you all along, but you chose to persist in your mistrust, in your mistaken belief that we wish to harm you. You must realize, for your own sake, that I sit in this chair for a reason, I'm here to help you. You are not as strong as you think. I know this for fact because it's my job, and I'm good at it. We're all of us weak, Sally, and we must acknowledge our weaknesses. We're all fallible human beings, we need each other. If you give me a chance, I'm in a position to help, but you must let me. I'd like nothing better, please believe me. You may not believe this, but I like you, Sally, I really do, I'm on your side. You're a little confused, that's all, I can see how you were pulled into this, and I want to help you out. Work with me and I'll meet you halfway, maybe two thirds of the way. You want your friend to rest in peace, don't you? If she rests in peace, you can rest in peace." "Daley," I said. "You're doing this again, you're waiting for me to crack, I know what you're doing, it won't work." "My name is Conn," Conn said. "I only want what's best for you and for Elsbeth." "Daley." I choked on the name. "He used the same spiel, the same exact words. Then you walk in here, giving me your version of the good cop." "I am a good cop," Conn said, his face breaking into a crooked smile. "I want my lawyer," I echoed emptily, "how many times do I need to repeat this?" "Didn't you tell me," Conn scolded, "that you didn't have one?" "But I do," I said, "I have friends." I let my face drop into my hands and began to sob. Conn was right, I was weak and confused, I needed to lie down somewhere and go to sleep. If only I could slide down to the floor and keep warm and quiet. An image flashed in my mind and I tried to remember where it was from and if and when it actually took place. It was the three of us again, in a restaurant, or Elsbeth's dining-room table, and Drew, more jovial and open than usual, was saying that men, all men, had visions of themselves on death row, ordering the last meal before their execution. "Only men have this vision," Drew stated. "Women don't have it because they're less likely to end up on death row. They're more lenient with women in our so-called justice system." "What would you have?" Elsbeth asked, mocking. "Do you think they keep gourmet chefs on call for death-row inmates?" Elsbeth, help me! I begged mutely. They seemed determined to put me away, and I had to extricate myself. Maybe it was a game they played to fill up the hours to the end of the shift when they would go out to the parking lot and get chummy and drunk before going home to the wife. "Why are you doing this?" I asked, wiping my tears with the back of my hand. "It's my job," Conn replied evenly. "Your job," I said, "is to find the real killer." "It may surprise you, Sally, but that's exactly what we're doing." Again I winced at the sound of my name in a detective's mouth. "But you're making a mistake, an awful mistake," I cried, putting my heart in my words. "You don't know what it feels like to be wrongly accused. If you knew, you wouldn't have the heart...." "Yeah, yeah," he said, unmoved. "We hear all kinds of stories." I stared at him, trying to think. We were going in circles again. I would never penetrate through to him, to the person under the mask, to the person who had a wife and possibly kids. "You can't hold me here," I said. "I know my rights, I want a lawyer." "Here." He pushed the black telephone across the desk. "Call him." "I have to think," I said. "I don't have a lawyer. I'll have to call a friend and see if she can recommend one." "I'll tell you what." Conn rose to his feet. "Why don't you use the pay phone outside?" "Outside, where?" "Just make a left turn in the hall," he said cordially, "you'll see it." I pushed up from the chair and hesitantly made the few steps to the door. It must be a trap, I thought, suddenly entranced by the belief that I was naked. I quickly glanced down at myself and tapped my pants, my shirt, making sure I had clothes on. I walked out to the corridor and turned left. It felt strange to be on my feet again, and I tried to figure out how many hours I had spent in the room with Conn and with Daley. It had to be four or five o'clock in the afternoon—another beautiful day shot, wasted. I walked through a corridor of shut, gray doors, and I wondered what went on behind them: the place felt eerily empty and quiet. I'll call Lydia at work and ask about lawyers. Hopefully, she'll be forthcoming and won't start preaching and asking too many questions. It distressed me, if only for a moment, that Lydia had become so important in my life. I had devoted too much time, had invested all my love, in just one person, Elsbeth, now dead, and the source of all my troubles. I reached a small landing and the exit stairwell, but there was no pay phone in sight. I turned around. Nothing, I was all alone. A trap, for sure. Conn was inviting me to take the steps—and then what? Was he allowing me to disappear, or would he be waiting for me downstairs with open handcuffs, accusing me of trying to escape? It would be my word against his, a situation

I had got used to. I took the stairs. If they stop me, so be it, I was beyond caring. What could they do to me? Kill me? Tears began to roll down my face. How did I get myself into such a mess? Oh, Elsbeth, Elsbeth, look at what you're doing to me. From beyond the grave. I kept going down, down, then saw an emergency exit and pushed the heavy steel door. I was outside, on the street, and the air felt warm and newly familiar on my skin. I was free. They had nothing on me and they let me go, but without so many words, without admitting defeat, keeping me instead in a state of suspense to make me feel like a thief, stealing my way. Their sick egos wouldn't permit them to say: We made a mistake, go, you're free, you're innocent. How I yearned to be the tourist again. As if in a daze I pushed through the rush-hour crowds. I was one of them, and yet I was set apart. A pregnant woman came toward me, her belly big and hard, her bellybutton visible under the white tunic; all at once, I felt vulnerable for the woman and for her unborn child. At home, I lowered the shades and crawled into bed and in the confusion of half-sleep saw Elsbeth stand before me, Elsbeth, tall and beautiful as ever, with a string tied around her neck like a delicate necklace. A small bottle was nestled against her white throat, and that's where her blood collected. "Oh, Elsbeth," I said, reaching to touch the string, wet and pinkish with Elsbeth's blood. "What is this for?" My hand reached for the bottle, then recoiled with aversion. Not aversion to Elsbeth, but to Elsbeth's blood. I wanted to hug her and show her how sorry I was, but the blood, I didn't want the blood on my hands and clothes. "Elsbeth," I whispered, then awoke, covered in sweat. I remembered the detectives and, to spite them, wanted to rise and wash up and continue to go about my life, make dinner, watch TV, maybe go to the park and watch the chess players, but I didn't have the strength. How happy I felt to have seen Elsbeth again, Elsbeth so real and so angelically beautiful, with the small, red bottle, like a jewel, nestling at her throat. I felt a vague need to cry, yet no tears came. I turned on my side and hugged the pillow close to my chest. If only they left me alone and let me stay in bed, I felt peaceful in bed, lulled to sleep. More likely, they would knock on my door in the middle of the night to terrorize and frighten me. I could fool them all and kill myself and so the case against me would be effectively closed. And so would Elsbeth's. The angry, disappointed hunters would pull a rubber band around the folders—Elsbeth and I bound together—and toss them in a metal filing cabinet. No proof, no accused, no guilty parties. Just two dead women, a few forms and scribbled notes, neatly secured with a rubber band.

DAYS PASSED. No one knocked on my door in the middle of the night and my answering machine, except for a few hangups, was clear of messages. Gradually, I began to climb out from under. They had given up on me, I thought, and tried to resume my routine in the park. But, I found, I was too restless to sit there for long. I saw Tom a couple of times, but didn't tell him anything, afraid he'd spread the word and people in the park would guard themselves from me. In my dream, a cat bit off a piece of a mouse's head, near its eye, yet the mouse was still alive, even moving a little across the floor trying to get away from the cat, but the cat followed, reaching a tentative tongue into the mouse's wound, sort of licking/tasting its blood. I retched at the horror of it all. My psyche, I thought, was damaged, perhaps permanently warped. Upon waking, when I moved my hand down my side, down my stomach and thighs, I felt dissociated from my own warm skin. All day long I walked the streets and, to give myself something to do, I counted and catalogued smokers into gender camps. They had a furtive look about them and my expert eye spotted them instinctively, zooming down to the taut fingers holding the maligned object. The females I watched with special interest, lingering on those who sucked long and hard, hungry for the stuff, drawing on their insatiable appetite for life. They seemed more desperate than the males but where was it decreed that women had to be cheerful all the time? It was the end of the millennium, life rushed at me, the streets reeked of urine. Everybody talked but nobody listened. Men in suits shook hands as if important matters were at stake. It was all a game, Elsbeth had said, but with consequences. A man in a horse-drawn carriage loudly chattered on his cell phone, while the woman at his side sat stone-faced and empty-eyed. On Fifth Avenue a man bent under the weight of a burlap sack advanced toward me like a dark cloud. As he came near, he blew a kiss to my crotch, automatically, as one making the sign of the cross upon sighting a church. It is only us, the loonies, who still pay attention, I thought. No one called me, no one knocked on my door in the middle of the night, yet it didn't mean I wasn't being watched. I walked the streets, humming to myself moody little tunes I made up on the spot. Every now and then, at the gym or on the street, I'd suddenly turn around to surprise the one following me, and, at the same time, to ascertain that no one was following me. Every so often I thought I heard my name called. Every so often I thought it was my mother's voice, calling my name. More and more, as I gathered into myself, I felt whole compartments shut down in my brain. I went to the river, past a new glass tower that was going up with amazing speed. To ease my fears, I excused the cops. The cops, I reasoned, mistreated me because they had to, that was how they dealt with everyone. Their perceptions were skewed because every day of their professional lives they came in contact with people who lied for one reason or another, and so, naturally, they were coarse and brutal with everyone alike, even with someone like me, so obviously clean and blameless. I took myself to the movies and held my breath with all the other spectators as the couple on the screen went at it. The camera zoomed in on the woman's tongue going into the man's mouth, and I tried to remember the last time I pushed my tongue into a man's mouth and what it felt like. A cinematographic minute later the two lovers fell asleep, and I admired the artful arrangement of limbs and sheets on the bed, revealing the man's arm, the woman's thigh, as they lay side by side, the man harboring the woman from behind. How beautiful they looked in the soft, gelatine light! In the steam shower I devised new ways to pamper myself and, like Elsbeth, rubbed my skin with lemon peels. In the sauna I spread warm honey all over my body and lay down on my towel. Groom, groom, groom, I chanted, raising my legs straight up in the air to admire my toes and the brilliant sheen of my skin. Ah, I thought. Beauty tips were nothing to sneeze at. Lydia, I knew, regularly shampooed and conditioned her pubic hair to keep it soft. Once a week she smeared sour cream on her face and throat and covered her eyes with slices of chilled cucumber. Things mixed in my head. Like a cocktail, I thought. Every time I remembered the detectives and the tricks they tried on me, I was filled with rage, but also with a sense of vindication. No doubt they had hoped I would succumb, adopting the lamb-like, passive frame of mind they were trained to instill in those they questioned. No doubt they had hoped I would accept the prescriptive fate they had assigned me, but I fooled them, didn't I, I beat them at their own game. I took a deep, yoga breath. "Murder is my business," Daley had said, and I despised him in my heart. A guy went past, rhythmically pummeling a pack of cigarettes into his palm just like Elsbeth used to do and I remembered with longing the diamond in her bellybutton and the rings on her small pink nipples. Now Elsbeth lived in my head together with the detectives. The questions they put to me still roiled in my mind but with fading urgency. Phrases repeated in my head like a loop of Indian music, a mantra, the instructor called it. The day I left the precinct the sun was setting and the streets thronged with people going home from work. A man sat in his airconditioned car and bit into a bulky sandwich. Everything seemed so normal, so ordinary, and yet so alien. The next morning I went to the park, determined to resume my life in spite of the detectives. Soon, I thought, I'd finish my dissertation and look for a job. I'd already begun browsing the Internet and considered teaching positions in the anthropology department of colleges in small towns in the Midwest. I would relocate, I thought, and start afresh. I would relinquish my loner status and maybe re-remember how to kiss and fall in love. Tom arrived on his bike. Tom of the many wives and the Chinese girlfriend. He told me stories and I listened, laughing with him but silently siding with the wives. He complained some more about his shrewish third ex-wife and I thought it had become his mantra, a monologue he couldn't get out of his head. "When she talks to me nice, I worry. I bought my daughter a cell phone and told her: Every night, from seven to nine, you keep that cell phone on, I'm paying for it." He adjusted the bandanna on his forehead. "The woman used me, and I didn't even know it. She heard I make good-looking babies and smart too. I didn't want to marry her, she conned me into it." Tom took off on his bike. Autumn approached in tiny steps, the evenings grew cooler, the men at the chess tables wore jackets over their shirts and scarves around their necks. I sat next to Frenchie and observed his round face, his bulging blue eyes: a cheese merchant and a stranger, in love with a game. Summer was dying and I chose hot, bright colors to call attention to myself. Summer was dying and the blue sky was filled with white fluffy clouds. Respectable men gave me serious looks, older women gave me haughty, uncertain looks. In a dream I painted my nails black because my cousin, whom I was visiting, was also painting her nails black. She leaned forward in front of the mirror and I asked her if she'd been losing weight. As a child, I feared the cousin who was fat and older and bossed me around when the adults weren't looking. One day she called me into the bathroom and locked the door. She led me to the sink and pointed to the reddish-brown water, with clots of blood floating in it. She was menstruating, she told me proudly, and I wanted to throw up, the stench was unbearable. I turned to leave but she wouldn't let me, until someone knocked on the door and I was released.

I SIPPED MY COFFEE. Since the weather turned chilly, Franklin had disappeared. On a nearby bench a man nibbled on his sweetheart's ear; in between nibbles, he whispered sweetnothings in her ear. The sweetheart, her eyes half shut, inclined her head and smiled. In the restaurant, Elsbeth cooled her face with a wet napkin. She was warm, she said, flushed with wine. "You drink too much," I chided. "Don't worry," Elsbeth said, "I know what I'm doing." Day after day the air got colder and I stood before the open doors of my closet, wondering what I should wear: a sweater or a jacket? Life went on, very much as before. When I met my Chilean neighbor, he gave me a big smile. "You must be in real trouble," he said. If I'm in trouble, why is he smiling? I wondered. Unless this opening was meant to lead to a joke, some sick joke. More and more, I felt, in some way or other, people around me were disturbed, deeply ensconced in their private cocoon of hurt. I was nothing special, I was one of the pack. "What trouble?" I asked, also smiling. "The police came around and asked me questions. Don't worry, I didn't say anything incriminating." As if he could—I stared, waiting for the grimacing Chilean to continue. But he didn't. "What did they say?" I asked. "Oh," he said. "They wanted to know what kind of neighbor you are, what kind of clothes you wear. I told them I see you once in a while, in the elevator, and so on. They also questioned my wife. We both said the same thing." "What?" I demanded, losing patience with his slow ways, his slow delivery. "What did you say to them?" "We said that we don't know who your friends are, and we hardly know you." "They're ruining my reputation," I said, more to myself than to him. "This," said the Chilean, "should be the least of your worries." He was right, of course, the least of my worries. The rains came, and I napped and dozed, and, my mouth closed, I heard myself snore through my nose and throat. At the supermarket checkout line, women complained about the rain. "It knocked on my windows all night," said a white-haired woman. "I couldn't sleep." "In my country," said the checkout girl, "women go out to wash their face with rain water. They say it makes you look young." "Where is your country?" I asked, thinking maybe I could go there. "The Dominican Republic," said the girl. "Come here," Elsbeth said. "Look." She was pointing at a new shoot on her Pearl plant. She had just moved into her new apartment and the plant had survived the move. In the old apartment she had a huge and unruly philodendron she had decided to leave for the superintendent. But, the day before she moved out, the plant crashed to the floor. "The plant knew it," I said. "It committed suicide." "Don't say such things, it brings bad luck," Elsbeth protested, yet perhaps a little pleased that a plant would commit suicide because she was going to leave it behind. My nights were difficult, my skin was on fire. In bed, I tried various positions that normally soothed me, curling on my side and hugging the pillow or the down cover, or lying spread-eagle across the bed. Still hot, as if with high fever, I turned on the airconditioner to make the room very cold so I could bury myself under the cover, but the motorized noise hummed in my head and I had to turn it off. Even my brain worked against me and as soon as I woke, as if following a picking-at-scabs mechanism, it took me to memory sites where pain and shame were stored. The only striking event during those days was the morning I came face to face with the birdboy. At first I thought he was wearing a mask, a half mask that covered his forehead and nose, but as he and his mother approached I realized that no, it wasn't a mask, it was his real face, the long, hard beak jutting out from between the small eyes; the skin, pasty-white, must have been grafted from other parts of his body. I was horrified and yet enchanted by our brief encounter, and as the day progressed and in the days that followed I thought of him as a rare exotic flower, and where I previously saw horror I now saw beauty. From my memory, I culled detail after detail about this teenage boy, his slender build, his nonchalant stride. He had adorned his deformity with tiny silver rings and a delicate silver chain rested across his beak like a necklace. The boy, I thought, was amused by the face he was given. He had a healthy sense of humor, and pride, and in my thoughts I envied the courage it took to walk among the blind. My perceptions sharpened and focused. More and more I sat in the park and immersed myself in works of fantasy and dream; I fared much better in the world of fable than in the world of fact. The park calmed my soul, the oak and sycamore trees stood tall and serene. When the sun came back for a day, I went to Brighton Beach to say goodbye to the ocean before it was stowed away for the winter. I called Lydia to see if she wanted to come with me, but Lydia was busy with a new boyfriend she had met on the Internet. He was very handsome, she said, but damaged. "How is he damaged?" I asked. "He has mother issues, he's too sensitive. Every word out of my mouth upsets him. It takes me hours to convince him I didn't mean to hurt him." "Must be difficult," I said. "Very," she agreed, "but

I like the give-and-take." So I set out on my own, sitting on the train and reading a book. Once in a while I looked up and observed the other passengers, grateful to be on a train going to Brighton Beach. I felt mellow, even optimistic, staring at a young girl who tried to hide from me in her mother's lap. She was stunning, and I admired the smooth mulatto skin, the thick lashes, the green eyes. Accidents of beauty, like the girl, like the birdboy, were sparks from the unknown. "She is beautiful," I told the mother, and the mother smiled, stroking the girl's head. Feeling like a tourist, I sat on the beach, drinking my beer and smoking a cigarette. Nearby, a middle-aged man peeled off his bathing trunks; I glimpsed his dangling genitals under the mini-skirt towel he had tied around his waist. European, I guessed, probably Russian. I had never thought of Russians as water-enthusiasts but it was a fact that waves of Odessa Russians had taken over Brighton Beach with their borscht and knishes, mingling with leftover Hispanics, blacks, and old-time Jews. Now fully, dandily attired, except for the socks and sandals he held in his hand, the Russian stood and watched the ocean. I wondered what was going through his head, and found comfort in the thought that men, too, had their poetic moments. They, too, wrote and sang songs, kissed, laughed, fell in love. They built bridges, they collected the garbage. When I came out of the subway, night had fallen. I went past restaurants and watched diners bend over their plates, sticking forks in their mouths. I nodded hello to doormen idly surveying the street from their doors. Everywhere, it seemed, the city was being dug up and men in helmets stood in shoulder-deep tunnels. Smoke rose from holes in the ground. A huge crane pointed at the sky, and the full moon, just like in the movies, glided in and out from under the clouds. I felt a sudden uplift as if I, too, understood it all and was part of it. I sipped my coffee and wound my leather jacket tight around me. There was a chill in the air, a few leaves still clung to the trees, and I welcomed the tender feelings that cruised in me. I missed Franklin, I longed to see him wrapped in my comforter, rising from his cardboard bed to face the new day. Mrs. Williams called again and sweetly told me it was time to confess. I let out a cry. "I didn't do it, Mrs. Williams. I tell you, Drew did it. Why do you want to believe him? Why won't you believe me?" "The police," Mrs. Williams said wearily. "Drew has an alibi." You can't be that stupid, I wanted to shout. "If he gets two guys to lie for him, does it make him innocent?" I asked, and Mrs.

Williams sighed. "Some things," she said, "must forever remain a mystery." In yoga class, the instructor taught us how to balance our moon and sun breaths. She said there were no enemies, only the self. She gave us exercises to conquer our self-animosity and I succeeded, at least for the hour. I hadn't heard from the detectives but one day, I feared, they would appear at my door. That's what my neighbor had said, grimacing. They had nothing on me but, like the Chilean said, they'd come anyway, following their hunters' instincts. "Once they've got your number in their computers," he said, "they never leave you alone. What did you two have, anyway?" "What do you mean?" I asked. "You and the dead woman," said the Chilean. "We had a friendship," I said, overcome by the simple clarity of my own words. For now, at least, I felt safe, secure. A fine, luminous mist filled the air, and I had a memory flash of Elsbeth and I running home in the rain. Upstairs, I got down on my knees with a white towel in my hand. From the rain, smudges of dirt and tiny rivulets of mud had formed along her slender calves, and I, lovingly, rubbed out the stains, while Elsbeth, ticklish, laughed and twitched on the bed. The sun re-appeared, washing away the clouds, and I sat on my bench, admiring the trees, so solidly grounded, so tenaciously holding onto the earth. All things are corruptible, all things are generable, I remembered Newton's words. People emerged from their homes and sleepily went to work. Tom arrived on his bike. He was going to the gym, he said, and was stopping for a moment to tell me his good news. I looked up from my book and waited, wondering what it might be. "I'm getting married," he said, grinning. "Again?" I exclaimed, and Tom laughed. "I'm incurable, kind of an optimist, I guess, but she is different, she doesn't bug me," he said and drove off. In the distance, the fountains roared up to the sky, then came down in a loud, greenish splash. Life, I thought, was a marvel.

TSIPI KELLER was born in Prague, raised in Israel, and has been living in the U. S. since 1974. Her short fiction, and her poetry translations, have appeared in many journals and anthologies; her novels, *The Prophet of Tenth Street* (1995) and *Leverage* (1997) were translated into Hebrew and published by Sifriat Poalim. Keller's translation of Dan Pagis's posthumous collection, *Last Poems*, was published by The Quarterly Review of Literature (1993), and her translation of Irit Katzir's posthumous collection, *And I Wrote Poems*, was published by Carmel (2000). Among her awards are: A National Endowment for the Arts fellowship, a New York Foundation for the Arts grant, and an Armand G. Erpf award from Columbia University. Her novel, *Jackpot*, was published by Spuyten Duyvil in 2004.

SPUYTEN DUYVIL

All Spuyten Duyvil titles are available through your local bookseller via
Booksense.com

Distributed to the trade by
Biblio Distribution
a division of NBN
1-800-462-6420
http://bibliodistribution.com

All Spuyten Duyvil authors may be contacted at
authors@spuytenduyvil.net